DRAGON SLAYER:
RISING

Book 2 of the Dragon Slayer Chronicles

Carey Green

Dragon Slayer: Rising

Carey Green

Dragon Slayer: Sacrifice © 2015 Carey Green

Cover Artwork:
Reggie Caturay Achevarra - 12TWENTY4 Creative
https://12twenty4.us/

Scripture quotations:
The Holy Bible, King James Version. New York: Oxford Edition: 1769.

The Dragon Slayer Chronicles Series can be found at

www.DragonSlayerBook.com

Dragon Slayer: Beginnings – Book 1
www.CareyGreen.com/DS1

Dragon Slayer: Rising – Book 3
www.CareyGreen.com/DS3

*****†*****

More books by this author

NON-FICTION

The Marriage Improvement Project
a devotional study for couples
www.CareyGreen.com/mip

The Elder Training Handbook
a leadership assessment & training tool for the church
www.CareyGreen.com/eth

RECHARGE
Spiritual devotional methods to recharge your spiritual life, improve your spiritual health, & grow your intimacy with God
www.CareyGreen.com/rechargebook

Moving Toward God - a 19-lesson workbook covering the basics of the Christian faith
www.CareyGreen.com/MTGbook

FICTION

The Great Smizzmozzel Bash
a rhyming, rollicking adventure for kids
www.CareyGreen.com/Smizz

Through Heaven's Eyes
a Christmas drama for the local church
www.CareyGreen.com/heavenseyes

*****†*****

To everyone who has so patiently waited for the release of this book. I trust it was worth the wait.

To my wife, who daily increases the joy of my life.
To my children and grandchildren; may you slay every dragon you face in the strength of the LORD.

To Jesus, who has equipped me for every good work.

*****†*****

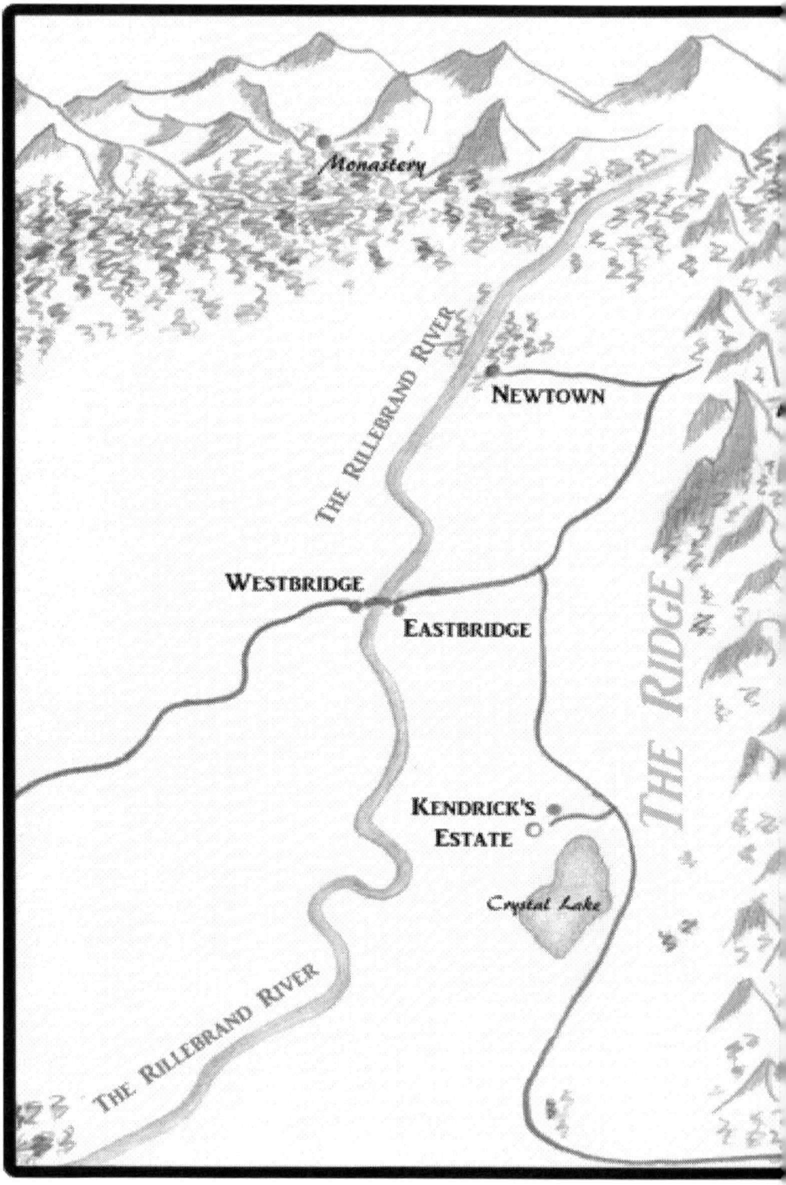
Monastery
The Rillebrand River
Newtown
Westbridge
Eastbridge
The Ridge
Kendrick's
Estate
Crystal Lake
The Rillebrand River

The North Country

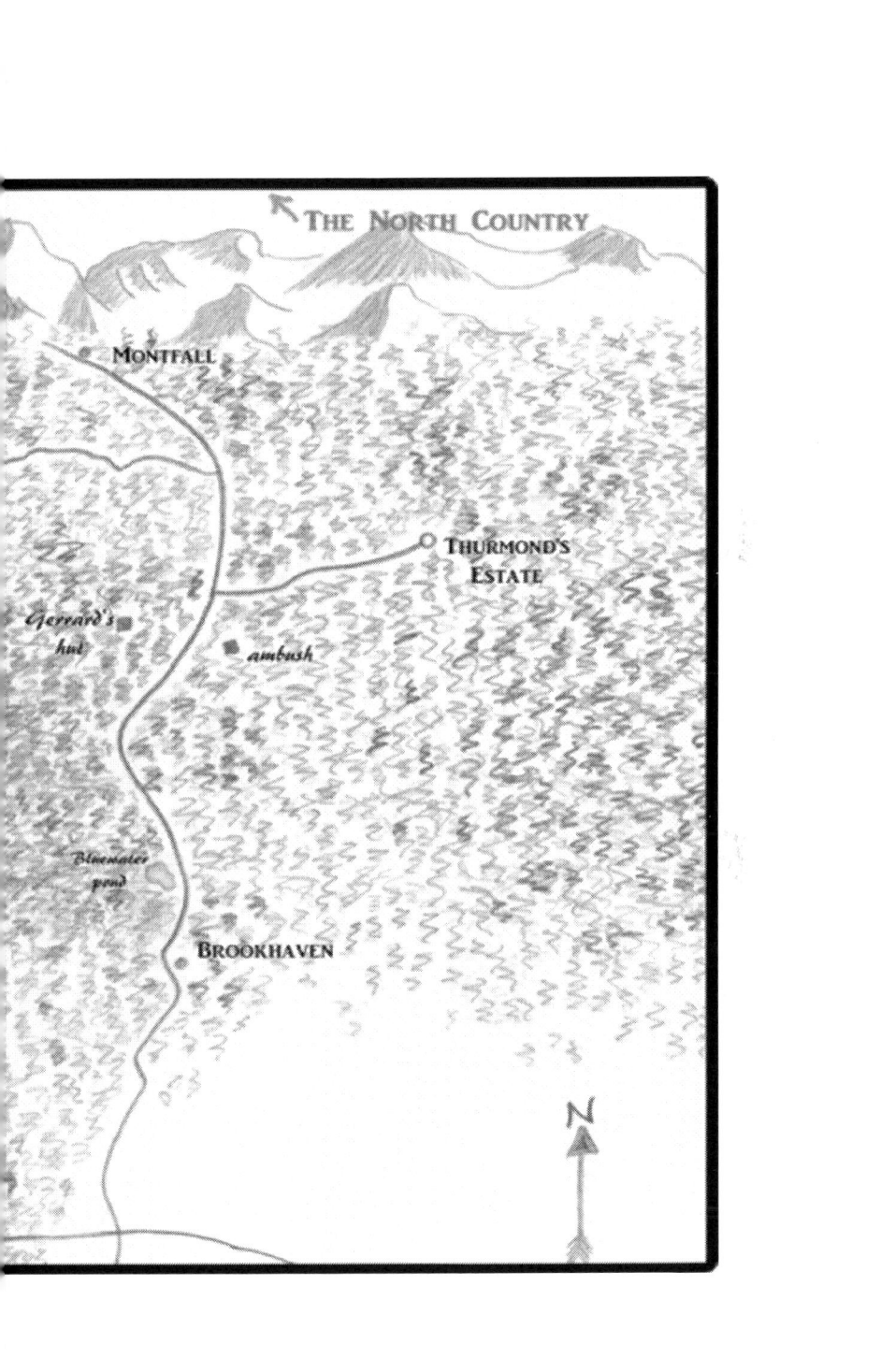

Montfall

Thurmond's Estate

Gerrard's hut

ambush

Bluewater pond

Brookhaven

N

PROLOGUE

From the fifth and sixth days, dragons have been. The first pair was glorious, emerging from nothingness at the command of their Maker. Their wings stretched wide as they yawned to life in mid-air, the crisp atmosphere of the garden splitting as their graceful forms shot through the newborn sky. Row upon row of shield-like iridescent scales glinted brilliantly in the sunlight, reflecting every color of the spectrum.

Opening their mighty jaws in cries of worship each reveled in the discovery of the magnificent breath-effects they possessed; flames, shimmering black liquid, a greenish mist, and a white, sparkling crackle of electricity.

As gentle as lambs they softly landed before the first man; they were to receive their name. He called them "Tannin" in the ancient tongue, meaning "great serpent." As centuries passed they would be known by many names; leviathan, wyvrn, and dragon among them.

Some say it was one of them that was inhabited by the enemy of all that is good and used to deceive the woman. It may be so, only the Maker knows. That great deception led to rebellion in the human heart and rebellion led to the fall of the human race. Paradise was spoiled, creation was tainted, and the two great beasts, like the rest, fell prey to its effects. They became ruthless predators perched at the pinnacle of the beastly realm. Through size, strength, and the devastating power of their breath they became terror itself, wreaking havoc on man and beast alike. None could withstand them. All creatures hid from the shadow of their ravenous hunger.

As the curse had its way mankind began the slow and slippery slide into the pit of depravity, victims of a self-inflicted sickness of the soul. Selfishness took its only possible course and over more than 16 centuries mankind plummeted into an existence devoid of moral restraint. The patient love of the Creator was put to the test, His great heart vexed beyond measure.

In His loving anger the Maker once again created but not as He had before. What He created was a plan of salvation for man, through a man. In one of the greatest ironies of history that man constructed the means of deliverance from the wrath of his greatest Love. Through a long and tedious season of labor a vessel of salvation was prepared for the man's family... but they were not alone. The seeds of a new world went with them in the form of the beasts of land and air, each miraculously docile as they were before the fall. Among the beasts were two dragon hatchlings, a male and a female, each so new they still bore supple folds of skin instead of an impenetrable armor of scales.

As the Creator shut the man and his family safely within the vessel the world outside was torn apart. Tremors came from below, the first indication of the mighty earthquakes to come. The fountains of the deep burst forth, splitting the land into continents and flooding everything with the first of a seemingly unceasing flow of water. Adding to the already flooded plain, a deluge fell from the heavens, covering the earth until water rose over the highest peaks. The vessel rose upon the waters, weathering the deluge day after day, month after month for over a year. The beastly cargo remained docile, even compliant as the man and his family cared for them within the confines of their boat home. The small family marveled at the sovereign influence of their Maker as the lions showed no hint of aggression and the lambs no sign of fear.

After more than 12 months the sun broke through the blanket of clouds overhead and the boat lurched hard, striking an object beneath the waves. With another jolt it lodged in a crevice on what they would later know was the highest peak for as far as the eye could see. The waters receded inch by inch for three months until finally the rocky tips of mountains peaked above the surface. Over time a muddy bog emerged in the plains below. It bore nothing but the earthy tones of dirt,

PROLOGUE

stone, and driftwood. The green of life was gone, an eerie stillness filled the air.

As months passed the beasts and their caretakers became restless, hoping the time to leave their haven would come soon. Already filling their cage were the two sleeping dragons. They, along with many other creatures, had fallen into a hibernation-like sleep shortly after the vessel first rose on the water. The tannin were fully mature and fearsome to behold. The youngest son stood over them, admiration in his eye. They were powerful, strong, and to be feared, clearly the uncontested rulers of the beastly world. He glanced up at the high window as the waning light of day shone through.

There is a new world out there, he thought, and a new beginning. Though we are a small lot now, rulers will rise. He bowed his head to look at the child snuggled in his arms. He had been born just days before. I must see to it that you and your sons are among those rulers.

The next morning, the patriarch of the small clan called his sons together.

"Our God has spoken. It is time. Tomorrow we will release the animals and leave the ark."

The three brothers looked at each other eagerly. They had wondered if the day would ever come. Though they had been skeptical when their father first revealed the plan to build the vessel, they had complied out of duty to the aged man. Though it seemed strange that he heard from their Maker while they did not, the risk of disbelief was too great. What if he was right? What if a flood was coming? As they worked alongside him for decades they were astonished at his knowledge of carpentry and tools, angles and dimensions. Those were things he should not know, being a man of the soil, yet he did. Now that the promised flood had come and gone they were fully convinced of God's existence and their father's communication with Him. Their father continued.

"You must prepare yourselves. Tonight, before you sleep, you will hear the voice of God for yourselves."

The mouth of the youngest fell open. Did he hear his father rightly? They would hear from God themselves?

"How, father? What must we do?" he asked with a trembling voice. The old man smiled.

"He is holy, we are sinful. It is by His grace that we breathe at all. All I can advise is that you remove every bitterness, sinful thought, and unclean motive from your heart and trust in His mercy that it will be enough."

That evening as promised, they sat around a dim lamp in their father's berth and heard the voice of their God.

Be fruitful and multiply and fill the earth. The fear of you and the dread of you shall be upon every beast of the earth and upon every bird of the heavens, upon everything that creeps on the ground and all the fish of the sea. Into your hand they are delivered. Every moving thing that lives shall be food for you. And as I once gave you the green plants, I now give you everything. But you shall not eat flesh with its life, that is, its blood. And for your lifeblood I will require a reckoning: from every beast I will require it, and from man. From his fellow man I will require a reckoning for the life of man. Whoever sheds the blood of man, by man shall his blood be shed, for I made man in My own image.

"And you, be fruitful and multiply, increase greatly on the earth and multiply in it. Listen now, I establish My covenant with you and your offspring after you, and with every living creature that is with you, the birds, the livestock, and every beast of the earth with you, as many as come out of the ark; it is for every beast of the earth. I establish My covenant with you, that never again shall all flesh be cut off by the waters of the flood, and never again shall there be a flood to destroy the earth. This is the sign of the covenant that I make between Me and you and every living creature that is with you, for all future generations: I have set My bow in the cloud, and it shall be a sign of the covenant between Me and the earth. When I bring clouds over the earth and the bow is seen in the clouds, I will remember

PROLOGUE

My covenant that is between Me and you and every living creature of all flesh. And the waters shall never again become a flood to destroy all flesh. When the bow is in the clouds, I will see it and remember the everlasting covenant between God and every living creature of all flesh that is on the earth.

The next morning after many of the beasts had already been released the youngest stood outside the cage of the tannin. As if on cue they woke, stretched their mighty wings and moved to the door of their cage. He stood aside as the door swung wide. He watched in awe as the mighty beasts made their way peacefully toward the massive door of the vessel. They launched into the sky of the new world, heading straight for a high peak on the edge of the horizon.

The youngest son watched as the beasts grew small in the distance, taking careful notice of the mountain to which they flew. Watching their mighty forms fade into the brilliant blue of the sky, he whispered a promise to his son who was sleeping peacefully in his mother's arms down below.

"They are the most powerful beasts the Lord God has made. In them will be your strength and that of your sons after you. It will be so, my son. I give you my solemn word."

Within seven days he departed, his wife and son with him, determined to find the lair of the beasts and make himself their master. He knew there was not much time. It was only the miraculous hand of the Lord that kept them at bay during the journey. He knew that divine enchantment could already be waning. He wanted to reach them before the image of man became unfamiliar, before instinct made them predators once again.

The journey was long, the way rutted and uneven. The powerful currents had fashioned a harsh landscape over which the green of new life sprouted in isolated places. The foothills ahead grew greener with each day of travel. It was an encouraging sign. After two weeks the mountains were reached but the necessity of building shelter and gathering food prevented an immediate search for the beasts. Then their first winter in the new world came hard and cruel, delaying the search for another 5 months.

By the time the man left his crude hut on a cold spring morning it had been six months since he had last seen the beasts. He was desperate to find them. Shouting an impatient word over his shoulder at his frustrated wife he ventured into the brisk air and drove himself up the mountainside.

Just after evening fell, one week after leaving his wife and son, he found the lair. The beasts had made their home in a large cavern high in the side of a lower peak. He recognized the familiar stench of their dung from outside the gaping hole. Into the darkness he went, torch in hand. He was determined to gain the respect of the beasts before it was too late.

The dancing shadows grudgingly revealed the dragon's lair, stuffy and dank. The beasts had gone on what he suspected was a nocturnal hunt. Not a good sign. The docile nature he'd witnessed at their departure was likely long behind them. He would be viewed as prey, nothing more.

There must be something, some way... the man tried to convince himself as he waved the torch side to side in an effort to assess the cavern's interior. In the far corner, partially hidden behind a large outcropping of stone he found what he did not expect. A nest.

A combination of small trees, reeds, and a sticky black substance had been interwoven to form the circular shape large enough for five men to stand inside. In the back of the nest, hidden under broken reeds was the unthinkable; four eggs, each twice the size of a large melon. They glimmered in the torch light. He had to be quick.

Removing a rough, oversized bag he lifted the first egg, dull red in appearance. The uncommon warmth of the egg in his cold hands caused him to flinch and he almost dropped it. With a deep breath to calm his nerves he carefully wrapped the egg in a blanket and eased it into the bag. He repeated the process with a black egg and again with a green one. Reaching for the remaining egg, a shimmering white one, he stopped. Something in his gut held him back.

PROLOGUE

With a sigh, he removed the green egg from his bag, laid it back inside the nest and covered the two eggs with the reeds.

"I have a child," he spoke aloud to the absent beasts, his voice echoing eerily in the expanse of the cave. "It's only right for you to have a few of your own."

With that the man hitched the heavy bag over his shoulder, retrieved his torch from a crack in the wall, and moved into the night.

CHAPTER ONE

For the first time Silas was fearful of Hestia, the dragon he'd hatched, raised, and labored to train. He had good reason to be. The beast was hurtling across the sky spewing flame in an uncontrolled rage and Silas was perched precariously astride her neck. The old man was almost certain the wild ride would end with him falling to a rocky death on the mountains below. She dove, writhed, and twisted in every conceivable contortion. He knew she was trying to rid herself of the fiery pain that throbbed in her bloody left eye but there would be no relief apart from his intervention.

"Hestia! Down!"

Deafened by pain the monster flew on. The wind caught in Silas' long outer cloak. The increasing force caused by every beat of Hestia's leathery wings threatened to tear him from the dragon's scaly hide. Silas removed his dagger from the inner pocket of the cloak and slipped it into his belt. Clinging desperately to the beast's neck with one arm he struggled to free his other arm from its sleeve. Once that arm was free he struggled to free the other. Finally, the cloak fluttered free with a last rush, tumbling downward toward the jagged peaks.

I must get her to the ground. The wound must be treated and dusk will be upon us soon.

Silas went to work, forcing the tips of his fingers under the tight edges of the rock-hard scales along the back of his dragon's neck. Her scales were hard and close-fitting; they cut the old man's knuckles terribly but he continued shoving his hands further into the narrow opening between scales. When he felt his hands had attained enough depth to achieve the needed leverage, Silas pressed upward on the underside of the scales with the back of his wrists

"Down!"

The dragon began a begrudging descent past the craggy mountain peaks toward the tree line far below. Thankful that his solution had worked, Silas guided the dragon to a clearing he had used long ago during her training. It was high on the mountainside. Nearby was a small cave that yawned out of the mountain's rocky face. He knew the cavern would be a tight squeeze for his now fully grown dragon but it would have to do.

"Hestia, there! Down!'

The dragon complied with a mournful growl, flying straight and true toward the meadow. Upon landing, Silas pulled his bloody fists from under the merciless scales and leapt from the dragon's back, narrowly avoiding the flailing wings of the beast as it pawed at its bleeding eye. Under normal circumstances he would approach her boldly, submitting her immediately to his will. But she was injured and therefore unpredictable. He eased toward her large head speaking soft words of reassurance.

"Hestia... calm. Calm, Hestia. You must let me see it."

The dragon craned her neck to view him from her good eye, snarling all the while.

"Hestia, down!" he commanded, resuming the confident tone of the master.

Continuing to paw at her left eye the dragon flopped to her belly in deference to him. Silas crept toward her, resuming the soothing tone. As he neared her head the beast turned to keep him in view, making it impossible for him to assess the severity of the injury.

"Stay!" he commanded and turned toward the cave.

As he had hoped, the remote location had prevented the cave from being looted. Nothing had changed since his last visit. In the back of the cavern, hidden under a stack of pine needles was a bag. Inside it was a dagger, flint and steel, a corked water bottle, and a heavy coil of thick rope. Silas returned to the dragon, rope and bottle in hand. Upon his return the dragon raised its head and hissed.

"Hestia! Down!" Silas commanded, extending his hand toward the rebellious beast.

CHAPTER ONE

Hesitantly, the dragon complied and Silas went to work, attempting to bind her powerful jaws. He caught glimpses of the bloody gash where once the yellow of her eye shone brightly. With her jaws bound Silas attached two long ropes to her makeshift muzzle, one on either side of her jaws. Each was stretched to its length and tied tightly to a tree, preventing the animal's head from moving side to side.

"Good girl, Hestia. You know that I do this for your good," Silas said, stroking the side of the beast's head.

Walking around the dragon Silas saw the full extent of the injury. The eye socket was a mess of blood. The thrust of the sword combined with the weight of the man who had dangled from it momentarily had rendered her blind for sure. He suspected that as the beast's body did its slow work of healing what remained of the eye would be expelled from the socket. Silas cleaned the wound as best he could, continually consoling and rebuking his resistant beast.

"Hestia, stay! I will return."

The old man wandered across the meadow and into the woods, bottle in hand. His keen eye soon spied what he was looking for; nettle, chickweed, and comfrey leaves. On the way back to the beast he snatched up a few early marigold flowers. He made a final stop at a large birch tree. Brandishing his knife, Silas gouged the point deeply into the tree. Waiting for sap to ooze from the notch he emptied the bottle of its contents then held its mouth to the gash. Once the bottle was full of sap Silas sat against the tree and placed it between his feet. Methodically rubbing each of the plants between his palms until each was ground finely, he placed them one by one into the bottle. He walked back into the clearing, his thumb over the bottle top, shaking the concoction vigorously.

"Hestia. We are almost finished."

Cutting a large swath from the bottom of his shirt Silas folded the cloth into a square-ish lump. He poured the homeopathic solution onto the cloth and worked it in until the bandage was saturated. The old man rolled the soaking material into a tight cylinder the size of his fist and moved to the wounded side of the dragon's head.

"Hestia. Stay!" Silas commanded as he worked to pry open the squinting eyelid of the writhing beast.

Without hesitation he thrust the dripping cloth into the hole. The monster howled, straining at the ropes as flames issued from between her clenched teeth. Silas weaved and ducked, avoiding her flailing fore-claws. He stayed close until he was sure that the material would remain packed inside the socket.

Leaving the beast writhing he went back to the cave, started a fire to the right of its entrance and cleared room for the dragon to lay half inside and half outside the small cave. By the time Silas returned to the dragon night had fallen. Hestia's temper had subsided and she was fitfully resting.

Drawing his knife, Silas prepared to cut the ropes that bound the dragon's snout on each side.

"Hestia. Den! Den!" he insisted, pointing toward the flickering campfire. When he felt sure the dragon understood his command, Silas cut her free. Shaking its head side to side and glaring at her master, a low rumble rose from her throat.

"Fine. Be angry. But I remain the master," the old man grumbled.

The dragon rose to its full height, snarled at her master again and tromped toward the cave.

*****†*****

With no proper weapons and in the blackness of the evening, Silas found it impossible to scrounge up food worthy of a dragon. In the end she had to be satisfied with what amounted to much less than a mouthful of squirrel while her master went hungry. The old man sat awake long into the night, brooding as he stared into the flames of his small fire ring.

I hope Kendrick is dead. Hestia trampled him soundly as she ran from the cavern. If not, I'll see to it that he is soon enough. He and all his family. They cannot escape me.

He tossed another stick into the fire.

CHAPTER ONE

How did he find me? I've been well hidden for over a decade, since the day I stole away his daughter.

The old man laughed aloud.

I wish I could have seen his face the day she vanished, to revel in the pain I caused him. Now that would have been delicious.

Silas, known as "the Screw," rose to check on his dragon. She was sleeping soundly. Despite her clawing the eye was still packed with the herbal compound.

The letter. Only the letter I sent could have led him to me.

He sighed.

Had I not given in to the urge to taunt him, to make that overbearing wife of his suffer even more, I would still be undiscovered.

He looked to his sleeping beast and kicked at a rock as he moved back toward the fire.

Kendrick is easy enough, but the other man who attacked Hestia in the cave, he is of greater concern. Who is he? One of Kendrick's soldiers, perhaps? He had the courage of a soldier but the stealth of a cat. Even Hestia did not know he was there until it was too late.

The fire crackled as Silas strained to recall the face of the man he'd only seen once in the deep shadows of a cave.

I do not know him. Who is he?

CHAPTER TWO

Hon's dark eyes scanned the horizon. Sunlight streamed across the plains, illuminating the rich green fields in streaks as it shot through craggy gaps in The Ridge behind him. He and his companions had been forced to travel slowly due to Lord Kendrick's injuries. It had been a long journey for everyone.

He looked over his shoulder to check on the rest of the group. Rowan, his mentor and friend brought up the rear. His dark eyes were alert, constantly scanning the rocky shoulder of The Ridge on either side. As always, he took on the responsibility for the well-being of those he was with without having to be asked. He was a natural leader and a caring friend.

In front of him was the cart, purchased in Montfall, which bore the injured Lord Kendrick. Though Hon had struck the most significant blow in their battle with Silas' beast, leaping off a large pile of rocks to thrust his sword into its eye, Lord Kendrick had been wounded most severely as the shrieking dragon trampled him on its way out of the cave. An ordinary man would have been killed but Kendrick was no ordinary man.

Riding on each side of the cart were two of Lord Kendrick's best soldiers; Rupert, captain of his guard and Gregory, a young but capable man. In front of them, leading his limping mule was Gerrard, the heavily bearded woodsman who had quickly become both mentor and friend to Hon. His hound Angus trotted alongside. Next to Hon rode a painfully thin but beautiful young woman a few years his senior. She was Camille, Lord Kendrick's daughter.

"There it is," Hon said, pointing to a small grove of trees set against the Rillebrand river. "Newtown. It's nothing like you are used to m'lady, but you will like it."

"Hon, I've told you that you don't have to speak to me so formally." Camille smiled. "I am a person, just like you. You forget as well, I am not accustomed to the finery of my station. Compared to what I've experienced for most of my life Newtown will be a haven."

Hon *had* forgotten. Camille had spent the past eleven years as a slave. Silas had kidnapped her as a child, an act of betrayal against her father. Newtown, though a humble village would definitely seem an improvement to her.

"I know you're eager to be returned to your mother and brother but I hope you can stay for at least a little while. Newtown is a peaceful place and the people are more family than neighbors, at least to me. I can't wait to introduce you to Victoria and her mother, Abigail." Hon grew quiet.

"What is it, Hon?"

"I just remembered… Abigail was injured when the dragons attacked the village, do you remember me telling you?" Camille nodded. "I pray she's well. When we left she was barely clinging to life. If she dies… Camille, she has been a mother to me, really. She raised Victoria and me like siblings, with equal love for both of us even though I was an orphan. If she dies…"

"They both mean a great deal to you, don't they? Abigail *and* Victoria, I mean."

Hon sighed, a deep longing stirring in his heart.

"Yes, they do. They've been so good to me, God's hand of blessing, in fact. Were it not for their kindness and Rowan's, I would undoubtedly be a street urchin in some filthy corner of Eastbridge. But anyway, Newtown is a wonderful little spot. I hope you like it."

"I'm sure I will," Camille responded. "I am eager to meet Victoria and the others but I must admit I am nervous too.

"Nervous, why?

"It's hard to explain the strange mix of emotions... I long to be in the company of women so that I can know them, and in so doing, to know myself I suppose. But I am afraid at the same time; afraid that I will seem silly, or course, or awkward

CHAPTER TWO

to them. It's painfully obvious that I do not have the benefit of... ohhh, it's so hard to explain."

"Please, go on," Hon said.

Camille sighed heavily, knotting her fists in her lap as the horse shifted its weight down the west side of The Ridge. She was clearly struggling to put her feelings into words.

"I've grown into a woman all alone, without the benefit of an older woman to, to show me what it is to actually be a woman. I feel I don't know how to be what I am if that makes any sense?"

"It makes perfect sense," Hon reassured. "But don't worry, Camille. The women of Newtown are some of the finest, most accepting women you will ever meet. They will not only welcome you, they will also understand what you've been through. Everyone in the village knows your story and has been praying that we would recover you. And we have," he said with a smile. "They will rejoice over you."

Camille smiled at Hon demurely.

"Thank you, Hon. I am sure of it."

Hon pulled up at a clearing alongside the road and dismounted. The group had been taking regular breaks to allow Lord Kendrick times of reprieve from the rough bouncing of the cart and to enable Gerrard's limping mule, which had been injured during a furious journey over The Ridge, to get periodic breaks from the rocky road.

"Newtown is in sight, at least," Rowan said as he dismounted. "I think we would do well to camp here for the night. I'm sure we could all use the rest and there is very little light remaining. We have just enough time to gather wood and get some food in us. Come sunrise we can be on our way and make a short day of it."

"I know you've all been going slow on my account," Lord Kendrick said as he hobbled away from the wagon on crude tree-branch crutches, "and I greatly appreciate the consideration. But if it is all the same to the group I would rather take a brief rest then continue on." His face grew somber. "Silas' threats against my family spur me forward. I've been long enough away and would prefer to be there sooner rather than later."

Camille moved to her father's side. He draped his muscular arm over her shoulder as she tucked her head under his chin.

"Any objections to Lord Kendrick's suggestion?" Rowan asked the group.

"Aye," said Gerrard, "but not the sort that need delay the whole party. Me old girl is spent from these 3 days on the road," he said, nodding toward his mule. "I feel I must rest her or lose her, and me heart is not ready for such a blow. You good folk travel on. We shall stay here the night. Me Gertie needs her rest and I shall give it."

*****†*****

The village dogs announced their arrival as the weary party of travelers rode into Newtown. Among the welcoming crowd was Victoria, who rushed to Hon and embraced him as only a sister could. But there was something more to her hug, Hon could feel it. She lingered there beneath his arm, clinging to him as if her soul would crumble if he were to release her. So with Victoria under one arm Hon continued his greetings to others, thanking them for their prayers and concern. As the crowds dispersed Hon turned Victoria's chin upward and their eyes met.

"What is it Vickie? Tell me…"

"I'm so weary Hon, so tired. Mother hasn't improved at all and there's only Hampton and me to sit with her at night. I feel like I haven't gotten a full rest since you left. And, and…" she hesitated.

"Go on. I want to hear it," Hon encouraged.

Burying her head in his chest again Hon heard the words he half-expected.

"I've missed you, Hon. I need you."

Hon leaned her away and looked into her green eyes. There he saw what he recognized in his own heart for the first time.

"Victoria, I'm not the same boy who left here. I've looked into the fiery hot face of death itself. If I'd have died I

CHAPTER TWO

would have gone to the grave with many regrets... and I don't want to have any. Victoria, I need you, too. I love you. I was too proud and immature to admit it before."

Her eyes glistened as she looked into his.

"Welcome home, Hon."

*****†*****

Hon believed with all his heart that Gerrard's words from long ago were true. It was his destiny to hunt down and destroy the dragons. The beast he had faced in the northern mountains was a terrifying creature. All he had to do was close his eyes to feel the heat of its breath against his face and the rough, rock-hard texture of its scales against his skin. It was as real now as it was then.

And since his first-hand encounter with the beast his childhood dreams had returned. Once again, nights were filled with torment and his mornings with a battle to overcome the frenzy of emotion brought on by the dreams. The red monster's mark on him was certain.

Lord Kendrick had called him "fearless" and "brave" as he described his assault on the dragon. But Hon knew differently. He was afraid when he attacked the beast and he was still afraid as he thought of it.

He also believed the outcome of that battle had nothing to do with him. The gracious hand of God had been with him. There was no other explanation. The dragon could have easily spotted him an instant earlier and jerked its head around to snap him out of the air as he hurtled toward it. But it hadn't. He had been protected. Among all the reasons he felt certain that he was to become a dragon slayer that was the most powerful.

There was also the fact that there were at least three other dragons out there, each of them kept and directed by an evil master. The odds seemed overwhelming. How could he, an orphan boy from a small village defeat such impossible foes? Hon didn't know the answer but knew nonetheless that in spite of the fear and the odds, it was his destiny.

But now another, powerful reality had dawned which he couldn't deny. It was the source of the conflict that was growing within him. He wanted nothing more than to be with Victoria. As he sat next to her, keeping watch at her mother's bedside, his heart ached. He held the tender hand of the one he loved but was driven to seek out the beasts responsible for her mother's injuries.

"A group of us will be meeting this afternoon at the stables," Hon said, noticing that Victoria did not look at him. "We've got to determine what can be done about the dragons."

Victoria fidgeted on her stool.

"I know," she said, forcing out a weak smile. "Hon, don't mistake my hesitance for weakness. I know something has to be done and I know that you are right in the middle of it. I just don't like it, that's all."

"I don't like it either," said Hon. "It's like I'm being pulled by an ox on one side and a mule on the other. I want to stay with you, Victoria. I do, honestly. But I can't leave the risks to others. And there's more than just that… I, well… Gerrard thinks that I'm the one to lead the entire effort. And Victoria, I'm beginning to agree with him."

Victoria's chin dropped to her chest and she sat still for what seemed an eternity to Hon. He took her hand but she pulled it away. When her eyes finally met his a single tear ran down her cheek.

"I don't know what to say to you. I'm barely more than a girl. I only know what I feel."

"What is it you feel?" Hon asked.

"I don't want you to do it. I will miss you, and be afraid for you and die a little every second you're away." She paused, her face flushing red. "And what about me? *I* need you, Hon. *I* need you!"

"Victoria…"

"Don't," she interrupted, "I know what you're going to say. You're called to it. Gerrard says it's your destiny, I know. But what does Gerrard really know? He's just a woodsman, Hon! He doesn't know about love, or us." She stopped,

CHAPTER TWO

obviously still a bit embarrassed at the thought of their love. She smiled. "I feel the pulling of the mule and ox myself, you see?" She sighed heavily. "But it's not animals that pull at me, it is the Lord on one side and my selfish, ignorant heart on the other. We both know which must win so let's leave it be. More talk would only stir up the losing side."

With that Victoria rose and moved toward the door of the small hut. She turned before exiting, wiping another tear from her cheek.

"Would you sit with mother while I find Hampton? I want to ask if he can sit with mother this afternoon while we are at the meeting."

Hon nodded, with a smile.

CHAPTER THREE

Lord Hugo Champlain's frosty breath formed thick in front of his fat face, its moisture crystallizing in his heavy beard. His horse labored through the hard drifts of snow that had formed across the road, a difficult job for any steed under normal conditions. But the work was made all the more difficult due to Lord Hugo's mass. He was a mountain of a man, not quite as wide as he was tall. His thick fur coat, made from the hides of three arctic bears, was raised high around his ears to ward off the icy bite of the wind. Though the rest of the world enjoyed the warmth of summer, Lord Hugo's land far north of the great mountains was a realm of perpetual winter.

Following behind, two armed guards rode on either side of a covered, ox-drawn sled. Inside were two maidens Hugo had chosen for this particular journey. It was his custom to choose from among the commoners two, sometimes three maidens to accompany him to the snow caves. It was an "honor" no maiden desired for herself because none who had gone before had ever returned. They huddled together inside the tent, strangers just days before but now companions facing the unknown together. They cried silently, fearfully, their minds fabricating all sorts of horrendous ends for themselves, but none so terrible as what reality would bring. It would come at dawn a few days hence. Hugo would take them deep into the snow caves and watch with demented delight as the beast he referred to as his "ice dragon" played a cat and mouse game with them before devouring them. Rounding the shoulder of the jagged rock formation known as "The Needle," Hugo saw the ice caves in the distance.

"Almost there, ladies!" Hugo shouted, his high pitched voice carrying over the wind. "Almost there!"

*****†*****

Lord Hugo sat over his noon meal, savoring the roast seal along with the sport of the morning. The maidens had proven feisty, a worthy diversion for his aging dragon. The two had not been like many of the pitiful young girls who had gone before, screaming and cowering helplessly as the dragon came at them. The two had fled in opposite directions, one even hurling rocks at the beast. Boreas, his mighty white beast had enjoyed the hunt. Hugo was pleased with the trip for his dragon's sake but on the same note carried a great frustration.

The dragon council continues to wait, urging patience. But time is something I do not have.

He gazed down the dark cavern to his left, hearing the sounds of his beast breathing heavily after its meal. With his fat finger he absentmindedly traced the deep scar running from his beady right eye into his thick beard.

Boreas has only five, maybe six years left. He is a predator who has already waited too long. If the dragon masters are to rise and if I am to have a place in it, something must be done soon.

Wine spilled down his jowls as he greedily drank his fourth tankard. He slammed the oversized mug on the tabletop.

I will not wait any longer! I must force their hand. If they are too cautious to take action I must be the one to do it. The trick is for me to instigate the action without appearing to be the cause. I must be the pebble falling into the pool, causing the ripple that will become the wave while I sink away unnoticed.

Hugo pushed away from the table violently, pacing the torch-lit cavern as his mind raced. Removing a torch from the wall he strode down the dark corridor toward the sounds of his dragon's breathing. The glow of his light fell across the graceful head that was almost as large as Hugo's entire body. The long, sword-like bones protruding from the heavy scales atop its skull arched backward, creating the appearance of a hood over the beast's upper neck.

CHAPTER THREE

He is beautiful... a creature unequalled.

Hugo shuffled his feet. One of the dragon's eyes popped open. The man wiped the last traces of wine from his beard with the back of his hand.

The entire council knows from experience that our beasts can be unpredictable. Their nightly hunts often range farther than we expect. Suppose Boreas happened to range further south than usual... if he made his presence felt in a place where the effect would be too great to undo? The council would have to forge ahead then. Hmmm... what was the name of the Lord to the south, the one Silas was trying to subvert? Kensing? Kendall? Kendrick. Yes, Kendrick's estate is the place. He's the last obstacle anyway. The council would welcome his "accidental" destruction.

Hugo's broad face stretched into a grotesque smile, his beady eyes barely visible above his bulging cheeks.

"Well my terror, the time has come." Boreas raised his head, curious at his master's tone. "Kendrick's it is."

*****†*****

The two men stood toe to toe, one tall, muscular, and dark, the other short, thin, and pale. The older man stared up into the other's dark eyes, determined not to be the one to give way. He would have dominance, he must. Though he was bound to the other man by a century-old covenant made by their ancestors he would not be subject to any man.

"You have been careless Silas," the younger man insisted. "The four of us agreed that the time was not right for our brotherhood to rise, at your insistence. Now you dare risk our discovery by coming to me here in my own stronghold with news that your beast has not only been discovered but is seriously wounded? I should kill you where you stand."

"You would be a fool to try, Rajic," the old man said evenly. "Many have made the attempt before you so why not add another corpse to the count?"

In a flash, Rajic drew the matching pair of katar from his thick leather belt only to have one wrist clamped immediately in the old man's strong left hand and the other blade blocked by a long, rusty blade that had been drawn simultaneously. Silas' eyes never broke contact with those of Rajic. Once again, they were locked in a battle of wills.

"We are one, Rajic. Whether we like it or not our paths are intertwined. The ancestors have decreed it to be so. The news I bring is *not* good and I do not like it any more than you do. But it is reality and you must deal with it. I am still unsure how Kendrick discovered my dragon's lair but he did. There is nothing to be done about it now. We would be better off to determine what to do about it rather than squabble like a pair of alley cats."

Rajic relaxed, lowered his weapons and stepped away with a smirk on his face. He backed toward the elevated platform at the end of his great hall. He sat in an ornately carved high-backed chair in the center of the platform. Next to him in a smaller chair sat an olive-skinned beauty dressed in exquisite silks from the far east. A sparkling gold amulet rested on her forehead, dangling from a bejeweled headdress. She had dispassionately observed the encounter between the two men. With a glance at her, Rajic spoke again.

"How do you even know Kendrick lives? Did your dragon trample him or not?"

"It did," Silas responded plainly, "but when I returned to the cavern his body was not there. I assume the other man took him away but whether as a man or a corpse, I do not know."

"And who is the other man?" the woman asked, leaning forward in her chair. "Do you know him?"

Rajic's jaw tensed as he glanced in her direction through narrow eyes.

"I do not, Queen Amla," Silas answered.

Rajic leaned close to his queen, whispered tersely in her ear, then backed away slowly. The queen leaned back in her chair.

"We must reconvene the council. You and I cannot make a decision alone."

"Let's not play games, Raj. Just now you were ready to kill me without so much as a word from the council. You

CHAPTER THREE

don't expect me to believe that their tepid opinions suddenly matter to you, do you? We both know that of the four of us, we two have the true influence, the power to see things done. Hugo is nothing but wind and arrogance and Sanniya is a shriveled old hag. We are the ones to determine how the rise of the dragon masters will happen."

The Queen laughed. Rajic shot her a smoldering look.

"You are a crafty old man," she said, leaning away from her husband. "You play to my husband's vanity well but it does not escape my notice. Though I would enjoying watching Rajic kill you, I am beginning to like you."

"I am touched, your highness," Silas snipped, "but spare me the tearful embrace just now, your husband and I have work to do."

"On with it then," Rajic snapped, motioning to his queen to be silent.

Silas paused deliberately, deliberating how much more to reveal.

"I also have reason to believe that our council is no longer hidden."

"What? Is there a traitor among us?"

"Not a traitor, a fugitive." Silas hesitated, but there was no advantage to be gained in keeping the secret any longer. "Years ago I snatched Kendrick's daughter away from him. For over a decade she's been my captive. After the confrontation with Kendrick in the cave I returned to my dwelling to find her gone."

"You told this girl of our plans?" Rajic threatened.

"Don't be foolish," Silas snapped. "I told her nothing. But she is a keen young woman. In ten years who's to say what she's perceived through observation and inference? We must assume she knows all and act accordingly."

Rajic steamed visibly. His voice rose with each phrase.

"First you dare come here to confess that your dragon's lair was discovered and now this? What other incompetence am I to be subjected to?"

Silas did not respond, calmly eyeing the couple. He'd learned long before that dominance could be maintained by controlling the pacing of a conversation. He waited.

"Well?" Rajic demanded, the red flush of rage rising up the sides of his neck.

Silas looked to Queen Amla.

"You really should help him get control of that temper. He's going to do himself harm."

A barely visible smirk appeared on the Queen's full lips.

"Do not address the woman!" Rajic screamed. "She is nothing! You must contend with me and I've wasted enough time on such incompetence."

Rajic shot from the throne and rushed toward Silas who stood unflustered. Upon reaching the old man Rajic towered over him, breathing heavily. The older man waited, unmoved, his hand on his dagger.

"You have spies, I assume?" Silas asked.

"Of course I do," Rajic answered through gritted teeth.

"You must send out your most skilled spy to discover what is known about us and to identify the man who was with Kendrick. That man is at least as much a concern to us as Kendrick, possibly more."

"Why?"

Rajic's head snapped around at the sound of his queen's voice. Silas continued, amused at the tension between them.

"Don't you see? Kendrick confronted me in the hopes of recovering his daughter. A futile gesture but understandable for a father. But the other man… he is a different case entirely."

"What do you mean?" asked Amla, who ignored her husband's irritation.

"What do I mean? Queen Amla, what kind of man assaults a dragon? Alone? With only a sword?" He paused to let his words sink in. "I've never met such a man… until now. If we do not kill him immediately he will be our undoing."

*****†*****

The throne room of Rajic, ruler of the eastern side of The Ridge brimmed with tension as the large door closed behind Silas. The dragon lord had not moved from the place

CHAPTER THREE

where he had confronted Silas. Behind him, his wife remained seated on the raised platform, dreading what was coming. Through a clenched jaw, Raj spoke.

"If you *ever* disrespect me like that before others..."

"I did not mean any disrespect, my lord," Amla said. "I meant to protect you."

Rajic spun around.

"Protect me? From what, that old man?" he said, waving his arm at the door.

"From yourself," she answered. Rajic stormed up the platform stairs, yanking her from her seat.

"I do not need your protection!" he shouted into her face. "What I need from you is your silence. You think I am vain, prone to manipulation by a doddering old man. But I have him in the palm of my hand, ready to squeeze him to dust! He is nothing. You are nothing."

The queen tumbled into her seat as he shoved her backward. His words wounded her deeply and she was frightened. But her silence had not proven helpful in the past so she continued.

"Raj, if you were more willing to heed my words in private I would not need to speak them in public. But no, you are always right, always the one who knows best. Even *you* don't notice everything. I see things, I perceive things... you may not believe it but I desire to be an asset, not a thorn in your side. Why can't you see that?"

Rajic bent low, thrusting his finger in her face.

"You will hold your tongue or it will be cut out. Do you understand?"

She nodded.

"And if you *ever* disrespect me before others, in any way, your life will become a pit of misery. Believe me."

His eyes bored into her until she looked away in tears. He spun away and disappeared through a doorway behind the platform.

"It already is," she whispered.

CHAPTER FOUR

Seated inside the barn on stools, logs, and overturned milk buckets were most of the residents of Newtown. They had come to discuss what had come to be known as "the dragon problem." Everyone had been affected by the attack weeks earlier and were eager to hear what could be done to prevent another. Hon looked around the room, surrounded by the familiar faces, sounds, and smells of the village where he had grown up. It was good to be home though he did not know for how long.

Rowan began the meeting just as Lord Kendrick entered, hobbling in with the aid of crutches and his daughter's shoulder. His broken legs were freshly and tightly wrapped with plaster-soaked strips of linen that had hardened into an immovable shell surrounding his legs.

"Lord Kendrick, I see that Leechy was set loose upon you," Rowan joked.

"Yes, and I was defenseless against him. I thought the splints I had to wear on the journey from Montfall were uncomfortable. These 'casts,' as he calls them are like wearing hip-high boots made of granite! Quite annoying, but I am thankful, nonetheless. He insists my legs will heal without any problem."

"He is the best surgeon I have ever met," Rowan replied. "You can trust his assessment."

Kendrick nodded as he leaned awkwardly against the barn wall. Camille took a seat on a stool between him and Victoria.

"When do you plan to start the journey home?" Hon asked.

"Tomorrow," Kendrick said. "Camille insisted that I take a day of rest to recover from the journey and one day is all the cooperation she will get from me. I am eager to be home to Patrice and our son, Cedrick. We have much to celebrate, having our dear Camille back," he said, looking at his daughter over his shoulder. "But I am also eager to prepare a defense against what I am convinced will be an all-out assault. Silas promised as much. We've sent Gregory ahead to announce our approach and to get the preparations started."

"We have the same concerns, you and us," Rowan said, "So I'm glad you are here for this discussion." He turned from Lord Kendrick to address the entire assembly. "I suppose that some of you have not heard the full account of what we discovered over the past few weeks, so let me begin by summarizing. You all know that we left three weeks past to search for Camille and to find and destroy the two dragons that attacked our village. You also know that Lord Kendrick had already traveled this far tracing the route of a messenger who delivered a letter to him from Camille's captor, Silas. Together, we made our way up The Ridge and along its top until we reached the northern mountains. Then we headed east. One night, camped high up on a cliff, Hon noticed something in the sky. It turned out to be the dragons that attacked Newtown. They were 'dancing' as Hon likes to call it, diving back and forth in front of the full moon. It was an amazing sight. When dawn came they parted company, the black one flying into the woods far to the east, the red one disappearing over the mountaintop where we were camped.

"Hon suggested that we search for the red dragon first since Silas, who had taken Camille was its master. The thought was that if we found the dragon we might find Camille. So we split up, searching the mountain all the next day. Myself, Rupert, and Gregory, Lord Kendrick's other man, all returned to camp that evening as agreed, having found nothing. But Lord Kendrick and Hon did not return. Both of them had discovered the dragon's lair from different entrances and did not know the other was there.

To make the story brief, Lord Kendrick bravely confronted Silas single-handedly in spite of the dragon's presence. Just as Silas loosed his dragon to attack Lord Kendrick, Hon leapt from atop a pile of boulders that had

CHAPTER FOUR

fallen against the cavern wall and plunged his sword into the dragon's eye."

The room exploded with a combination of gasps, cheers, and applause. Victoria squeezed Hon's hand, smiling proudly but uncomfortably. Rowan continued after the commotion settled down.

"In a bewildered rage the dragon rushed for the exit, charging over the top of Lord Kendrick. As you can see, Lord Kendrick bears the injuries of that encounter."

"It's one I'll never forget," Lord Kendrick interjected. The crowd laughed nervously.

"Sadly, Camille was not in the cave and we were forced to make our way down the mountain to Montfall, a nearby village. Unknown to us she had escaped on her own and was already past Montfall, actually heading in this direction on the forest road on the other side of The Ridge. That is where Gerrard found her, collapsed from exhaustion in the middle of the road."

"Who is Gerrard?" a woman asked. Rowan paused, casting an overwhelmed look in Hon's direction and gesturing in Gerrard's direction.

"There is so much to tell, please be patient. Gerrard here is a friend of Hon's father. He is the woodsman who came among us last evening."

"What?" the same woman interjected, "Hon, I thought your father was dead?"

"No," Hon replied, "While we were at The Twins I received word that he was alive, living in Brookhaven. I made my way there immediately."

Murmurs went up from the group.

"I'll leave it to Hon to recount that story another time," Rowan resumed. " Gerrard decided it would be an easier journey for his injured mule to travel downhill to Montfall and by the hand of Providence our paths crossed there. There is nothing more to tell except for a long journey home."

The villagers applauded.

"Now, you may have heard rumors so let me put the facts before you. As you know from the attack we suffered here last month, we are facing more than one dragon. What is more, they have masters who to some degree are directing their movements. Camille has informed us that there are four of them, three men and one woman."

A gasp went up from the crowd.

"Each of them has a beast of their own. We are not sure, but the black one that attacked Newtown is suspected to belong to Rajic, the new ruler of Thurmond's lands over The Ridge. One of the other dragon lords is known to Gerrard, a man named Lord Hugo. He resides in the far northern country beyond the mountains. The woman remains a mystery to us.

"As you can see, we are up against more than simply defending our town against mindless beasts. There is a purpose behind what is happening, one that some of us feel we must somehow stand against. Hon? Would you like to take it from here?"

Hon stood up awkwardly, unaware that Rowan was going to ask him to speak. Victoria squeezed his hand as he rose, giving him a half-hearted smile.

"All of you know that I was snatched away from my home by one of these dragons when I was small. I don't know for sure but it could have been the very one we encountered in the cave." He shifted his weight nervously. "Gerrard has encouraged me to consider heading up a group of men to hunt down and destroy the dragons and their masters. I believe that I will. I think that I'm meant to. First we must prepare for the possibility of another attack on our village. Lord Kendrick will be doing the same at his castle.

"We know the dragon's hide can be pierced by the force of a crossbow bolt so we must buy or build as many crossbows as we can. But Lord Kendrick has another idea; we should be able to fashion crossbows on a larger scale: six, or possibly even ten feet across. They would operate on the same principle as a normal crossbow but make use of a crank to draw them. We would mount them atop a cart or wagon for the sake of mobility and design a way for their base to spin and be raised and lowered. With a weapon of this kind we could conceivably take down a dragon with one well-aimed shot."

CHAPTER FOUR

Murmurs of interest and approval made their way around the room.

"Does anyone have questions? No? Then, I believe we are finished."

A handful of craftsmen made their way to Rowan as the rest headed back to their daily chores. Gerrard approached Hon, speaking quietly.

"Nicely done, lad. A significant plan for the defense of yer townsfolk. And might I add, yer wise to mention nothing of the men you intend to recruit. If word of it got out then all you seek to gain by it would be lost."

"Yes," Hon replied, "but how do I recruit men for a covert purpose when it's too dangerous to speak of the purpose at all?"

"That, lad is a trick you've gotta' be figuring out."

*****†*****

At Gerrard's suggestion Hon had invited a small, but select group to meet by the river after dark. He sat alone on a large boulder beside the river, watching as a handful of torches moved his way.

God, I need Your help. How do I determine who is to be trusted and who cannot be? How do I find men who are strong enough to bear the weight of secrecy and the danger of what we must do? He sighed, seeing the torch bearers almost upon him. I will trust You. It's all I can do.

The first to arrive were Rowan and his son Frederick. Hon and Frederick had grown up together, playing, hunting, and discovering the new land around their village. As they got older they had trained together under Rowan to be a part of Newtown's defense.

Next was Gerrard, the old woodsman Hon had met at his father's house across The Ridge. The wisdom the old man possessed, along with his quirky personality had captivated Hon immediately. Preston, one of the soldiers who had served with Rowan under Lord Thurmond before the group settled Newtown was next to arrive.

The last to come were Camille, Lord Kendrick, and Victoria. Hon smiled. Without delay, he began the meeting.

"I asked you to meet me here where the rush of the waters can mask our discussion. We have crucial matters to discuss that must remain private. Before you leave you will be given a choice to join a small but important band of people in a mission that I hope will save the region from the dragon lords. No matter your decision I ask that everything that is spoken tonight be kept entirely secret. If anything we discuss reaches the dragon lords our efforts will be entirely wasted. Agreed?"

Every head nodded in agreement.

"What I spoke of this afternoon was for the defense of Newtown. But more must be done than simply mount a defense. I mentioned the possibility of finding and destroying the dragons and their masters and that is exactly what we must do.

"The dragon lords will not be dissuaded from their plans. Camille has informed us that they are bound together through a long-standing generational pact of some kind. They view conquest as their destiny, a fate foretold by their ancestors. They will work to overcome every defense we develop. For that reason we cannot be defenders only, we must become aggressors, disruptors, and destroyers of their plans.

"But we won't be able to do it through strength of arms. We are greatly outmatched in that kind of battle. Though Lord Kendrick has an army we know that at least one of the dragon lords also has an armed force. And they have the dragons, besides. What is more, were we to begin amassing an armed force we would draw too much attention and would quickly become a target. So even though we are outmatched, we are not outwitted."

He paused and looked to Rowan before continuing. The older man nodded.

"We must think differently. We can equip a small group who will learn the specialized skills needed to become dragon killers. We will also develop a network of trusted spies, men

CHAPTER FOUR

or women who will work to get close to the dragon masters somehow, to discover their plans before they are implemented. And, though I hesitate to say it, some may be asked to serve as assassins."

The group looked uncomfortably from one to the other.

"It is an unsettling thought but the evil we face is great. If one of our people gets close enough to make the attempt on a dragon master's life it seems we must."

Victoria spoke up.

"I understand the reasons and agree, mostly. But I struggle to know if it is truly the right path. Killing a person in defense of Newtown is one thing but to stalk and kill a person in cold blood, even one of these dragon masters... it seems to be different somehow."

Hon wished Victoria was not the one to bring up the objection. He did not want to disagree with her in front of the others. He was relieved when Rowan stepped into the conversation.

"How is it different?" Rowan asked. "Were they marching into our village, leading an army of ruffians we would not hesitate to let arrows fly. Were they astride their dragons, flying overhead as their beasts spewed fire and poison, we would do all we could to shoot them from the sky. In moments like that the choice is clear because the danger is near us. But here, sitting beside the river in the moonlight it seems far removed. But the danger is not removed from us, it only seems to be." He waved his arm toward Newtown. "Like Abigail who lies fighting an unseen poison within her body, we must realize that these dragon lords are a poison across the land. Though unseen, they are a very present danger to us all.

"Camille, you have spent eleven years in Silas' company. You tell us... am I speaking the truth?"

Camille looked up through watery eyes.

"Yes. You are right. Silas has killed men simply for the pleasure of it without any sign of remorse. My years in his cold hut were those of continual suffering and deprivation. He enjoyed making it so." She wiped her eyes roughly. "I do not tell you to gain your pity. I want you to know what sort of man he is. I'm convinced the others are the same. Their overarching desire is to dominate all lands through force and the strength and power of the dragons."

The weight of Camille's words and experience settled over the group in a hush. All eyes were on Victoria.

"I understand that," Victoria said. "I don't doubt that you have suffered and that he is… that they are evil. I just struggle to know what is right when it comes to killing in cold blood."

Hon spoke up.

"Since the day our town was established we have sought to be on the side of right. We have been decent people, God-fearing people. I believe that we still are."

Victoria nodded her head. Hon continued.

"The question before us is this; Can we still be decent, God-fearing people yet be violent aggressors against evil men? I believe the Lord gives us some guidance in finding the answer. I've never been a good reader but Abigail has often read us the ancient stories, Victoria. You know the ones I mean, where God commanded his people to wipe out entire races that were evil.

"Don't miss that point, God commanded that His people wipe out entire races as they sought to inhabit their promised homeland. They were to kill men, women, and children. The only reason I can fathom is that those races were entirely corrupt. They even made human sacrifices of their own children."

"You may think it strange in light of what I just shared," Camille interjected, "but I struggle, just here. I have no doubt that Silas deserves death. But I do struggle to know my own mind in the matter… whether I feel that way out of hatred for the man who kidnapped and abused me or if I feel so because it is just and right."

"Aye lass," Gerrard answered. "I understand yer quandary. I felt the same in the months after Hugo murdered me wife and daughter. I asked meself, 'Am I only hatin' the man who done me wrong or is the purity of righteousness present in me anger somehow?' What I come to know is that

CHAPTER FOUR

good folks like us can be capable of both at the same time, hatred and righteousness. The tricky part is in knowing how to let the latter of the two be the motivation fer our actions 'stead of the first."

"I appreciate that Gerrard," Victoria said, her lower lip quavering, "and I agree. The only way we can tell the difference is to answer the most important question: Is God directing us to do this like He did His people in the past?"

"Though I do not like the thought of being labeled 'assassin,' or 'murderer,' " Hon said, "and I'm not even sure I would be able to do the deed when the moment comes, I do sense a conviction that this is the right course for me. It may be a choice each person has to make for themselves, before God."

The group nodded with understanding.

"I think we've all known that there was a special purpose for you, Hon," Rowan agreed, "though I wasn't sure what form it would take. This makes sense to me. It seems right. As for me, I am in full support of the cause. But don't feel I can be one of the men who are out seeking inroads against the enemy. My place is here. The village needs me and my family needs me. I'll do all I can to support from this end and to serve as another set of ears to help consider ideas and strategy but I won't be joining you on the road."

"It comforts me to hear you say so, Rowan," Preston said. "I was feeling that I'd be seen as a coward to say it, but I feel the same. My heart is with you Hon but my place is here among those who would defend Newtown."

"Well, I'm with you all the way," Fredrick spoke up. "I'm of age and ready to do my part. It frightens me to think of it and I'll need more training but I feel I must join you, Hon."

"Thank you, Fredrick. I'm happy to have you alongside," Hon replied. "And I completely understand what you and Rowan feel," Hon said, nodding at Preston.

"Lad, I'm clearly not the one to be leading the charge against dragons but I can help in other ways." Gerrard said. "I know the woods and tracking and I know me share of folks who would be sympathetic to yer cause. I know a wee bit about that rascal Hugo, too. So when it's time to face him down I'll be able to add a fair bit to the mix. And I've just thought of another way the hand of Providence may have afforded me to help. Me pigeons. I took a fancy to the wee birdies years ago and have been sending messages back and forth with some acquaintances fer some time. There's a coop down to the south near the edge of the desert lands, another up at the monastery, and one over to Montfall. Within three to six months we could do the work to establish one here. 'Twould be a much quicker way to send communications."

"Gerrard, thank you. I know it will be a great help to us," Hon replied.

"And another thing," Gerrard continued. "Once you've found yer mighty men you'll need a hidden place to do some trainin'. Me forest home is available."

"Thank you," Hon said.

Lord Kendrick spoke up.

"Men like Rajic and Hugo undoubtedly have enemies. You need someone who can teach you how to find them and how to determine whether they can be trusted. Hon, I am happy to introduce you to Quinn, the man who heads and trains my spies. He is a loyal man and wise in the ways of stealth and intrigue. If you feel the time is right you are welcome to join us as we travel home tomorrow."

"I am grateful," Hon answered, glancing at Victoria, whose eyes were cast down. "I will consider it tonight and let you know before you leave. But I like the thought of being home at least a few days. I could come later."

"Whatever you feel is best," Lord Kendrick said. "Just know you are welcome."

Hon searched the faces before him. Nobody seemed hesitant or unwilling with the exception of Victoria.

"Victoria? What are you thinking?" he inquired.

She replied with a roll of her big eyes.

"I don't know. I guess I'm afraid. I'm afraid of us…" she paused and looked directly at Hon before continuing, "…of you, doing the wrong thing. I know there is much to be done before any of the truly dangerous things need to happen but

CHAPTER FOUR

I'm still leery of the whole thing. Gerrard and Rowan, I have heard your words about the rightness of the cause. They make sense up here," she said, touching her temple, "but I haven't come to grips with them in here," she finished as her hand went to her chest.

Hon knelt in front of her and reached up, touching her cheek with the back of his fingers.

"You take all the time you need, Victoria." he said.

CHAPTER FIVE

Though it only took three days, the journey home seemed eternal to Camille. Her desire to see her mother and her younger brother whom she'd never met was torturously strong. But her father's injuries required that they travel at a slower pace. The dawn of the third morning she awoke feeling as if she would burst from the suspense. Each beat of her horse's hooves marked the slow passage of time until at last she saw the towers of her father's castle rising before her on the horizon.

"There it is, father! It's been so long but I still remember that silhouette! I can hardly wait anymore!"

"I have no doubt," her father replied from the cart behind her horse. "I've missed your mother and brother but I can only imagine how you must feel. If death could come from too much joy I would be burying both you and your mother this evening. It's going to be a glad reunion."

"What is he like, father? Cedrick, I mean. It breaks my heart that he is approaching twelve years old and I have never even seen him."

"He is a fine young man, full of energy and curiosity," her father answered. "Honestly, I've had a hard time restraining his eagerness. He reminds me a lot of you. Among those his age Cedrick is unrivaled with both spear and quarterstaff."

Rupert, captain of Kendrick's guard added to the description.

"He's even bested a few of the less experienced men. He has his father's skill for anticipating his opponent's moves and a keen mind to go with it."

Kendrick laughed.

"Were I to allow it he would already be in the field battling alongside the soldiers. Lately he's been pestering me to allow him to train with Quinn. Given what Hon is attempting to do it may not be such a bad idea, though I'm not sure his mother is ready for him to be in harm's way like that."

"Oh father, we have so much catching up to do, so much to rebuild. I wish time would move faster so that we could be there!"

She fell silent at her father's chuckle, knowing that he delighted in her eagerness. The towers rose slowly in the distance. Her mind returned to the secret conversation by the Rillebrand outside Newtown three nights past. She wanted to be involved somehow but didn't know how she could. She had no training for battle and the last eleven years had not afforded any opportunity to travel or be out in public. She felt awkward and uncouth, as if she would be sorely out of place in any setting.

Dusk fell and they had already turned west, down the road that led to the small village of Castlegate and then beyond to their home. Sensing the end of their journey the horses picked up their pace. The fresh air of freedom was intoxicating to Camille. There was so much to be thankful for: her rescue by Gerrard, her father and his patient love that pulled her back to sanity, Hon and Victoria and the people of Newtown, and the eminent reunion with her mother and brother. After eleven years in seclusion she couldn't believe that life could be so good. She turned her head toward the north, looking back toward Newtown. A movement caught her eye, far up in the darkening sky.

"Father! There, to the north," she said, pointing. "Do you see it?"

Her father followed her extended arm. There was a look on his face she couldn't remember ever seeing before. Fear.

"No!" Lord Kendrick exclaimed. "We've not been able to prepare. To the castle! Ride hard!"

Responding instinctively to her father's urging, Camille dug her heels into her horse and they set off, the cart that bore Lord Kendrick banging and bouncing along behind. She stole a look over her shoulder and saw what had filled her father with such concern. A dragon.

CHAPTER FIVE

Rounding a bend in the road, Castlegate came quickly into view but they did not slow. Kendrick shouted to the villagers as they barreled through the town.

"To arms! To arms! The beast has returned! To arms!"

Screams erupted amidst the scramble of the villagers, mothers directing their children inside, men reaching for pitchforks, spears, and bow and arrow. In a blur the travelers were through the town and charging up the hill beyond. Rupert pulled a brass horn from his belt and blew a piercing note as they bore down on the front gate. Within seconds the portcullis rose before them and the trio rushed through.

"A dragon approaches! To arms! To arms!" Rupert shouted.

Soldiers scurried to their positions atop the walls. Signal fires, stacked neatly atop each corner of the wall were lit to provide additional light. At that moment a powerful screech erupted from the sky and a blur of white swooped over the top of the east tower.

"It's not the same one," Kendrick yelled. "It's not Silas' dragon."

The horses came to a dusty halt outside the stables and Rupert leapt from his horse and hurried away, calling out orders as he went. Kendrick clamored over the side of the wagon, crutches in hand.

"Camille, get inside the manor house, now! Find your mother and brother!"

*****†*****

Camille ran into the keep in search of her mother. Her mind compared every face she encountered with the picture of her mother drawn from the annals of her memory. A mild panic gripped her as her eyes bounced from face to face. Amazingly, she remembered the layout of the castle as if she'd never been gone. At the top of the stairs she rounded a corner as the chaotic sounds of the attack drove her deeper into the keep.

She made her way down the wide hallway to what she knew to be her mother's sitting room. Rushing through the doorway she was shocked to find the small table, set for tea. The finest lace was spread, her grandmother's fine tea set was polished and laid out in proper order and a vase of her favorite yellow roses were the centerpiece. A familiar voice came from the next room.

"Madeline, they should be here any minute. I want everything to be ready just like it was that day, and…"

Her mother's words stopped short as she walked into the room to find her long lost daughter standing before her. Patrice's eyes pooled instantly as her hands went to her clenching throat.

"Camille?"

The two rushed together, collapsing into each other's arms as a flood of love, sorrow, regret, and joy overwhelmed them. They stayed locked in their embrace, their foreheads together until they were interrupted by wild sounds from the hallway. Patrice looked toward the doorway with a quizzical expression.

"What's happening out there?"

"It's a dragon! It appeared just before we came through the gate. Father is still outside helping Rupert direct the troops."

"But Peter said that your father has broken both of his legs! How does he think he will be able to…"

"Mother, he will be fine. I've watched him these past few weeks and I believe he knows his limits. And the men will need the reassurance of his presence. The monster is huge and they are frightened."

Patrice burst into tears.

"We prepared your birthday tea just like it was on that day when he took you. I hate that man. He's still bringing his rot into our lives. I want to see him burn in…"

"But mother," Camille interrupted, "this dragon is white."

*****†*****

CHAPTER FIVE

Another screech pierced the air as Kendrick turned to see the beast descending talons first into a cluster of archers atop the east wall. The men scattered like chaff, the few arrows they were able to release bouncing from the dragon's impenetrable hide. The pale monster rose high with a shriek, tossing the men it had clutched in its huge fore-claw to the ground far below.

"Crossbows! Call for the crossbowmen!" Lord Kendrick shouted.

Soldiers spilled from every doorway, some still pulling mail over their heads, many turned toward the armory to comply with Kendrick's command. Shouts rose and multiplied across the lower bailey as men recognized the voice of their Lord.

"Lord Kendrick has returned! Our Lord has returned! Look alive men!"

High above the beast continued its assault, diving time after time upon the battlements, scraping men from the parapets like crumbs from toast. Kendrick was amazed at the power of the monster as it ripped men and stone alike from the top of the castle. He felt helpless, hobbling up the stairs in an effort to get closer to the fight.

"Crossbowmen, to arms!" he shouted again.

After what seemed an eternity men bearing crossbows appeared one by one atop the walls. Kendrick directed them.

"Make every shot count, men!"

A surge of men bearing crossbows rushed past Kendrick, almost toppling him from his crutches. A familiar young man was among them.

"Cedrick!"

The boy turned to see his father, waved with a grin, then focused his attention on the dragon as it made a wide arc to return for another attack. Kendrick's first instinct was to command the boy inside but he realized that in the heat of the action and with the blood rushing through his veins his son would never hear him. He watched as Cedrick tilted the weapon downward, placing his left foot in the stirrup at the front of the crossbow as he simultaneously attached the forked gaffle to the string. With a mighty pull using his leg on one end and arm on the other, Cedrick drew the string back until the "click" of the catch was heard.

Dropping to one knee the boy lifted the weapon and loaded a bolt in one fluid motion. He placed the front stirrup atop the wall and raised the back, resting the tiller on his shoulder. Cedrick cocked his head, sighting down the length of the weapon just as the dragon came out of its turn and headed directly toward him.

Soldiers let fly with arrows and bolts as the dragon bore down on them but Cedrick did not shoot. Kendrick was proud to see his son exercising restraint. Waiting for the right opportunity was critical. The closer the beast got the larger a target it became. Each flap of the dragon's huge wings unnerved the men. Some scrambled to reload after a missed shot, others backed away, their mouths agape.

Cedrick waited. The beast was almost on top of him before he let fly, just as the dragon banked to one side. The bolt sank deeply into its left flank, inciting a horrendous moan from the beast.

As the beast passed directly over the place where Cedrick was positioned, Lord Kendrick couldn't believe what he saw. Cedrick rose to his full height, raised his arm high, and let the beast's belly rub along his fingertips as it shot past, ducking in a flash as the massive hind legs rushed by. He watched as the monster arced high and far, away from the castle. Then the boy turned, flashed his father a wry smile, and began to reload his crossbow.

But there would not be opportunity for another shot. The beast continued to rise and floated gently away into the northern sky.

*****†*****

"Seventeen dead and countless more wounded," Rupert reported to his lord. "We've also lost the northern watchtower. The beast ripped it away like it was parchment," he said, still shaking from the rush of battle.

Pointing with a crutch, Lord Kendrick gave orders.

CHAPTER FIVE

"Get these wounded off the battlements and into the keep, immediately! And double the watch, every man bearing a crossbow. The beast may yet return. Summon the masons and every available carpenter to the great hall. We must discuss plans for new weapons and battlements. I'll be with them within the hour."

Rupert saluted and turned away. Kendrick scanned the area, seeking his son. He spied Cedrick helping a man lug a wounded soldier down the stairs. He waited until the boy was finished with the task then called to him.

"Cedrick!"

The boy smiled and came up the stairs two at a time and almost tackled his father with a strong hug.

"I'm so glad you're back! How are you? Mother told me you were injured."

"Recovering nicely. There's an old troop surgeon from Thurmond's day who lives in Newtown. He's fixed me up so well I'm tempted to ask him to attend me here."

Cedrick was listening and gathering scattered arrows from the ground at the same time.

"Cedrick, leave this work to others. We need to return to our chambers," Lord Kendrick said. "Your sister is home!"

A smile stretched across the boy's lean face. He tucked a handful of arrows into his own quiver and walked side by side with his crippled father, helping him down the staircase and into the keep. The boy was tall for his age, and handsome, already filling his tunic with the muscular physique of a man. Surprised faces bowed again and again as household servants recognized their master and the nature of his injuries. Kendrick smiled, thanking each one for their service.

"I saw what you did, Cedrick. It was an amazing shot."

The boy smiled, soaking up his father's affirmation.

"Thank you, father. I told you I am ready. I was born to be in the thick of things."

Lord Kendrick laughed.

"I'm beginning to believe you. You are naturally gifted, there's no arguing that. But I also noticed what you did as the dragon passed overhead. Son, you must guard yourself. There is a fine line between confidence and cockiness."

A confused look came over the boy's face.

"Cockiness?" He stopped to look his father in the eye. "No, you misunderstand father. Seeing it fly so, so gracefully, so closely overhead… It was beautiful… amazing. Father, I was compelled to reach out. It was like the urge to lift a rosebud to your nose… or, or the desire to dive into a cool spring on a hot day. Father, I had to touch it. I *had* to."

Lord Kendrick looked at his son curiously. He'd forgotten for a moment that his son was still very much a boy, able to be intoxicated with the wonder of the world even in the heat of danger. In a way, he envied him.

He smiled and tousled his son's hair as they turned again toward the keep. His thoughts went to his wife and daughter. Though they were inside for the duration of the battle he wanted to make sure they were unharmed. He found his two ladies huddled in the sitting room arm in arm, talking in rapid whispers.

"Is it over? Is it gone?" Lady Patrice asked. Upon noticing the large casts on her husband's legs, Patrice extended her arms to him.

"Oh James! What you have endured to bring our Camille back to us!"

"I am only one of many," he replied. "You must meet them all so they can be properly thanked."

At that, Lord Kendrick pulled away from his wife's embrace, directing her attention to Camille and Cedrick. They were locked in a tight embrace, both of them weeping.

*****†*****

Far to the northeast on an outcropping of rock jutting from the western side of The Ridge, Lord Hugo Champlain watched his pale dragon land gracefully atop the stony shelf. The beast was obviously winded; a sure sign that Lord Kendrick's people were given the fright of their lives.

CHAPTER FIVE

"Well done Boreas, well done," his high-timbered voice assured. "The Dragon Lords rise... they rise! The council will have to take action now and you will have your day, my pet."

The dragon moved toward him and Hugo immediately noticed the beast favoring its left, rear leg. He moved to assess the damage. The well trained beast endured his prodding hands, wincing but never making a sound.

"The flesh has already closed up around the shaft and the bleeding is nearly stopped. We can get you home before we take further action."

With that, Hugo retrieved a leather harness from a nearby rock, threw it over the base of the beast's neck and cinched it tightly in place. The dragon dipped its long, graceful neck and Hugo lugged his massive frame up and into the makeshift saddle.

"Up my pet! We fly home to prepare for war!"

The dragon rose, limped to the edge of the cliff and cast itself into the sky, its widely spread wings bearing it northward.

CHAPTER SIX

Hon couldn't believe the destruction. Though the parapets and towers of Lord Kendrick's castle were already being repaired, the damage wrought by the dragon was immense. Stones the size of his hut in Newtown lay on the ground at the foot the castle walls. Wooden frames rose around the crumbled top of the eastern tower.

"It's unbelievable," he said to Gerrard, who had agreed to accompany him.

"Aye lad, 'tis quite a site. Powerful strong the beasts be. 'Tis good fer you to be here so soon after. Ya need to know yer enemy well and this should help you do it."

Hon and Gerrard were detained by the guards at the front gate but upon reciting the passphrase Lord Kendrick had supplied in his message, they were admitted. The parchment from Lord Kendrick had come at the hand of a rider four days earlier. As Victoria had read the letter to him Hon's heart sank into the dust. The message confirmed what he did not want to be true; staying in Newtown for a time to enjoy his newly discovered love for Victoria was impossible. The attack on Kendrick's estate was only the beginning of the havoc the dragon lords would bring and he was already behind in his preparations.

With a tear in her eye Victoria had agreed that he must go and Hon rode out with Gerrard early the next morning.

The gatehouse guards sent word to Lord Kendrick and directed Hon and Gerrard to the keep. Upon entering, a chamber maid led them to the great room where Kendrick and his family were seated around a long table. Camille rose and ran to them, throwing her arms around Gerrard.

"Mother! This is him, the man who found me on the road!" She took Gerrard's hand and led him to the table.

"I am grateful to you, sir," the teary-eyed mother said. "You don't know the blessing you have given to our family."

"Not to be disagreeable m'lady, but methinks I do know. I too have lost a daughter... at the hands of the man who holds the white dragon's leash. In me mind's eye I've experienced a glad reunion with her many a time and if it were possible to bring her back, I know how I'd feel toward the one who did it. It pleases me to no end to have been of such service to you, m'lady."

"And let's not forget Hon," Kendrick said, not rising from his place at the table. "I enjoy the breath of life because of his bravery."

Lady Patrice turned to Hon, gracefully taking his face between her dainty hands.

"How could I thank you enough, young man? James has told me what you did. You saved his life, you know?" She looked from Hon to Gerrard as her voice cracked. "My family is a family again because of the two of you."

Hon shifted uneasily.

"I'm glad I could help," he said. "In the rush of the moment you don't always think, you just act. That's all it was."

"You do yourself a discredit," Kendrick replied. "Many act in panic or fear. You did not. You acted with courage."

"Thank you," Hon said, wanting to be done with the conversation.

"Come, sit. Have you taken breakfast yet?" Kendrick asked.

"We've not," Gerrard replied, "and me stomach is telling me so!"

Hon was glad for Gerrard's wit. It eased the discomfort he felt. Lady Kendrick called for more food and the room was soon abuzz with servants.

"Gerrard, you are very welcome here but I didn't know you would be coming," Lord Kendrick said.

"Aye sir, me and Hon got to chattin' about the subject and thought I might come along to see if I could set up one of me message stations here. The pigeons, you know."

"Pigeons?" Patrice asked.

CHAPTER SIX

"Oh yes, mother," Camille answered, "Gerrard uses pigeons to send messages far and wide."

"We thought it good to establish message centers in sundry places," Gerrard continued, "and if you don't mind, this would be a good one."

"Absolutely," Patrice said, then flushed with embarrassment. "Pardon me, but I have forgotten to introduce our son Cedrick. Cedrick, Hon and Gerrard."

"Happy to meet you," Gerrard said, thrusting out his long arm. "You are the image of yer good father."

"I take that as a compliment," Cedrick replied with a smile. "I must offer my thanks as well, Gerrard. You have returned the sister I never knew. And Hon," he said, offering his hand, "I would love to hear about your encounter with the dragon first-hand. The one we faced earlier this week was a thing of beauty and terror, all at once."

Hon was impressed with the boy's manners and maturity. He seemed much older than his eleven years.

"I would have to say the same," he answered.

The conversation continued as the meal was served. Hon heard glad accounts of the Kendrick family's reunion and shared his own feelings about returning to his village. He glanced at Camille as he spoke of his newfound love for Victoria. The princess sat motionless, a faint smile on her lips as she stared at her folded hands. Soon, the conversation turned to the dragon masters.

"I would love nothing more than to be of help!" Cedrick exclaimed. "Father, what do you think? I am ready for more and feel I could be of use to Hon."

"Cedrick," Lady Patrice interrupted, "I know you believe are fully capable as a warrior and that you need to spread your wings, but this... this is the most dangerous thing I can imagine. I don't feel easy about it. You've not even reached your twelfth year."

"But he does have the abilities of a man," Lord Kendrick inserted. "No doubt there is still much for you to learn, Cedrick but I am willing to explore the idea."

Patrice shot her husband a worried look.

"How about this," Kendrick offered. "You can accompany Hon to see Quinn this afternoon. Learn all you can. Ask questions, get a sense of what is ahead. And Hon, would you help me in assessing Cedrick's readiness? An outside opinion would be much appreciated." Hon nodded. "We can speak of it again tonight, at supper."

"Thank you father!" Cedrick beamed. "I will do all you ask!"

Kendrick patted his wife's hand sympathetically, giving her a knowing look.

"Mother? Father?" Camille asked. "Would it be alright with you if I tag along when they meet with Quinn? I'm curious what my place in all this might be and I'd like to begin exploring the possibilities as well."

Lady Patrice's mouth fell open, clearly at a loss for words. Lord Kendrick put his arm around her.

"I appreciate you seeking our counsel on the matter and we will gladly give it. But you are a young woman now, Camille," her father answered. "I see no harm in it. You have as much invested in these matters as anyone and given your experience, you have much to offer. Patrice, what do you feel about it?"

Lady Patrice stammered out a reply.

"Please forgive me, Camille. I am in shock, I suppose. After all you've been through I am surprised that you are interested in getting into this messy business at all. I imagined that the two of us would cloister ourselves away from the wickedness of it and take time to heal, together."

There was a hopeful tone to her voice.

"I do want that mother, more than anything," Camille said. "I have missed you most of all. But Hon is just beginning to make his plans, isn't that right, Hon?"

Hon nodded.

"So we will have time to do exactly as you said mother, with the exception of the 'cloistered away' part." She smiled. "I think we'll have plenty of time to reconnect *and* for me to find my place in the world."

Lord Kendrick released a soft laugh.

CHAPTER SIX

"She is your daughter, Patrice. Strong, yet sensitive. And ready to take on the world if need be." Lady Patrice blushed.

Hon liked their family immensely.

*****✝*****

Cedrick led the way up the winding stairs, high into the west tower of the keep. Quinn's quarters were specially arranged for him, allowing him a secluded place to provide training and the secrecy needed to speak freely with his subordinates. Hon and Camille followed close behind, both eagerly chatting about what lay ahead.

"I'm excited to hear more of your ideas, Hon," Camille said as they approached the door.

"If anyone can help you understand what you're up against, it will be Quinn," offered Cedrick. "He's a genius."

Hon and Camille looked at each other with raised eyebrows. Responding to Cedrick's knock, a wooden peep hole in the door slid open. A set of narrow, close-set eyes peered out the slot, barely reaching the bottom of the opening. Without a word, the peep hole slammed shut. The rattling of many locks and bolts reverberated through the heavy wooden door, ending in a long silence. Cedrick smirked as he glanced at his companions. The door cracked open with a creak and the same eyes peered out again through the crack. The door finally swung wide with a loud complaint.

"Quinn, it's good to see you," Cedrick said to the short, thick, middle-aged man who had opened the door.

"I'm happy for you," he said, turning toward a large, immaculately clean work table.

"My father told you we were coming?" the boy asked.

"Naturally," Quinn replied.

"This is Hon. He's going to be gathering a group of men to go after the dragon masters. Father said you would be a great asset to him."

"I'm sure I will," Quinn said succinctly, busying himself with two sheets of crimson parchment taken from a neat stack on a nearby shelf.

"I appreciate any help you are able to give," Hon stammered. "I'm afraid I don't know much about what I propose to do but you'll find me an eager student."

"I already have," Quinn responded.

"I'm sorry, what?"

"I *have* found you to be an eager student. You took to military training easily enough and have excelled."

"Wha… how do you know that?" Hon inquired, looking curiously at Cedrick who shrugged his shoulders and smiled.

Quinn moved around the table and faced Hon directly. The top of the older man's head barely cleared Hon's shoulder. He spoke clearly, his head tipped back to look Hon in the eye. His hands continued to fold the parchment he had brought with him.

"Hon, or should I say 'Honor'?" The older man cocked his head to the side. "If there is anyone on the rise in this land or the neighboring ones, I know about it. That includes you. You were snatched by Silas' beast at age six. The worm dropped you along Thurmond's forest road and a Sergeant Rowan found you, who by the way is becoming quite the mayor of your little community, isn't he? Thurmond adopted you as his own but only after attempting to kill your father. When Thurmond took his own life his housekeeper brought you over The Ridge into these lands. There's not much else to tell, until recently. You were a wild child, a bully, and had to learn the hard way that it wouldn't do. Since then, you've been quite the traveler; boating to The Twins, leaving to find your lost father even though it was you who was lost, and seeking out damsels in distress," he waved his arm toward Camille, not looking away from Hon.

Quinn stopped his biography to offer the parchment to Hon. He had folded it into the unmistakable shape of a dragon, wings outstretched and mouth wide.

"Do the nightmares still haunt you?"

Hon was dumbfounded, looking at the intricate sculpture in his hand.

"Uh, they aren't as frequent…"

CHAPTER SIX

"Good. I've made a note of it," Quinn said, tapping his forehead with a stubby index finger. "Nightmares are a waste of mental energy. Good you're rid of them."

Cedrick laughed behind his hand at Hon and Camille's expressions while Quinn turned back to his table. The older man stopped mid-stride, turned, and faced Camille.

"Over 4000 days in cruel captivity is a long time, lady Camille. I apologize. The protraction of your suffering is my fault."

Camille furrowed her brow in confusion. Quinn's demeanor softened as he saw her response.

"My role is to know things and if I don't know, to find them out." His head hung low and his voice dropped. "I could not find you. You became a wisp of smoke and blew away. No matter my efforts, Silas kept you hidden. The false leads and fruitless tips he concocted were quite effective. You suffered long because of my failure."

"Quinn, it's alright," Camille reassured. "You did your best."

"I did," the master spy sighed, "but sometimes best is not enough. And no m'lady, it is not alright."

"Quinn," Cedrick changed the subject, "would you have time to hear what Hon is hoping to do? He would appreciate your counsel. Father also wants you to assess my readiness to come alongside Hon, to be a help to him."

The older man smiled for the first time, then it was gone.

"I've all the time you need. It is your father's will so it will be done."

The four gathered around the table, each perching themselves on a high stool. A row of slender slits in the tower wall bathed the room in dim light. Quinn sat across from Hon, staring at him. Hon shifted in his seat.

"Begin," Quinn said.

"Oh, well, my thinking is that these dragon masters, we believe there are four of them, cannot be defeated by force of arms. It would raise too much attention. We need to form a small, well-trained, secretive force that can move quickly and quietly. But not all would be involved in battle. Some would gather information…"

"And some would be assassins," the older man interrupted, his eyes closed in thought.

"When necessary," Hon said. Quinn opened his eyes.

"Oh, it will be necessary. They will not form ranks to face you in open battle. There is no advantage to it. If one of you gets close enough to strike, you must. It is the only way to deal with those who are truly evil." Quinn closed his eyes again. "Continue."

"If I may," Camille interjected, "could I ask you a question, Quinn?"

"If you must," he replied, not opening his eyes.

"How is it that you did not know of these dragon masters until now?"

After a long silence Quinn opened his eyes.

"It vexes me to say it but these four are like vapors. Of course I know of Rajic and Hugo and Silas, and I have heard of this Queen Sanniya from the south, but I knew nothing of them as dragon masters. Here and there have been reports of dragon attacks, which I did not doubt. But there has been nothing to suggest that the beasts were connected to masters. Logic itself militates against the thought, yet it is true."

"Well, we know who they are now," Hon said. "I want to stop them from doing even more harm before they have a chance." Hon replied.

Quinn sat, staring Hon in the eye for almost a minute.

"If you will dedicate yourself I will teach you the basics of observation, asking questions without arousing suspicion, disguise and covert movement, and will instruct you in establishing listening posts in various areas. This can be accomplished within a few weeks. But you will also need someone trustworthy and capable to serve as the hub of the wheel, gathering and distributing the information you gather."

"I *will* dedicate myself. I must," Hon said. "Can you recommend someone to take on the other role?"

Camille cleared her throat, quite obviously. Hon turned to her with a smile.

CHAPTER SIX

"Did you have someone to suggest?"

*****†*****

Hon rose early for his departure. The dim glow of the rising sun was just beginning to brighten the eastern sky. Storm stomped impatiently as Hon tightened the cinch and secured his pack.

"We'll be off in a bit," Hon said. "You just be patient. You've been cooped up in the stable too long, I know."

"So laddie, off you go, eh?" a familiar voice asked from behind.

"Gerrard, you needn't have gotten up to see me off."

"Oh, I didn't laddie. I was up as it were. Years of early rising has me fixed to the practice. I couldn't sleep longer if me life were depending on it."

"Well, I'm glad for that," Hon said with a smile.

"Laddie, I was thinkin'..."

"Uh oh," Hon joked, "this could be trouble. Last time you said something like that we wound up in a gale on the Widows Peak."

Gerrard laughed, his thick beard blowing out from his mouth in great puffs.

"Well me boy, I doubt it will be quite that much fun this time but I could think up something to add to the recipe if you'd like."

"No, there's plenty of fun ahead," Hon answered. "I don't need you contriving any for me. So what is it you've been thinking about?"

"There's a man I met a time ago, a man from the east who might be willing to join yer little band of mighty men. He's got no love for Rajic, fer certain."

Hon was intrigued.

"Tell me more."

"He's a wiry lad, yer senior by about 10 years and every bit the fighter. Handles a sword like the best of 'em and like I said, has plenty of motivation to see old Raj put down."

"What's the story there?" Hon asked. Gerrard chuckled.

"I'll let him tell you… when you find him. He'll do a better job of it fer sure and if you don't find him ya won't need to know, now will ya?"

Hon shook his head.

"Gerrard, you sure enjoy stringing a person along, don't you?"

The woodsman smiled.

"How else are you gonna' have any excitement in yer life Laddie?"

The two friends laughed, exchanged a bear hug, and Hon moved to mount Storm.

"One more thing, Laddie," Gerrard called after him. Hon turned back.

"Would you take this?" Gerrard extended his hand. He held a green and red plaid cloth. He unfolded it to reveal a white square with a colorful green and red crest embroidered on it. It bore a lush tree and a sword with a crown angled across its tip. Atop the shield was a helm of armor, surrounded by a flourish of ornate garland.

"What is it?" Hon asked.

"Me family crest."

Their eyes met.

"What's this about, Gerrard?"

"Remember me tale about Hugo's betrayal and slaying of me family?" Hon nodded. "This is the sash I wore the day the scoundrel stripped me down and cast me out. The friend who slipped me food and clothing included this in his bundle." Gerrard stopped and rubbed his shaggy beard. "Laddie, what I told you about giving up me revenge is still true. It's long been entrusted to the hand of Providence. But as certain as I feel that the good Lord will give Hugo his reckoning at the right time, I also feel certain the scoundrel is to have a clear remembrance of the evil that's led to his fate. I know yer not seeking him out straight away but if you do come to face him down, would you make sure he sees this before you do him in?"

Hon took the swatch of thick fabric and tucked it inside his vest.

CHAPTER SIX

"You know I will."

CHAPTER SEVEN

A week had passed since Boreas' attack on Kendrick's castle and Lord Hugo Champlain was delighted. The effect was exactly as he had planned. The messenger bearing Rajic's invitation had just departed with his reply. Hugo laughed as he unrolled the parchment again, deciphering the century-old, cryptic code used by the dragon lords.

The council must meet. You have much to explain. Witnesses confirm it was your beast that destroyed a good part of Lord Kendrick's estate the week past, accelerating our plans beyond what we had desired. We will meet the third day after the full moon, one hour past sundown. Enter my lands through the Montfall road and follow it south. Pass the eastern road and continue south. Once you reach the western road to my fortress follow it until you come to two boulders at the base of a large elm. You will find a game trail behind it which you are to follow until you reach the meeting location.

R

He chuckled to himself. *This will be tremendous fun.*

*****†*****

Lord Hugo arrived at his destination shortly after the designated time. Sanniya's spotted mule was already present as was a small gray horse he assumed belonged to Silas. Rajic's dark horse was not visible but they were meeting so close to his fortress he wasn't sure a horse would have been necessary.

The path ended at the entrance to a small cave set into the side of a sheer cliff. It was the perfect meeting place tucked into a dense part of the northern woods. Flickers of torchlight emanated from within. Hugo passed through the entrance and found the other three dragon lords already seated around a rough table. There was no greeting and no formalities were exchanged. The moment he sat Silas got right to business.

"At our last meeting we all agreed to wait until the time was right, until the people were sufficiently agitated against Kendrick to welcome our rise. What have you done?"

Hugo poured wine into the heavy mug before him and drank greedily, intentionally making them wait. He did not like being accused even though the accusation was warranted.

"It *was* my Boreas. I will not deny it," he almost yelled, his shrill voice echoing off the cavern walls.

Silas stared at him.

"You admit to subverting the will of this council?"

"I admit to no such charge!" Hugo screamed, intentionally elevating the tone of the meeting. "You accuse before you know the facts, you old fool. If you would hold your tongue long enough to learn something you would know better than to make such a baseless claim."

Hugo paused, measuring the reaction to his outburst. Sanniya had not moved. She was seated in the shadows, a gray hood over her head, her bright eyes reflecting the flame of the candle. Rajic gripped his cup tightly and waited. Silas continued to fume.

"Boreas went on his nightly hunt. His normal habit is to snag a polar bear or caribou and he always returns by morning. But the morning in question he did not return. I was not worried. He is a well-trained beast and I knew he would return in good time. I suspected he had ranged farther than normal, which appears to be the case. It was evening before he came home. He was injured; a crossbow bolt stuck into his flank. That is when I knew that he had hunted for more than wild game. When I received your letter it was obvious what had happened."

CHAPTER SEVEN

"Why do you not have a stronger grip on your beast, you fat fool?" Silas replied, viciously.

"Don't pretend that such a thing has never happened with your beast," Hugo whined. "I know for a fact that your Hestia has taken a hit from a bolt or two in the past. They are predators, not puppies. We do well to subject them to our bidding at all! This kind of thing is to be expected from time to time, or didn't your senile old grandfather pass along that information?

"And what of you, Rajic?" Hugo continued with disdain, "Did you not know the beasts have wills of their own? Oh, but you didn't receive your legacy in the traditional, 'family' way, did you? No wonder you know no better."

Hugo's father had taught him of the lineage of his fellow dragon masters and had instructed him to use the knowledge to his advantage. Silas had inherited their commonly held legacy through his maternal grandfather since his parents were both unfit; his mother being an imbecile and his father a drunkard. Rajic's inheritance of his beast, Raat, had come by more devious means.

"As you see, I know a few things about this group." He stood, using his massive stature to accentuate his point. "I will not be blamed for a monster's instinctive drive to hunt and kill. It is to be expected by those with half a brain. If anyone is to blame it is the three of you." The tension in the room rose visibly. "Each of you insisted that we wait to reveal ourselves but our dragons do not understand such things, or even care. You might as well try to restrain a tempest."

A heavy silence descended on the group. Hugo knew that his points were valid, in a manner of speaking. What he did not know was whether they would follow his line of reasoning or reject it in favor of their suspicions. Sanniya's broken English pierced the tense silence.

"Dragons hungry for blood. Will not wait. Will of ancestors shows us way to go."

"You think the attack on Kendrick's place was some kind of fateful direction for us from our ancestors?" Silas questioned.

Sanniya nodded her head.

"That is a mad way of thinking!" Silas insisted.

Rajic entered the conversation.

"I am not one for mysticism." He clenched his teeth before continuing. "But what other choice do we have?" He glared at Hugo. "At least two of our beasts are known to the surrounding lands, perhaps even three. I hear rumors that your red and my black paid a visit to a village on the other side of The Ridge nearly a month ago, Silas. Did you know they had found each other?"

Silas shook his head as Rajic continued.

"The dragons are stirring apart from our control of them."

Silas stared at Rajic. Hugo could see that his anger was abating.

"If our two have discovered each other perhaps the others have made the same discovery?" Rajic said, looking from Hugo to Sanniya.

"As far as I know, my pale one has only ventured this far south the one time," Hugo replied coyly. He was happy for the turn the conversation had taken.

"No." Sanniya answered. "Galib, he is only in desert lands."

"Then perhaps the dragons themselves *have* determined that it is time for their masters to rise," Hugo suggested, still towering over the small table. "Imagine if the people did not hear of random attacks by dragons as they are now but instead heard tales of four dragons; black, red, green, and white working in tandem to bring castles, lands, and lords into submission. it appears my white dragon did a great deal of damage, presumably not only taking lives but wreaking havoc on a well-built castle. What would have been the outcome if all four of our beasts were there, attacking at the same time?"

The group pondered his words as they echoed through the cave.

CHAPTER SEVEN

"What you propose is risky," Rajic said. "Our beasts have been alone their entire lives. Putting them together will be unpredictable."

"Two already together," Sanniya observed in her calm, hypnotic way. "Is natural, as for all animals. Dragons know how to live together. It is masters who do not."

The cavern was silent as each member of the ancient council pondered the old woman's words.

She is right, Hugo thought. We are the ones who have a problem working together. I can see Rajic's anger smoldering even now. But no matter; in time the dragon masters will rise.

Hugo noticed a faint smile on Silas' face. The old man turned in his direction and spoke.

"I apologize, Lord Hugo," he said sarcastically. "It seems the dragons have spoken."

*****†*****

As the last sounds of the departing dragon lords receded into the forest, Rajic heard the shuffling of leather on stone in the cave behind him.

"You heard everything?" he asked.

Queen Amla emerged from the darkness, her long robe flowing loosely around her.

"Yes," Amla responded as she inched closer. "What will you do?"

"I will do what the council has determined and watch that fat deceiver very carefully. One more false word from him and I will rid our group of his treachery for good."

"But it sounded as if his dragon acted on its own."

"A lie. Could you not see it?" Rajic jabbed. "His dragon's attack was deliberate. Hugo probably stood at a distance watching his beast tear the castle apart."

"But how do you know? It could have happened just as he said. Your beast has gone out of its own accord many times."

"His story does not fit the facts," Rajic responded with irritation. "My spies tell me that Kendrick's estate was attacked just after sundown. Do you hear that? Just *after* sundown. Dragons seldom leave their lair before dark. It's not in their nature. It would have been in the air while the sun was still high to have gotten to Kendrick's estate by then."

Amla hesitated, shuffled her feet, then replied.

"I see it now, my king. You are wise to perceive it."

Rajic glared at her.

"I grow weary of your patronizing, Amla."

She took a step backward.

"I do not intend to patronize you," she said, "only to be cautious."

"Cautious? What do you have to be cautious of?"

A thick silence gathered between them. Amla was clearly weighing her words.

"How am I to answer such a question?" she blurted. "When your anger is so near the surface the slightest breeze can stir it into flame… and you ask me what reason I have to be cautious?"

Rajic glared at her.

"Hugo has forced your hand and it infuriates you. I can see it, so I tread lightly."

His hot eyes had not left her face.

"You speak as if I have no reason to be angry," he said, evenly. "That fat wretch has intentionally gone against the will of the council. He pushes us to do as he wishes and I will not be pushed."

Amla nodded, saying nothing. Rajic clenched his jaw. Her silence provoked him all the more.

"You act as if I am a snake, poised to strike at you any moment," he spit.

"Can you blame me?" she defended. "It is those who have already been bitten who are most leery."

"Watch yourself," he threatened.

"Or what? You'll hit me again? You think you are a strong man but what kind of man raises his hand against a woman? Not a man, an insecure boy."

Rajic flew across the cavern, grabbing his wife by the shoulders. Amla screamed at him through a rush of tears.

CHAPTER SEVEN

"Hit me! Do it! It will only prove that what I'm saying is true! Go ahead!"

He trembled with rage but shoved her away. She continued screaming at him.

"Why did you take me in the first place? Just because you could? If you didn't want me to be at your side you should have left me as I was."

Her words lodged in Rajic's mind just enough to make him pause, but not enough to make him care.

She just might be of use. Why haven't I thought of it before?

He turned away.

"You want to help me?" he asked.

"Yes," she sobbed.

He stood motionless, his back to her, his mind twisting through the possibilities.

"You are right," Rajic said, turning to face her. "I have not given enough thought to how you can help me. I am sorry. Will you forgive me?"

Her shocked expression revealed that he would have to tread lightly or risk frightening her away from carrying out his will.

"Ye..." She stopped and raised an eyebrow. "Yes, I do. What is it?"

"I've been a fool not to see it before. If you truly want to help me rise, then there *is* something you can do."

"Really?"

He smiled and motioned for her to come to him. She inched forward until she stood a few feet away. Rajic took her hands and looked into her eyes.

"You need some time away, my dear. Why don't you take the next week to prepare for a little trip?"

"I don't see wha..." he raised his finger to her lips and chuckled.

"You will be my personal emissary to Lord Kendrick. Think of it... my own queen, coming to seek the help of one assumed to be an adversary. I'm certain that with your charms you will be very convincing."

"But.. but it's a ruse?"

Another laugh.
"You understand me perfectly."

CHAPTER EIGHT

The dark, ale smelling room was not the kind of place Hon wanted to be but it *was* the kind of place he would find the type of men he was looking for. He needed tough, fearless men and from what he'd seen since entering the place there was no doubt that he'd find them. But would they commit to a task as dangerous and thankless as the one he had to offer, or were they too independent and self-serving? It seemed impossible but he asked his Lord to lead the way.

Hon nursed his drink and watched the activity in the musty tavern. To his left, four men gambled away their week's earnings, becoming more out of their wits with each swig of ale. Beyond them, a table of tradesmen laughed and shared stories. In the far corner, a man of approximately 30 years sat, eating his meal in solitude. With the exception of the barmaid who had refilled his tankard twice already nobody went near him or even looked in his direction.

Quinn had taught Hon the things that indicate a man who is better left alone, and the man in the corner bore them all. A deep scar traversed each of his cheeks. More than one weapon adorned his belt. His demeanor made it clear that he was not looking for company. All of that was enough to make Hon look elsewhere were it not for one thing; he matched the description of the man from the east that Gerrard had recommended.

Rising from his perch, his drink in his hand, Hon made his way across the dimly lit room to the corner table. The man did not raise his head though Hon was certain his approach had been noticed. He slowed his pace as he approached the table, keeping his hands where the man could see them. The stranger looked up briefly, catching Hon's eye then back to his plate. He scraped up chunks of meat with his knife and thumb, raising the bites to his mouth time and again with no further acknowledgement of Hon's presence.

"A woodsman named Gerrard sent me here to find a man named Sandip," Hon began. "From the description he gave me, I believe you are him."

The olive skinned man pushed his empty plate away and took a long drag from his mug, giving no indication that Gerrard's name held any meaning for him. He wiped his mouth and motioned to the bench across from him. Hon took a seat.

"What does the old man of the woods want from me?" he asked, in a heavy eastern accent.

"He doesn't want anything. He's recommended you to me for a… a job." Hon replied.

The man pulled out a dagger and began trimming his nails. He looked up and waited for Hon to continue.

"I need men who are fearless and brave. Men who are willing to sacrifice for the sake of others."

Sandip burst out laughing.

"Fearless, brave, *and* sacrificial? What you seek is a fairy tale then, you see?"

"Perhaps," Hon answered. "But I have to try."

"What is this job that requires such heroes?"

"A secret one," Hon said.

Sandip looked up.

"Oh? Not only fearless and brave but *naive* as well."

Hon rose, suddenly feeling foolish. "I'm sorry I bothered you," he said, moving from the table.

"Sit down," Sandip said. "I will hear of this job."

"How can I know you can be trusted to keep it quiet?" Hon replied.

The Easterner smiled.

"You don't. But you will have to, you see?"

"Easy to say, but I can't be too careful. Were I to be discovered trying to recruit men for this cause things would go very badly for me."

"Who are you hiding it from?" the man asked. "Kendrick? Rajic?"

CHAPTER EIGHT

Hon smiled and said nothing.

"Since the old man of the woods is involved he must approve of your cause, right?" Sandip asked.

"He does," Hon answered. "In fact, it was his idea."

"And what did he tell you about me? Surely not that I'm strong, brave, and sacrificial?"

"He told me what he remembered of you, but emphasized that he's not seen you for some time. Men change and not always for the better."

"This I know," he answered, sitting back in his chair. "Why does the woodsman think I will be interested in your job? I know there must be some reason, you see?" he asked.

Hon waited, choosing his words carefully. He leaned across the table so his words would be heard by no one else.

"He believes you may have reason to… uh, dislike a certain man on the other side of The Ridge."

Sandip clicked his dagger loudly into its scabbard and sat up straight, his lips pursed. His eyes bored into Hon's. He clasped his hands tightly on the tabletop and leaned in Hon's direction.

"What is your name?"

"Hon."

Sandip paused, then spoke in sharp but hushed tones.

"Hon. I must tell you… the word 'dislike' cannot begin to describe my feelings. Rajic is the vilest of my race and a shame upon it. The man who rids the world of his putrid breath would bring great blessing, you see? If you are making plans to go against him," Sandip stopped, clenched his jaw, and sat back, "I would be interested in hearing more."

Hon smiled.

"Then we should speak in a place that is more private."

"Come with me," Sandip replied, tossing a few coins on the table as he rose.

*****†*****

The two left Westbridge by way of the road that linked it to its twin but before crossing the bridge they took a narrow path toward the river's edge. The trail led away from the bridge for some distance and ended in a small circle of large rocks, concealed by trees. The roar of the Rillebrand provided a perfect place in which to talk.

"You are young to attempt such a thing," Sandip began. "You too must hate Rajic greatly."

"It is not hate," Hon answered, "it is duty."

"Duty?" Sandip said, raising one eyebrow. "He has offended you or done something shameful to your family?"

"No, nothing like that. He and some of his associates must be stopped. For the good of the land and its people."

Sandip shrugged.

"Rajic is a seasoned and vicious warrior. But this you know, right? That is only the beginning. He has," Sandip paused, "he has another advantage that makes him difficult to defeat. You see?"

Hon paused, then went decided to play his hand.

"If you mean the dragon, I know."

Sandip's face showed his surprise as Hon continued.

"I also know Rajic is only one of four dragon masters. They have joined forces to dominate all the lands."

"Four?" Sandip questioned, a leery look in his eye. "How do you know this?"

"One of our group overheard their plans."

"Who heard this?"

"I can't say," Hon said. "For the sake of safety."

"You still do not trust me?" Sandip asked. "Right. It is a wicked world, full of traitors and deceivers. Rajic is the worst of all."

"What has he done to fill you with such hatred?" Hon asked.

Sandip's face clouded. His eyes burned with malice.

"He is a betrayer of the worst kind. He murdered my parents, plundered their home and stole away my inheritance and my betrothed. She is not the kind of woman to silently abide an arrogant fool like Raj, so I suspect she is dead by now. For all of that, he does not deserve to live."

Hon didn't expect such a dramatic reason for Sandip's hatred but was not at all surprised.

CHAPTER EIGHT

"When I discovered my parents lying in their bed in a pool of their own blood, I knew instantly that it was Rajic. Each of them had only one wound, a deep thrust to the heart. Katar leave an unmistakable wound, you see? When I found him he did not even wait for my accusation. We were tigers, equally matched and equally desperate. To this day each of us bear the marks of the battle," he said, running the nails of his index fingers down the scars on his cheeks. "When I began to gain advantage, my sword against his katar, he threw sand into my eyes, slashed across my face from both sides and fled. By the time my vision cleared he was high in the western sky."

"The sky? You mean he had the dragon even then?"

Sandip looked at Hon, confused.

"The dragon was my father's. Rajic's ambition poisoned his mind to the point of betrayal and he took the beast."

Hon's head spun as he tried to make sense of what he was hearing.

"So you are the true heir to the dragon?"

"Yes."

"And you knew about the other dragon lords?"

"I knew they existed but did not know their identities or the purpose of the group. Such things were closely guarded, kept in scrolls in my father's chamber, you see? I was to be told everything when I received the inheritance."

"How did Rajic know of these things?"

"Did you not understand? Rajic is my younger brother."

CHAPTER NINE

Exhausted from hours of intense concentration, Cedrick flopped onto his bed. Quinn was an insistent and unforgiving teacher. He and Camille had spent hours at Quinn's side observing and absorbing everything they could. The intricacies and details involved in spy work was taxing to the mind, but Cedrick was invigorated by it. Quinn had remarked more than once how the boy was taking to the role naturally. A knock at the door roused him just as he was fading into sleep.

"Yes? Come."

The door swung wide and Lord Kendrick entered, handling his crutches as if it were the most natural thing in the world.

"You're getting around on those things pretty well," Cedrick said "You'd better be careful or you won't know how to get around without them."

"Don't think it for a moment," his father said, sitting on the bed beside him. "My armpits are aching from these cursed things. I'll be very glad to be rid of them. How is the training going?"

"I love it," Cedrick beamed. "I'm a 'natural born sneak.' Those were Quinn's exact words!"

Lord Kendrick laughed.

"Well, I don't know if I like what that says about the family tree but I'm glad he's pleased. He's expressed the same to me."

"Really father? What did he say?"

"He says he's never seen a man take to the concepts and skills as quickly as you have and he marvels all the more because you are a boy."

"I knew it!" the boy exclaimed, "I could feel it!"

"I felt the same way the first time my father allowed me to join him in the training field," Lord Kendrick replied.

"When I saw the men drilling, the swordplay, the jousting, my heart burst to be out there myself. I knew at that moment I would be a leader of men."

Cedrick smiled. He enjoyed hearing his father talk of his childhood.

"And how does your sister fare with the training?" Lord Kendrick asked.

"Fine, I think," Cedrick answered. "She's grasping the concepts and doing well at applying them to situations but she's not as eager as I am to get out there and put it into practice," he said, waving his arm toward the window. "But she's sharp about it and will be a great one to keep information flowing as it comes in."

"I agree," Lord Kendrick said, "I just hope she's not taking on too much so soon after her return. Cedrick, when we first found her she was delirious, panicked. She didn't know me and was fearful of everyone. It broke my heart. She came to her senses quickly but I fear that more damage has occurred than she knows... than any of us knows. Silas was cruel to her, to a degree she's not yet expressed. She can't keep it inside, it's not healthy."

Cedrick didn't know what to say. He had no experience to help him understand such things.

"She'll be alright, father. She has mother to guide her."

Kendrick laughed.

"Yes, that is true. Your mother is able to draw things out of a person that they didn't know were there. She is the best medicine for our Camille."

A knock at the door interrupted their conversation. It was Camille.

"I just received a message from Hon," she said, lifting a parchment. "He's found a man he thinks may be of use and has a few leads regarding others. But he feels things are moving too slowly, that by the time he gets his group assembled and trained it will be too late. He's asking for help. The same message has been sent to Rowan at Newtown, and to his father over in Brookhaven. He asks specifically if Gerrard and you, Cedrick, can come to The Twins to help."

CHAPTER NINE

Cedrick's head whipped toward his father.

"Well," Kendrick said, "I can see his point." He glanced at his son. "Cedrick, I will speak with your mother and with Quinn. In fact, why don't we all talk about it over our evening meal? Camille, could you have one of the servants pass the word to Quinn that I would like him to join us for supper this evening?"

"Yes father, I will," she said, flashing a smile in Cedrick's direction.

*****†*****

"Yes, the boy could be of help. He is a natural," Quinn said as he sliced a piece of roast pork on his plate.

"But he's still so young," Lady Patrice interrupted. "James, he has yet to reach his twelfth birthday. How can you even be thinking of sending him into this wickedness?"

Cedrick looked nervously from his father to his mother. Lord Kendrick measured his words carefully.

"Patrice, I know he is young. It is the main reason I hesitate at all. But even boys need the opportunity to prove themselves."

"Which he did when the dragon attacked," Patrice responded. "And I'm not altogether happy about that."

"Mother!" Cedrick whined.

"It's not that I'm ungrateful for what you did, Cedrick. I thank the good Lord that you were able to make the shot. But it is a merciful thing that you were not injured. You shouldn't have been up on that wall in the first place!"

Lord Kendrick interrupted.

"Quinn, what are your thoughts regarding Cedrick's age?"

"Inexperience is the issue, not age," the spymaster stated bluntly. "I was engaged in difficulties of similar nature when I was younger than he is now. But I had been raised to it. The boy is capable but lacks experience."

"But I have experience!" Cedrick insisted. "When the dragon attacked I was the one who had the composure to stand my ground and take the shot."

73

Lord Kendrick looked to his wife, eyebrows raised. "He has a point, Patrice."

"I don't care!" she insisted, in an uncharacteristically angry tone. "He is a boy, not a man. He is yet to become a warrior and I do not want him in harm's way!"

Cedrick slumped in his chair, visibly upset. Lord Kendrick wanted to give him an opportunity but completely sympathized with his wife's concerns at the same time. Cedrick was very young, especially for a dangerous role like this.

"I know the weight of a parent's concern fer his young," Gerrard said. " 'Tis a heavy weight, indeed. If 'twould be of help, I offer meself as a possible solution to the quandary."

"What do you have in mind?" Lord Kendrick asked.

"I'll be going to meet our young dragon slayer and would be pleased for the lad to come along, his safety me utmost concern, m'lady."

Lord Kendrick looked to Lady Patrice.

"Patrice? What do you think?"

"I don't know." She raised her eyes to Gerrard. "While I am thankful for your willingness to look after Cedrick, I still feel hesitant. It would be dangerous and he is inexperienced in such things."

"I have no bone to pick either way," Quinn interjected, "but it will be dangerous at home too. The dragon will return."

"Yes, and we all know how safe Cedrick was during the last dragon attack," Lord Kendrick chuckled.

Patrice shot him an angry look.

"I thank all of you for your counsel," Lady Patrice said briskly. "My husband and I will consider it."

*****†*****

"Why can't you understand how I feel about this?" Lady Patrice begged her husband.

CHAPTER NINE

"Patrice, I do understand. I would hate for any harm to come to Cedrick. But dear, he's on the verge of manhood and must be allowed to spread his wings."

"That is not the issue, James. Against my better judgment I relented when you wanted to allow him to compete in the tournament last year. And I didn't stop him from accompanying you when you journeyed west to better our relations with the rising clans over there. You talk as if I've been a hovering mother hen but I *have* let him spread his wings. But this, this is too far, too soon!" She began to cry. "I've already lost one child and only by a miracle of God have gotten her back! I don't want to repeat the mistakes of the past, James."

Lord Kendrick hobbled across the room and eased himself down beside his wife, setting his crutches aside. He felt her fear in his own heart.

"Patrice, I still bear a heavy weight of guilt over Camille's disappearance. Eleven years is a long stretch of our daughter's life to lose, especially when I could have prevented it. I am struggling with the same fears you are but I want to be careful that I'm not basing this decision on regrets and fears from the past."

"I'm not talking about letting fear control us," Lady Patrice answered. "I'm talking about gaining wisdom from what we've experienced, there's a difference. We both feel that we should have done more to protect Camille from Silas. If we could go back and do it over, we would. I know that this situation with Cedrick is entirely different. There's no conniving old man trying to slither into our home. But we still have to protect him from his own youthful zeal and perhaps from his father's zeal to see him become a man." Kendrick looked into her large, dark eyes. "James, he's only eleven years old. Why in God's name would you want to send an eleven year old boy into such an evil business?"

Lord Kendrick pondered her words, feeling afresh the regret over Camille's abduction. She was right. It would be a mistake to push Cedrick into the wicked world too soon.

"Alright Patrice, I agree. He is young, and we should hold him back for now."

Patrice released a deeply held breath and smiled up at him.

"I don't want you to feel that I've coerced you?"

"Not at all, Patrice. I've learned that your zeal on matters concerning the children usually has a very good cause, even if I can't see it myself. I don't feel coerced, just convinced," he said, with a wink.

"Should we call him in?" Patrice asked.

Lord Kendrick looked out the window.

"It's very late, Patrice. I'm sure he's already asleep. Let's talk to him first thing in the morning."

*****†*****

Outside their chamber door, Cedrick rose from the stone floor beside the doorway, a tear trickling down his cheek. In long strides he made his way down the hall to his quarters. He quietly closed the door behind him and without giving himself time to reconsider began packing a bag.

*****†*****

A knock at the door woke Lord Kendrick. He glanced out the window to see the approach of dawn. After some whispering at the door, Lady Patrice approached, a rolled parchment in her hand.

"What is it Patrice?"

"Madeline noticed Cedrick's door ajar this morning and peaked inside. She found his bed undisturbed and this lying on his pillow."

Kendrick sat up, wide awake. They opened the note to find a curt message in their son's hand.

I know you don't think I'm ready, but I am. I am sorry, but I must go.

Your loving son, Cedrick.

Lady Patrice looked up at her husband, her mouth agape. Lord Kendrick rose and moved to the window. He gazed into the misty morning for a long while.

CHAPTER NINE

"It is youthful foolishness. He thinks himself to be misunderstood and mistreated. Were it a simpler matter, I would understand and let it play out. But he is walking into the greatest danger any of us has faced. Gerrard is leaving in a few hours to meet up with Hon. I will send a message with him instructing Hon to send Cedrick back to us immediately."

"But do you really think he'll return, James? If he's done this what's to keep him from ignoring the message and continuing on the path he has chosen?"

Lord Kendrick turned to her, taking her hands in his.

"Despite the wound this is we both know Cedrick to be a good-hearted, obedient boy. I'm confident this is a temporary lapse in judgment provoked by youthful zeal and disappointment. It's the kind of impetuous decision that all children are prone to as they move toward adulthood." He raised her chin until their eyes met. "Patrice, we are the adults, and as such we must be the ones to let truth and level heads prevail. You can't tell me that you never rebelled against your parents when you were his age."

"I did," she confessed, "and was sorrowful afterward." She sighed. "But James, this is so serious, so much is at stake."

"And it will be dealt with seriously upon Cedrick's return," he assured.

Another knock interrupted and the maid, Madeline, cracked the door and poked her head in again.

"Sorry to disturb again m'lady, but it appears to be the morn for messages!"

"What is it?" Kendrick asked, hobbling toward the door.

"A rider came in moments ago, hard and fast, sir. He was carrying this."

Madeline presented a second rolled parchment bearing the seal of Kendrick's guard commander from the southern outpost.

"Thank you, Madeline." The maid slipped from the room.

Lord Kendrick's upraised eyebrow told his wife that he was just as curious as she was. Opening the scroll, he read aloud.

Lord Kendrick,

We have intercepted a party from Lord Rajic's realm in route to your estate. The soldier in charge claims that his litter carries Queen Amla herself. He is insistent that there be no delay in her meeting with you. I spoke with the Queen, who did step from her enclosure briefly. From the descriptions I've heard, I do believe it is her. I have confiscated all weapons and dispatched my best soldiers to escort them the remainder of the way. You should expect them within three days.

Commander Collen

"What in the good Lord's name is this about, James? Why would she be coming here?"

Lord Kendrick shook his head.

"I don't know. It's definitely unexpected. I wonder if it has anything to do with Hon's plans?"

"How could they know anything about it?" Patrice questioned. "Everyone has been so secretive, it couldn't have gotten out."

"I hope you're right," Kendrick said, stroking his beard. "But we have to assume the worst. There is deceit in this someplace, or treachery."

"What do you mean?"

"Patrice, we could have a spy in the mix."

CHAPTER TEN

The slow breathing of her mother wheezed from the pallet next to her. It made sleep impossible. This sound was different than what she'd become accustomed to over the past month. It was strained, belabored, painful. Victoria rose to light a candle.

Since the day the black dragon had spewed its acrid mucous over her Abigail had not moved on her own. The month-long bedside vigil had caused Victoria to feel that her mother was already gone... only she wasn't. Abigail lingered, unmoving, the stuffy air of the cottage suffocating all hope. Her mother's life dangled on the passing seconds, its grip weakening with each one. Victoria knew the time was coming. Death was the uninvited guest that could not be refused, bullying its way in, demanding a place in their lives. At that moment, a gift from God rose to Victoria's consciousness in the form of a childhood memory.

When she was around seven years old she and Abigail had a conversation, it was the day she had finally come to understand what it meant that her father and brother had "died." She was afraid then, a child who was terrified that she might be next to die. But Abigail had noticed her uneasiness and inquired about what she was feeling. Victoria could hear the conversation clearly, as if it had just happened.

"Victoria, what is troubling you?"

The youngster was timid, afraid to even speak of death for fear that the words would somehow make her its target.

"I'm afraid," she hesitantly volunteered.

"Afraid? Of what, my dear?" her mother had asked, moving close to her.

"I'm afraid that I will die," she blurted. "Papa and Brice died and Hon's mamma and papa died. I'm afraid to die mother, afraid to disappear and never come back."

Her mother had hugged her, the soft warm hug she remembered so well and longed for still.

"I understand Vickie, death is a frightening thing because we don't understand it."

"What happens when you die?" she asked her mother, fidgeting in her arms.

She remembered her mother's comforting smile.

"Let me ask you a question, Vickie. I think it will help you understand. When you walk through a doorway, where do you go?"

"Which doorway do you mean?"

Abigail laughed.

"That is a very good question, Vickie. You don't know where you're going to go unless you know which door you're walking through, right?" Victoria nodded. "When a person dies, they go to one of two places; Heaven, where they get to live forever with God, *or* to a terrible place called 'Hell,' where they live forever without God. Victoria, like choosing a doorway every person gets to choose where they will go when they die. And God is so loving; He tells us exactly how to choose the right door. When we trust that Jesus took the punishment for all our sins, we move through the doorway that leads us to heaven when we die."

"But isn't Heaven for good people?"

She recalled her mother's wrinkled brow as she pondered how to answer.

"No, Heaven is a place for humble people who admit their need and accept God's forgiveness."

"We can't go to Heaven unless we're forgiven?" Victoria asked.

"No, we can't, because heaven is a perfect place and only sinless people can go there. But we are not sinless people, are we?"

Victoria shook her head in agreement.

"Jesus willingly took our sinfulness upon Himself. When He died on the cross it was like He was the worst sinner who ever lived because He took responsibility for the sins of everyone. God killed Him for it because sin is wrong

CHAPTER TEN

and must be punished. But after He received God's full punishment for our sins, He came back to life. He says that if we will receive His payment for our sins He will forgive us and give us His righteousness so that we can go to heaven when we die.

"So Vickie, it's like the two doors. If you believe that Jesus took your sin and gives you His righteousness, you go through the door that leads to Heaven. If you refuse to believe it or can't believe it, then you have to pay for your own sin. That means that when you die, you go through the door that leads to Hell where you will be punished for your sin. Does that make sense?"

Victoria nodded her head, deep in thought.

"What's it like to die, mother?"

Abigail sighed.

"Do you remember the times when we've been out by the fire of the evening and you've fallen asleep?"

Vickie nodded.

"When you woke up, were you still out by the fire?"

"No, I was in my bed."

"How did you get there?" her mother asked.

"You carried me."

"Victoria, dying is like going to sleep and waking up in another place. You close your eyes in this life and wake up in another life, a much, much better life if Jesus is the source of your hope. That doesn't sound so frightening, does it?"

The memory was vivid. She could hear the tone of her mother's voice and feel the warmth of her embrace. It lofted through the chambers of her mind, an echo from years ago that faded into the silence of the room. Victoria looked down at her mother's still form and tears filled her eyes.

Her mother was gone, to a better place.

*****†*****

"Has a message been sent to Hon?" Rowan asked.

Victoria shook her head.

"Would you like me to take care of it?" he offered.

"No, I will do it," Victoria replied.

Hampton stood beside Victoria, one arm around her back and a hand gripping the shoulder nearest him. Both of them were crying. Rowan glanced past them to see Abigail lying peacefully on the same pallet where she'd been for over a month. He remembered the night the dragons had attacked. Abigail was one of the first to step outside and was instantly covered with a sticky black substance as it spewed from the black beast's mouth. Within minutes she had succumbed to its numbing effects and had not awakened since.

Looking back to Victoria and Hampton, Rowan mourned in his own way.

The village will suffer greatly over this loss. Abigail was an anchor to all of us. But for Victoria — a mother is a difficult person to lose.

He looked at Abigail's peaceful form, knowing that for her, faith had become reality. A sound from the other side of the room caught his attention. Victoria was seating herself at the table with a quill pen and sheet of parchment. He knew it would be the most difficult letter she had ever written. Rowan had noticed the growing bond between Hon and Victoria and from his own experience as a soldier, knew the difficulty it had to be for them to be apart. A loss like this would add to the burden immensely.

"Do you know where he is?" Rowan asked.

"I think so," she mumbled. "His last letter said he was going to be searching out The Twins, trying to find men."

"Good," he replied.

Victoria broke down.

"Rowan," she cried, "I need him. I need him home now, with *me*. I know how important his task is but this is too much. I can't bear it alone."

"I understand," he replied. "He will come when he receives your letter. Nothing matters more to him than you."

She looked up, surprised and a bit flushed.

"Has it been so obvious?"

Rowan touched her cheek tenderly.

CHAPTER TEN

"Yes young one, but we are all glad to see it. There is nothing to be embarrassed about. Julia told me just last night that she was surprised it didn't happen sooner."

Victoria blushed again and then spoke.

"Your dear wife; it doesn't surprise me that she saw what was going on. She probably knew it before we did."

"I wouldn't be surprised. She is much more insightful about these things than I am. Victoria, I just had an idea," Rowan said, changing the subject. "If you would like to finish the letter this morning, I could ask Fredrick to take it for you today. He would be willing to do whatever it takes to find Hon so that there is no delay."

Victoria looked up. Her sorrowful eyes communicated gratitude and peace.

"I would like that. Thank you."

CHAPTER ELEVEN

Lord Hugo Champlain did not return home after the meeting in Rajic's secret cave. He rode a fair distance behind until Silas and Sanniya turned south on the main road. He turned north as if he was heading back to his own land but led his stolen horse into the trees just beyond the first turn.

Over the past three months Hugo had been engaged in a covert plan. Once a week he took a midnight ride on his white beast. They traveled high over the mountains into Rajic's realm. Trusting to his beast's instincts Hugo had searched out the hidden lair of Rajic's black monster and after only three such journeys, had found it. Eight miles east of Rajic's castle, surrounded by thick woods he discovered a deep, rocky pit that yawned skyward. Far inside, concealed in the darkness, a deep cave wound away from the vertical wall of the pit. It was the lair of Raat, the black dragon.

Upon finding the pit Lord Hugo had released his beast, knowing that its acute sense of smell would lead it directly to its cousin. His Boreas was old and experienced. He had no fear that his dragon would be outmatched if things between the two males became hostile. He laughed to himself as he remembered the initial growls that had echoed from the pit. But in a short time the sounds had subsided and the beasts emerged, frolicking like kittens.

On his third trip to the black dragon's pit, Hugo remained astride his beast and entered the cave with him. He wanted the black monster to associate him with its new friend. As he had suspected, there was some initial reluctance because of his presence but it was mixed with curiosity. After one more visit the black dragon paid little attention to him.

With those memories urging him on, Hugo picked his way through the dense undergrowth for two hours until the trees thinned. He dismounted, secured his mount, and walked to the edge of the pit. Deep below he heard the sounds of a beastly feast; the two dragons had been hunting.

"Boreas!" he called. "Come. Eat."

The distant sound of leathery skin on rock became louder as his beast obeyed. The white dragon rose from the darkness and with a few strong beats of its wings, lit on the edge of the pit next to its master. Hugo turned, extending his arm toward the whinnying, frightened horse and spoke again.

"Eat."

One lightning-fast thrust of its powerful neck and the dragon snapped up the helpless creature. With the horse still flailing in its mouth, the dragon turned back toward the pit, looking to its master for permission to return to its friend.

"Go," Hugo said, and the beast leapt into the pit. Hugo sat on the edge of the yawning hole, his legs dangling, thinking about the plan he had set in motion.

They take me for a fool. It grates me to think of it. But they will see that they are the ones who have miscalculated. Rajic and Silas; they know how to dominate their beasts but they do not understand them. Sanniya may know her green beauty, but she doesn't see what I do. The power of instinct and nature is strong, stronger than the bond between master and beast. The dragons will be loyal to each other when the time comes, more so than to any human master. They are too ignorant to know it and I will use that to my advantage. I am already gaining the trust of this one. The others will follow. I will soon rule the entire dragon clan.

The beasts finished their meal and emerged from the pit. Lighting beside each other opposite the spot where Hugo sat, they cleaned their fore claws and faces with their long, thick tongues. Hugo rose and closed the distance. He knew the risk of pushing the black dragon to fully accept him before it was ready, but felt that time was not on his side. The council had determined to bring all of the beasts together within the month. He had to have influence over all the dragons when that day came.

Strategically, he moved to his own beast first, speaking in soothing tones and touching his hind legs as he moved

CHAPTER ELEVEN

toward its head. The beast turned to him, entirely comfortable with his presence. He had been its master since the day it hatched twenty years before. Hugo removed his dagger and used its edge to scratch the scaly underside of Boreas' neck. The beast stretched its chin high, releasing a deep, throaty growl almost like a cat's purr.

Hugo watched the other beast, careful to observe any signs of fear or aggression. It appeared more curious than threatened, sniffing the air and stretching its neck in his direction. Hugo turned toward the black dragon and extended his hand, speaking in the same soothing tones he had used with his own. Each action was practiced, calculated to win over the monster.

"All is well, boy. No problems. Boreas knows me and you do too. Calm. Calm. Good."

With his first step toward the dark beast it withdrew its head, growling faintly. The dragon master paused and raised his hand above his head, beckoning his own dragon with a familiar gesture. The white dragon extended its head over him, close enough that Hugo could place the palm of his hand on its chin.

"There. You see? I'm a friend. Your new master."

With that, he extended his other arm toward the ebony beast, coaxing it toward him with a soft snap of his fingers.

"Come," he commanded, gentle but firm. "Come."

The dark dragon hesitated, then inched its head toward him. It stopped just beyond Hugo's reach. Hugo smiled.

"Cautious still? Raat, you *will* obey. Come."

He snapped his fingers again and extended his hand, his palm open and upraised. He looked into the beast's eyes, knowing that the gesture could be taken either as an act of aggression or one of dominance. He hoped for the latter. After ten long seconds the dragon blinked its dark eyes, dipped its head low, and closed the distance between Hugo's outstretched palm and its chin. The cold, scaly hide brushed his palm then recoiled. Hugo smiled again.

"Good," he reassured. "Good, Raat. Good."

Hugo stepped backward, keeping his eyes on the black dragon as he moved beneath the shelter of his own beast's broad neck. A few more visits and the dark beast would fully trust him. He was satisfied, very satisfied. His weekly visits to the other two lairs were producing similar results. The power of the council was his and the others were entirely ignorant of the fact.

CHAPTER TWELVE

Hon and Sandip prepared to leave Westbridge the next morning. While Sandip spent the evening tidying up a few personal matters, Hon sought another man, one Sandip himself had mentioned. The man was a one-time mercenary turned trouble maker. Hector had a reputation as a brawler and a drinker, but most important to Hon, a man who was afraid of nothing. Sandip had crossed paths with him in a tavern and had taken two days to recover from the encounter. The easterner's words still rang in his memory.

"I am no stranger to fighting," he said in his heavy, articulate accent. "But Hector is the hardest man I have ever fought. When I hit him, I struck stone, hard and cold. He stared back with icy eyes, unfazed. I did not want to fight, you see? There was no reason. But his challenge was public and bold and it was a situation where I could not avoid the conflict. At his insistence we put aside weapons to fight with fists only." Sandip shook his head at the memory. "He is a man to be careful of."

"Why do you think he might help us?" Hon had asked.

"After we fought he did the unthinkable — he insisted we share a meal. I must be honest, you see; I could hardly eat, I took such a beating. But for Hector it was as if the battle invigorated every part of him. He ate like a starving man and spoke of his life freely. There are things in his past that I believe might make him sympathetic to your cause."

Hon shook his head as he remembered the conversation.

I must be mad. I should have waited until Sandip could come with me. Maybe then we'd have found Hector hungover and a bit easier to manage.

Turning the corner into a dark alleyway, laughter and cat-calls filled his ears as he approached a small, unruly knot of men.

"Come on my pretty, just a little kiss," a yellow toothed old buzzard was saying, "your papa won't know a thing!"

In the middle of the tightly packed bunch Hon could see a girl no older than fourteen who had been unfortunate enough to be caught outside. Immediately Hon felt the urge to step in, in spite of the fact that he couldn't handle all the men at once. Nevertheless, he was in the process of drawing his sword when a slurred but commanding voice spoke from the darkness behind the group.

"Let her go, Baboso."

As one, the group stiffened, obviously familiar with the voice. Hands immediately flew to their knives. The old man who had been taunting the girl was too drunk to recognize the voice and replied with far too much bravado.

"Who's that? Step out here where I can look in yer eyes as I kill ya'!"

The voice responded from the darkness.

"Aunque estuvieras sobrio, no podrias matar a una cucaracha!"

"What?" the old drunk said, looking side to side at his companions. "What did he say?"

The voice spoke again.

"I say, 'You could not keel a cockroach, even eef you were sober.'"

One of the group ran down a side alley, away from the mysterious voice. The rest drew their knives and turned toward it. Menacingly, the voice spoke a final threat.

"Eef you are stupeed enough to draw on me then you deserve to die. Thees ees your last warning."

The men rushed the dark corner, knives waving. The first two were immediately cut down by quick thrusts of a thin rapier flashing out of the shadows. As the man stepped into the light the group spread out to surround him. He was of average height but thickly built, and by all appearances a commoner. The only exceptional thing about him was the glittering, ornately handled sword he brandished. He loudly harassed the group in his native tongue as his sword sliced the air repeatedly between himself and the mob.

CHAPTER TWELVE

Hon moved to the girl, helped her up and sent her away from the crowd. Turning back to the scene he found the group backing toward him and he was quickly a part of their rearmost ranks. The rapier was flying, dazzlingly fast, cutting down opponents one by one. Hon pushed his way through the men toward a doorway, knowing that if soldiers came he would be mistaken for one of the mob. Just as he opened the door, a second crowd came pushing out, eager to see the fight. Before Hon knew what was happening, the entire crowd was randomly pummeling each other, the hard liquor of the tavern having its effect.

Ducking punches and delivering a few in an effort to get out of the throng, Hon caught sight of the swordsman again. He no longer held his blade and was trading punches with a large man who had come from the tavern. The large man clearly had the size advantage but the swordsman continued to take every blow and deliver one of his own in return.

This must be Hector, Hon thought.

Shoving combatants aside, Hon made his way toward the man, hoping to find some way to coax him away from the melee. Just as Hon reached him their eyes locked, then all went black.

*****†*****

The rattling of chains and the cold of the shackles around his ankles and wrists roused Hon from his stupor. His sword and dagger had been taken and he was in a long line of men seated against a wall in the alleyway. They were chained together.

"You there," Hon called to the first city guard to come near. "I was trying to help the girl move out of harm's way. I wasn't part of the fight."

"Is that right?" the guard retorted as he leaned closer. He was a bulky man with a grizzled appearance. "Then how do you explain the bruises on your face, little lamb?"

"I was caught up in the mob by accident."

The guard grunted, gave Hon a kick to the leg and moved down the line checking the manacles of other men.

Three men down the line, Hon saw the distinctive, floppy hat that Hector wore. He marveled that it sat atop his head completely undisturbed while men all around him were unconscious, bloodied, or both. Hector ranted in his native tongue, equally displeased at being shackled.

The prisoners were roused, raised to their feet, and led out of the alleyway into the main thoroughfare and past the market where Hon had been just months before. A heavy mist began to fall on the unfortunate line of men. In the next hour they made the circuit from one public square to another. At each stop, five to six of their number were released from their chains, seated on a wooden stool or stump and made to extend their hands and feet forward to be bound in the rough stocks.

The line before him diminished with each stop until Hon knew he would be in the next group, along with Hector. The dim light of the approaching morning revealed the next square before they reached it; a small clearing between shops. It would soon be bustling with the activity of the new day. Hon and Hector were placed across from each other. He didn't know how he was going to get out of the mess but decided to take advantage of the time in the stocks while he and Hector were so close.

"You are the man they call Hector?" he asked.

Hector craned his neck to look up, clearly shocked that a fellow prisoner was calling him by name.

"Si."

"I've been looking for you," Hon replied.

Hector chuckled.

"Theen you are either craysee, or stupeed. Leave me alone, boy."

Hon didn't want to make him angry but was emboldened by the fact that Hector was restrained.

"A man named Sandip sent me to find you. Do you remember him?"

With a heavy sigh, Hector answered.

"The man from the east. I remember. What do you want?"

CHAPTER TWELVE

Hon looked around the circle of captives, uncertain what was safe to share. Most of them were passed out.

"I'm searching for brave men. Sandip said you were afraid of nothing."

Hector raised his head again.

"I fear nothing. Though by the end of our fight, I almost fear Sandip. Almost." He shook his head back and forth violently, his floppy hat falling to the ground. "Damn." He looked across at Hon again. "Why you need thees brave men?"

"I'd like to talk to you about that when we are released."

Hector laughed again.

"Eef you can geet us released, I will leesten to what you say. Until you do, shut up."

"Fine," Hon said. "I will."

*****†*****

Cedrick had been to Westbridge with his father many times but on none of those trips had he been searching for one person out of the crowd. As he entered the city he tried to recall Quinn's instructions. His friend Jonathan, the stable master's son, had loaned him some common clothes so he felt he was blending into the crowds easily. He kept his sword, ornate and brightly polished, hidden within the folds of his outer cloak. He was ready for anything, determined to prove his mother's concern unwarranted.

The message Hon had sent to Camille had given directions to the "Boar's Head Inn," where Hon was staying. Cedrick made his way down the wide streets. He stopped at the edge of a public square to get his bearings.

"Cedrick?"

The boy sought the voice that had called him. It was familiar, but he couldn't place it.

"Cedrick. Over here, in the stocks."

Moving toward the center of the square, Cedrick was shocked to find Hon with head, hands, and feet bound tightly between the wooden slats.

"How did you get in there?" Cedrick asked.

"I'll explain it later," Hon replied. "Can you get us out?"

"Us? Who's with you?" Cedrick asked, looking for a familiar face among the other prisoners.

Hon nodded toward Hector as the other man raised his head in disbelief.

"A new friend," Hon said. "See what you can do."

*****†*****

The only way Hon could work out the kink in his back caused by the awkward posture enforced by the stocks was to bend over repeatedly. He knew he looked silly, but didn't care. He was glad to be out. He smiled at Hector as the guards released the baffled man from his wooden prison. He did his own stretching then ambled over to Hon and Cedrick.

"Gracias Amigo," Hector said, nodding at Hon and Cedrick. "Thank you."

"I'm glad I could help," Cedrick said, bubbling with enthusiasm as he handed each man his weapons.

Hector took his rapier and swished it through the air a few times before returning it to his belt.

"Eef you steel want to talk, come with me," Hector invited.

Hon and Cedrick followed him, talking as they went.

"I'm glad to see you," Hon said. "Where is Gerrard?"

Cedrick hesitated.

"He wasn't able to come right away. But he should be here in the next few days."

"Well I'm glad you're here," Hon said. "Who knows how long I'd have been stuck if you hadn't come along." Hon could see the boy swell with pride at the statement. "How did you manage to get us released?"

"My father insists that I carry a document, signed by him and stamped with his seal. It verifies my identity so that in case we are separated I will have no problems. I showed it to the nearest guard and he was quick to do whatever I told him," the boy smiled, then grew somber. "I'm sure the idea came to him sometime after Camille was taken."

CHAPTER TWELVE

"However it came about, I'm glad for it," Hon said. "Your father is a wise man."

"Yes. Yes, he is," Cedrick stammered.

Hector led the way, stepping around the characteristic piles of manure and refuse left by the animals that crowded the lanes daily. Hon and Cedrick followed him into the side entrance of a fueler's shop. He made his way past stacks of coal and wood and into the back room. The soot-covered boy working in the front room glanced up, and upon seeing Hector went back to his work. The Spaniard led them to the very end of a narrow, dark hallway and into a dank room. He produced flint and steel from a cabinet and lit the oil lamp on the table. The light revealed a sparsely appointed room containing a small cabinet, a table and two chairs, and a pallet in the corner. A shutter-covered window let in cracks of light.

"Eef your boy would watch the weendow, we can speak here," Hector offered.

Hon noticed Cedrick bristle at the comment but nodded him toward the window with an amused grin. Hector did not waste any time.

"Why you need these brave men?" Hector asked, as if their conversation from the stocks had never been interrupted.

"There is a danger rising across the lands," Hon began. "I and a few others have become aware of it and are seeking men who would help us destroy it. But our plans must remain secret or else all of our efforts would be vain."

Hector cocked his head.

"What ees thees danger?"

Hon decided to test the waters before revealing everything.

"Dragons."

Hector sat back, his face an unreadable slate. He stared a long while at Hon then looked toward Cedrick.

"How do you know?"

"I have seen them, myself."

"How many?" the Spaniard asked

"You believe me, then?" Hon asked.

"Si, I do. How many?" Hector asked again.

"I have only seen two," Hon offered, "but we believe there are at least four of them."

Hector sat motionless, his eyes unfocused and looking far away. His thick, dark eyebrows furrowed low, almost concealing his eyes.

"You seek men to keel thees dragons," Hector said, more of a statement than a question. "The ones who do thees would be heroes. I could do eet myself," he said with a wry smile, "and take all the glory. Why must it be secret?"

The moment had come. There was no way to keep Hector interested without revealing the existence of the dragon lords.

"The dragons are under the control of men… masters." Hector leaned forward, his eyes boring into Hon's. "Some of these masters are well-placed in the surrounding lands and will try to stop us the moment they hear of our efforts. That is why it must remain secret."

Hector pondered Hon's words, then shifted backward into his chair.

"Eet ees not my concern. I have problems of my own."

"How can you say that?" Cedrick exploded, coming away from the window. "This concerns every one of us! You might think you could simply go over The Ridge or to the south or west to escape it, but it extends far beyond my father's lands!"

Hon winced at Cedrick's words. He hadn't wanted Hector to know who Cedrick was but it was too late. Hector turned his head toward the boy, mumbling to himself.

"Tierra de tu padre? You are Kendrick's son… si, eet makes sense that you got us out so quickly." Hector shook his head. "Even more, I am not the man for you. I have many troubles — weeth your father and hees laws. We would find eet eempossible to be on the same side."

Cedrick looked to Hon apologetically.

"You're looking at it the wrong way. Lord Kendrick is a fair man. He will hear you out. We can promise you that. Whatever problems you have had with Lord Kendrick's laws, I'm sure we can at least assure you he will hear your side."

CHAPTER TWELVE

The Spaniard laughed.

"You don't even know my side. I have broken hees laws willingly. I have stolen. I have keelled." He looked to Cedrick. "Tu padre would return me to the stocks weeth no delay. I weel not geev him the chance."

"Lord Kendrick is a just man, but also a forgiving one to those who are repentant," Hon offered. "Isn't that right, Cedrick?"

"Uhhh,,, Ye…Yes… he is."

*****†*****

Sandip sat outside the entrance to the Boar's Head as the three approached. Upon seeing them, he jumped to his feet.

"I was wondering if you had run into trouble or if you were not as you led me to believe. I see from your bruised face it was the first."

"I believe you know Hector?" Hon said, gesturing toward his new companion.

"Si, we know each other," Hector answered with a wry smile. "I weel not forget thees man in all my life."

"Nor will I," Sandip offered. "You are a strong man."

"And this is Cedrick," Hon said, introducing the boy to Sandip. "Cedrick is the son of a friend of mine and has come to join us."

"I am pleased to meet you," Sandip said. "For one so young to join this quest, it is a brave thing."

Cedrick smiled awkwardly.

"Thank you."

"We need to get moving. There is a lot to do," Hon said as he headed for the door of the Inn.

Sandip reached for Hon's arm.

"I forgot to tell you. There is a young man inside waiting for you."

Entering the Inn, Hon immediately recognized Frederick sitting at a table near the doorway.

"Frederick! I'm glad to see you and glad you decided to come," Hon said, embracing his friend. "We will need you. Let me introduce you to some new friends…"

"Hon," Frederick interrupted, "I come with sad news. Abigail has died and Victoria asks for you."

CHAPTER THIRTEEN

A *week on the road in this infernal cart,* Queen Amla groused. The journey to Kendrick's estate had been boring and slow, the bumps in the road becoming more pronounced with every mile.

"The village is ahead," her lady in waiting informed.

"Thank the ancestors. I couldn't stand another day in this thing."

Peeking through the stitched curtains that hung over the cart she saw a small, wooded town at the base of the rise before Kendrick's estate. The keep and castle stood high on the hill in the distance.

"We rest here," she said to the nearest guard. "We will make the last leg of the journey before nightfall."

*****†*****

Lord Kendrick and Lady Patrice waited in the great hall. Servants dashed around the room, consumed in the last minute preparations for their royal guest. Deep concern showed in Lady Patrice's eyes. Lord Kendrick took his wife's dainty hand between his calloused palms. They spoke without words, his eyes reassuring her, giving her strength for what lay ahead. A maid servant hurried into the room and nodded at the royal couple. Lord Kendrick nodded in return. The floor-to-ceiling doors parted and the steward stepped inside.

"I present Queen Amla, of Rajic," he announced.

Amla entered, her flowing green robe trailing behind. A thin, eastern-style veil encrusted with jewels covered the lower portion of her face. The aroma of Jasmine wafted across the room.

"Queen Amla, we are pleased to welcome you," Lord Kendrick began. "It is an honor."

"Certainly," Amla answered, peering from behind her veil, from Lord Kendrick to Lady Patrice and back again. "I do apologize for the haste with which I have come but it is an urgent matter." Her eyes bounced from servant to servant around the room. "I must speak to you privately."

"Of course," Kendrick replied. The servants immediately retreated. Queen Amla removed her veil and moved closer to the couple.

"I come seeking your help. I appeal especially to you, Lady Patrice. I feel you will understand my position best."

Kendrick smiled at his wife whose shock was evident.

"How may I be of help?" she asked.

Amla's head bowed. Her eyes searched the floor as if the words she needed would rise from the stones. She sighed.

"I have been resolute the entire journey here but now that I stand before you, I hesitate."

"You mentioned a danger. Is it political or personal?" Lady Patrice asked.

Queen Amla looked up, clearly surprised at the question.

"You see more than most, my lady."

Lord Kendrick chuckled.

"Yes Queen Amla, she does."

"What can I do to assure you that we will help if we can?" Patrice asked.

Amla's eyes raised and she smiled.

"You are kind. I do feel that you will," she said with a smile. "Enough hesitation. I must be free." She sighed deeply. "My husband is a monster. I must be free of him."

Lord Kendrick and his wife stared at Queen Amla. Her revelation was the last thing they expected.

"His mood was sullen when we first married and I foolishly excused it. I attributed his behavior to a variety of things — an especially hard day or a frustrating situation. But it was… is, more than that. It has grown and now… now I am fearful for my life. He is evil, evil to the core."

Lord Kendrick could see his wife's womanly heart moved with compassion.

CHAPTER THIRTEEN

"You poor dear! What can we do to help?"

Amla hesitated.

"Please," Patrice urged, "we would truly like to be of help if you will let us."

"But you have no reason to trust me — and what I must ask will put you in a dangerous position." She clenched her teeth and raised her chin, resuming her regal demeanor. "I should not have come. Forgive me for such a foolish waste of your time." She turned to leave.

"Please!" Patrice called. "You cannot go, not like this."

Amla stopped, still facing the door. Patrice continued.

"You are right, trust is a precious thing and must be built over time. But a beginning must be made sometime, don't you think?"

Amla turned and Lady Patrice continued.

"You have come all this way. By now your husband must know you are gone. Will you turn back now? Back to the danger that awaits?"

Amla closed her eyes. Moments passed. In time she raised her chin and looked directly at them.

"I ask for asylum."

CHAPTER FOURTEEN

The tiny village of Brookhaven lie toward the southeast end of The Ridge, just within the edge of the forest. It was a humble town, populated with simple people whose hard work provided their livelihood. The afternoon sun dipped behind the aspens and pines and combined with the gentle breeze to create a sense of motion across the village. Children played, women lugged buckets of water from the well in the town square, and men worked in their shops and fields, providing their own sustenance through the work of their own hands.

Stewart sat on a rough bench, his back against the front of his hut. He was enjoying the sensations of the summer afternoon, thankful for every day the good Lord allowed him to see; he received each one as a gift. Motion on the road drew his attention. Horsemen came lazily up the road. Brookhaven had earned the reputation as a peaceful, safe rest stop along the main north-south road. Many travelers had come to rely upon the village's hospitality. The land had changed much in the past ten years with the death of Lord Thurmond and Rajic's rise to power. Brookhaven was one of the last known bastions of comfort for weary travelers.

The horsemen wore the black tunics of men indentured to Rajic. The lead rider was a powerfully built man of average height who had clearly seen his share of battle. His arms and neck were deeply scarred and his demeanor revealed he was a formidable man. The insignia on his tunic indicated he was the commander of the half dozen men who rode behind him.

"Good afternoon," Stewart said, as the men approached. "How can I be of help to Lord Rajic's men?"

The commander flashed a crooked, yellow grin at him.

"You can begin by pointing my men to a place to get some food and bed down for the night," the commander replied.

"There is a tavern across the square," Stewart pointed. "We don't have a proper inn so the best we can do is offer you lodging in a barn or shed, if that will do."

The commander jerked his head toward the tavern and his men moved across the square.

"Is this your hut?" the commander asked.

"Yes, it is. A gift from some dear friends," Stewart replied.

"A gift, you say? How so?" the commander inquired.

"I was injured some years ago while away on a journey. When I returned, my neighbors had built this hut for me. It was a tremendous blessing."

The commander stared down at Stewart from atop his steed.

"What did you say your name was?"

"I am Stewart."

"Ah, Stewart," he paused. "I am Commander Eadric."

*****†*****

"Are you sure this is alright, Fulton," Stewart asked for the second time as he helped Fulton's wife, Ida arrange a pallet on the floor. "I don't want to be a bother to you and Ida."

"Stew, I won't hear another word. You know you are family to us," the blacksmith replied. "It's no bother, ever."

"I just wish the soldiers would have at least asked," Ida said. "It's not a good sign of where our land is headed when the king's men behave this way."

"No, it's not," Stewart agreed. He peered out the window at his hut and then across toward the tavern. "If Rajic's men are willing to force a man out of his home for the night without the slightest regard, what does it say of Rajic himself?"

"I've heard nothing good," Ida said. "I'm becoming more afraid every time his troops ride into town."

"The commander you met," Fulton asked, "you said his name was Eadric?"

CHAPTER FOURTEEN

"That's right," Stewart answered.

The blacksmith scratched his head.

"I feel I know that name, but it escapes me, Stew."

"How would you know it, Fulton?" Stewart asked. "Besides the quartermaster who contracts arms from you, you have little connection with Raj's troops."

"I know, but it's nagging at me, right back here," Fulton said, tapping just behind his ear.

*****†*****

Morning broke, foggy and damp. Stewart watched through the window as Eadric and his men emerged from the tavern and made their way back to Stewart's hut to gather their things. Eadric himself came directly across the square to the smithy.

"I'm looking for Stewart," he called to Fulton through the open doors. Fulton put down his hammer and walked to meet him.

"He's inside," Fulton said, gesturing toward his cottage to the side of the forge. He led Eadric to the cottage and invited him inside.

"Stew, Commander Eadric would like to speak with you," he said.

Stewart rose from his chair by the window.

"How can I help you, Commander?"

"Step outside with me," the commander said bluntly. "You stay here," Eadric said, jabbing his blunt fingertips into Fulton's chest. By the time the two men emerged from the cottage the other soldiers had gathered their things and were waiting in front of the forge.

"We've come here in search of a fugitive, a young man who defied orders to return to my checkpoint some months ago. We have reason to believe he was headed here."

Stewart knew instantly who Eadric meant.

"I will help, if I can," he said.

"Stop playing games," Eadric said, with a sudden cruelness in his voice. He is your son."

"My son is no fugitive. While he was here he received word that tragedy had befallen his village on the other side of The Ridge. There was no time for him to return by way of the southern crossroad."

Eadric stepped close to Stewart, clearly trying to intimidate him with his size.

"I don't care why he didn't return, you old cripple," Eadric said with a shove. "I only care that he didn't come back when he was told to. That proves him to be one of Kendrick's men, come in to spy out our land."

"My son is no spy, he is…"

"Shut yer mouth," Eadric said with a backhand across Stewart's face. "You said he went to Newtown? Where's that?"

"On the other side of The Ridge, to the north," Stewart said.

"In Kendrick's land. Just like I said," Eadric responded smugly. "You can't fool me. Obviously, we can't go traipsing into Kendrick's land in search of him but we can force him to return here."

With a nod from Eadric three of the soldiers forced Stewart to his knees. Binding his hands behind his back they lifted him atop a horse. Eadric stormed over to Fulton's hut and kicked open the door.

"Get all your neighbors into the square, now!" he shouted.

Fulton and Ida hurried around the village summoning everyone to come outside. When the square was filled, Eadric spoke.

"This man harbored a fugitive and aided him in escape. He will be punished accordingly. The only hope of his life being spared is if the fugitive, Hon surrenders himself. Then, we may have leniency on this one," he said, with a spit in Stewart's direction. "If you are able to make contact with the son," he paused, with a chuckle and a look toward his men, "I suggest you make him aware of what's happened here."

With that, Eadric and his men mounted their horses. Eadric and two other men surrounded Stewart's horse and led

CHAPTER FOURTEEN

him away. The other three lagged behind to make sure the villagers did not follow. Then, like their commander and his captive the three vanished into the fog.

CHAPTER FIFTEEN

The week since Amla's arrival had been difficult for Patrice. Her soul was conflicted. On one hand she naturally felt compassion for Amla, knowing instinctively the vulnerable position she was in. But Lady Kendrick was also suspicious.

She could not help but wonder about Amla's motives. She spoke convincingly of her plight and the story was consistent each time they spoke. Rajic appeared every bit the beast. If it was true, Patrice couldn't blame her for wanting to get away from him. But knowing what she did of the dragon lords she couldn't fully trust that everything was as it appeared. Amla had not mentioned the black dragon or any of the dragon lords, details Patrice wished she would have revealed. But then again, it had only been a week. Trust was still being forged.

Lady Kendrick was also concerned about their safety. Amla was right when she said that granting her asylum would put them in a dangerous position. Amla's traveling party had departed the day after her arrival, leaving no doubt that Rajic would know where his queen had gone. Patrice expected to see the silhouette of the black dragon looming on the eastern horizon any day. But she pushed the thought away, more concerned for her counterpart than for herself.

And in the back of her mind, weighing continually on her heart, was Cedrick. There had been no word of him either through Hon who he was expected to meet, or Gerrard who had left days earlier to find them. It was all she could do to keep herself from being devoured by fear. Though she tried to be strong the worry nagged at her, gnawing away her optimism one bite at a time. A soft knock on the door roused her from thought.

"Come," Patrice answered.

Queen Amla entered, a very different woman than first graced their grand hall. She wore plain, loose clothes that hid her womanly figure and revealed none of her former station. Her face was drawn and tired.

"How are you today, my dear?" Patrice inquired.

"You must have thought I would sleep the day away."

Patrice smiled.

"Fear is a heavy things to carry and you have borne it for a long while now. It doesn't surprise me that you need rest. Any woman in your place would."

"Thank you," Amla said, "for everything. These past few days are the first I've felt safe in years. But I know it will not last. Rajic will come after me, with a terror you can't imagine."

Patrice feigned ignorance.

"What do you mean? Is he really so foolish as to launch an all-out assault on us?"

"Not foolish, confident. And he has reason to be."

Patrice led her along.

"Yes, well, I understand the confidence a wife has in her man. James too is a seasoned warrior and able leader of men. Though I think him to be invincible, I know he is not."

"It has nothing to do with those things," Amla stuttered, "It has to do with, with… he has an advantage, a…"

"Oh?" Patrice encouraged.

Amla hesitated, visibly shaken at her own transparency. Patrice pushed her over the edge.

"Amla, you and I have shared so much already. We can dispense with the guarded comments, can we not? The fact is that you have left your husband and are now the object of his wrath as much as we are. Isn't it to your advantage to tell us anything that might keep all of us safe?"

Amla's dark eyes softened.

"You will think me mad to say it, but it is true. Rajic has command of a dragon."

Patrice took Amla's hand.

CHAPTER FIFTEEN

"Not at all. Thank you for being honest with me. Now I must return the favor. We know about the beast. We have for some time."

"Wha… How did you know?"

"Villages within our realm have suffered its attacks. The construction you've seen going on outside is preparation for the day it comes here. You must have wondered."

Amla looked shocked. If she was pretending, Patrice could not tell.

"Yes, I did wonder about the weapons. I've never seen anything like them."

"To ward off beasts like the one Raj commands."

"I see…" Amla replied, a far-away look in her eye.

"Is something wrong?" Patrice asked.

"Wrong? No, no, nothing." She paused, breathing deeply. "I'm glad that you finally know, that I have been open with you. And I'm so sorry but I tire so easily these days. Do you mind if we continue this later? Perhaps after the evening meal?"

Patrice smiled.

"Not at all. Do take your leave. I will see you at table."

*****†*****

Falling on her bed, Amla realized that she *was* tired, exhausted by the mounting tension that had grown between she and her husband over the years. It had begun with her, resentful of being taken from her homeland by a man she hardly knew. But Raj had convinced her that marauders from the south had killed his parents and brother, her fiancé. He'd barely been able to get her away.

But that good deed didn't change the fact that the love of her life was dead. It didn't make it any easier to accept his callous older brother as a substitute. Rajic and Sandip were as opposite as night and day. One tender, caring, even noble, the other rough, insensitive, and full of insecurity cloaked in pride. Even though Rajic had saved her life, she resented that he was not her beloved Sandip.

Her feelings only provoked Rajic's already demanding nature. He insisted that they marry and became more forceful in his advances. Amla spurned him repeatedly until, unable to handle the rejection, he beat her almost senseless. A week later, wearing heavy makeup to hide her bruised face, she submitted to a forced marriage out of fear for her life.

    From that moment she became numb. It was as if her mind was able to fly to a distant land, away from the pain, away from him. But she could not maintain the distance. He would not allow it. He was a master manipulator and began to work his devious magic. Through seasons of kindness, flattery, and gifts Rajic would draw her close to him, almost convincing her that he was more like his dead brother than she'd realized. But then, unable to maintain his deception, he'd wound her again. Hers became a back-and-forth life, emotions rising in hope that things could be different, then plummeting under the intensity of his rage. She became conflicted, hating and pitying him at the same time.

    Lying among the pillows of the lavish guest bed, the cool breeze rustled the curtains as sobs erupted from Queen Amla.

    "Sandip! My love… I miss you so!"

    She cried for almost an hour, wailing over every loss and sorrow of the past two years. She mourned the dreams of the life she'd planned with her beloved. She mourned the loss of her homeland. She bemoaned the turn of events that had put her into the arms of a man who did not love her and had driven her to become a fugitive. Amla sat up, drying her eyes as she stared out the window. She rose and walked to the door with determination.

*****✝*****

    Lady Patrice was surprised when Queen Amla stepped through the door. She had barely been gone an hour. It was evident that she'd been crying.

    "Yes Amla, is everything alright?"

CHAPTER FIFTEEN

"No — I mean, yes. Finally, everything is alright, or it will be." She raised her chin with a confidence Patrice had not seen. "If it pleases, I wish to speak with you and your husband as soon as possible. You must know the whole truth of why I am here."

"Certainly," Patrice said, "I will inform James immediately. We can dine alone this evening so that you can feel free to speak."

"Thank you," Amla replied. "You are very kind."

CHAPTER SIXTEEN

He did not know it, but Gerrard arrived in Eastbridge three hours after Hon and his party departed for Newtown. Cedrick's disappearance had put a damper on his trip. He entered the city hoping that the boy had already found Hon and that he was well. Gerrard asked directions to the Boar's Head and upon inquiring with the Innkeeper, was given a message left for him.

Gerrard,

Frederick has brought news of Abigail's death and we ride for Newtown. Cedrick is with us. I also take along two men I've discovered who are willing to join us, Sandip, who you know and another named Hector. If you are able to find one or two more men and join us there, we should have a good start.

Thank you, Hon.

Gerrard secured a room for himself and a paddock for his mule, then sat down to eat. Scanning the room, he was the only customer.
One or two more men, aye? This should be interesting.
He finished his meal and walked outside. The mid-day sun was blistering on the uncommonly still afternoon. The sound of the mighty river murmured in the background. Gerrard began walking, looking for a tavern or inn, any place that fighting men might be found. Turning a corner he came upon a busy crossroads.
A line of carts, hauling hay from market were coming toward him, people of various races and economic status rushed here and there. A man leaned against a doorway across the street. Down the road and to his right sat a young

beggar, her hand out, hoping for pity from the busy crowds. Gerrard shook his head.

It baffles me that the lad has found two men already. I'll be blessed to find even one.

He decided to take a different approach. Moving down the street, he came to the place where the beggar sat. She was a thin, dirty, pale girl of around seventeen years. Both legs were obviously useless. Her thin blonde hair fell wildly around her shoulders. Gerrard stopped beside her and lowered himself to sit in the dust at her side. She looked sideways at him, clearly unsure what to make of him.

"I mean ya' no harm, lass. Just a visitor to this place tryin' to get me bearings. I was thinkin' you might be able to give me some direction."

The shock had not left her face since he had joined her in the dusty street. She stared at the hairy man as if a bear or skunk was speaking to her.

"Do ya' speak, lass?"

She nodded her head.

"Glad to hear it," Gerrard said with a smile. "What's yer name?"

"Fiona," she stammered.

"Happy to make yer acquaintance, Fiona. Me name is Gerrard Reginald McGreggor, the third. But me friends call me Gerrard. Would ya' answer a few questions fer me, lass?"

The young woman nodded, her eyes still wide.

"I'm looking to take on strong men for a job, but need the reliable sort, men that can be trusted. Do ya' know any like that around here, lassie?"

She nodded again. Gerrard released a hearty laugh.

"Then what would you advise, lass? Where can I find these men?"

Before the girl could respond, Gerrard felt an iron grip on his shoulder. The woodsman was surprised he had not heard the approach of one so strong. Turning his chin toward his left shoulder he looked into the blackest face he had ever seen. A tall, muscular man, clad in tall leather boots,

CHAPTER SIXTEEN

breeches, and a rough leather vest with no shirt underneath glared down at him.

"Why you speak with girl?"

Gerrard tried to rise but the iron grip held him where he was.

"I figured the lass would know the town better than me, seein' as I'm a stranger here. So I was askin' her for some guidance, nothing more."

"What you seek?" the black man asked, not releasing his grip.

"Men," Gerrard said. "Trustworthy and brave men."

The girl's protector released his grip and stood to his full height, his hand on a short dagger tucked into his belt. Gerrard rose. At six foot four inches, he still had to raise his chin to look the man in the eye. The giant looked at Gerrard suspiciously, clearly trying to make an assessment of him.

"Aye, I look rough, no doubt of it, friend. Living alone in the woods a man comes to care less o' such things. But under the beard and dirt you'll find a heart ready to receive all who are willing to be received." Gerrard looked in the girl's direction. "'Tis part of why I chose to speak to the lass. She's the type o' soul too many walk past without notice. I wanted her to know she was worth noticin'."

The man stared at Gerrard then looked to Fiona.

"He speaks true?" he asked the young woman, who nodded.

A wide, white smile spread across the man's face and he extended both hands.

"Bongani is me. I watch after Fiona. A debt to her father, my friend. You understand?"

Gerrard smiled in return.

"Indeed I do," he replied, taking Bongani's hand. "Aye, 'tis an admirable thing ya' do, lad."

"Come," Bongani invited, pointing to a nearby poulterer's shop. "My work. We speak. You will be fine, Fiona?" Bongani asked.

"As always," she replied with a soft grin.

The two men were an uncommon sight, full grown trees among saplings, moving through the crowd. Both had to duck as they moved through the doorway and Bongani had barely the space to stand upright once inside. The smell of blood, feathers, and entrails saturated the air. On the tall wooden work tables were chickens in various stages of preparation, some still to be plucked and gutted, others plucked bare, and still others fully butchered and wrapped in cloth.

"A man give Bongani work. I watch her from window," Bongani said, nodding toward Fiona, who was visible through the opening. "I would keep her here but she want to help."

"You are from the southern lands?" Gerrard asked.

"Yes, land of my birth, far from here across desert sands. Green place along the great river."

"You mean the southern Rillebrand?"

"No. *GREAT* river, where Rillebrand is eaten. My tongue called 'Araali,' - 'strength of thunder.'"

Gerrard was curious.

"That is a far ways from here. How did you get this far north?"

"As young boy, I sold to slavery. Bongani endured much and traveled far as slave, but in here," he said, thumping his chest with his closed fist, "Bongani always free. Grow strong in eastern fields until slavery too heavy." Bongani hung his head. "Master beat slave one day, Bongani's friend. Bongani strike master, kill him. No sorrow in here," Bongani said with another closed fist to his chest. "All slaves free that day."

Gerrard could not believe what he heard. Bongani had the heart he was looking for but he wondered if he'd have the willingness to face the terror of the beasts.

CHAPTER SEVENTEEN

Hon arrived in Newtown just in time for Abigail's burial. A cloud of sorrow hung over the village; a testimony to the impact Abigail's life had made on the tiny community. Victoria collapsed into Hon's arms as soon as he reached her.

"The Lord brought you home. I couldn't have borne this without you."

"And I wouldn't have wanted you to," Hon said, wiping a tear from her cheek as they walked together into the barn at the town stable. Inside, the village was gathered to honor the memory of their dearly loved friend.

"She was well loved," Hon said, taking a seat next to Victoria.

"I've always known that. She was a mother at heart, not just to you and me."

The barn was adorned with clover and honeysuckle from the surrounding fields, the latter was a flower Hon knew to be one of Abigail's favorites. Candles, though an extravagance when used in the daytime, were placed across the front of the room, each flame dancing its tribute of love for the dear woman who had gone to be with her Lord.

The morning after Abigail's death Victoria had sent a messenger to the monastery far to the north of Newtown. Brother Philip, a minister who had passed through the village many times came immediately. He arrived just a day before Hon and was asked to lead the ceremony. Abigail's neighbors and friends looked at Brother Philip with sorrowful eyes, seeking words of solace and peace.

The young monk stood before the townsfolk painfully aware of the depth of sorrow they felt. He knew how powerful a role Abigail had played in the formation and growth of their community, and he knew from the fine woman Victoria had become what a diligent and faith-filled mother she had been. He saw in Hon, Abigail's adopted son, what persistent, prayerful, patient love could do for even the most destitute. Abigail had been a source of strength indeed.

"I have no words," Brother Philip began, "to provide the comfort your souls need at this moment. For that, I am truly sorry. As the scriptures say, 'there is a time to every purpose under heaven,' including 'a time to weep.' This is such a time for all of you and I share only a small part in that sorrow.

"My soul was immediately blessed by Abigail the first time I came among you. Even though I know that Abigail would be quick to insist that the blessing I received was not her, but her Lord working through her, *I* must insist that both are true. Our Lord indeed does His will in this world and every good blessing comes from Him. But He uses a variety of means to bring about that blessing. One of His favorite tools is a faithful, surrendered servant, the kind we all know Abigail to have been. And now, the Lord holds one of His favorite servants in His arms.

"As I consider the vicious and brutal attack that came upon your village, I wonder at God's reasons for allowing such senseless things. Why was it Abigail who first stepped outside? Why did she do so at that particular moment? What would have happened if she'd stepped outside seconds earlier, or later? Why did she linger unconscious for so long and in such pain?

"These and many more are the questions that pass through our minds and plague our souls. The answers are slow in coming. And we must admit to ourselves that they may never come.

"In such times we are tempted, though we don't recognize it as such. We are tempted more powerfully than the temptation toward hatred, or lust, or greed. It is the temptation to doubt God. Is He truly good? Is He truly loving? And if the temptation to doubt God has its way, another temptation follows close behind. We become angry at God, resentful of the things He has ordained to take place. We put ourselves in the place of judge and condemn the Holy One of heaven.

CHAPTER SEVENTEEN

"But the same unanswerable questions that push us toward doubt can also urge us toward a stronger faith. For example: We could just as easily ask questions of a different sort — Why was Abigail not a victim of disease or death earlier in her life? Why was she given such a beautiful and faithful daughter? Why was she placed into a loving community like this?

"You see, our lives are filled with both sides of a mystery; want *and* blessing, sorrow *and* joy, and neither has an explanation beyond the fact that our loving God is sovereign and has willed our lives to be as they are. True faith does not believe Him to be good only when we can clearly see that He is. It believes Him to be good even when it cannot see, because He says that He is.

"The challenge to our faith is this; will we trust that what He says of Himself is true, no matter how life and circumstances may tempt us to conclude otherwise?

"My brothers, my sisters, I urge you as I must continue to urge myself; do not walk the path of doubt. Instead, choose to believe God. At other times He has *shown* us that He is love and that He is good. Let us not forget that He has also shown us through the Person and work of His beloved Son, Who sacrificed Himself in our place.

"Abigail, like few women I have ever met learned to trust God instead of doubting Him. She spoke of it. She sang of it. She showed it as she lived among you. Abigail now inhales the promised life of Jesus, breath after eternal breath even though her body lies lifeless here before us. Her faith that has held up so many of you at times holds her now. She is safe, and free."

*****†*****

After Brother Philip's words many from the town stood to share their memories and express their sympathy to Victoria and Hon. Hon found it strange that what would normally have been a very somber and sorrowful time was filled with a mixture of peace, happiness, and even laughter.

Nobody wept as one without hope. The assurance that Abigail was truly alright and that those she left behind would be as well, permeated the entire meeting. At the graveside Victoria and Hon thanked their friends and neighbors for their remembrances and words and the linen wrapped body was laid in the ground. Victoria dropped a bouquet of Abigail's favorite wildflowers into the open grave and began to sing.

Blessed cross, hail, holy Rood!
Death, by thee, was first subdued
When my God was crucified,
When my King and Savior died.

Queen of trees are through, O Palm,
For our wounds the sovereign balm,
Strong support when burdens press,
Solace in our sore distress.

Tree of life, O sacred tree,
Glorious sign of victory,
Christ thy fruit, O tree divine,
Never fruit so sweet as thine.

When before thy judgment-seat
Friend and foe at last shall meet,
Jesus then propitious be,
Son of God, remember me.

Hon found the song entirely appropriate and amazingly soothing to his own aching heart. Victoria's faith was strong like that of her mother. It gave him great hope to know that her aching heart, for which he cared so much, was cared for by One greater than him. He spent the rest of the quiet morning alongside Victoria; listening, holding her, and tending to her needs. But along with the grief, his heart bore another burden, the weight of a decision he would soon have to make. His choice would impact Victoria even more than it would himself.

CHAPTER SEVENTEEN

By afternoon the drain of emotion had taken its toll and Victoria lay down to rest on her pallet in the cottage. Hon took the opportunity to seek out Rowan, his mentor and friend. Rowan would understand the decision he had to make.

He found the older man, a retired soldier, in the fields outside town. He was busy working as always, for the prosperity and good of his family and friends.

"Rowan!" Hon called. His friend waved and smiled. Hon moved down the row of shin-high, leafy greens where Rowan was pulling up the last two good-sized turnips in the row.

"Hon, how are you?" the older man asked, genuinely. "It was a beautiful time this morning. Abigail was honored well."

"Yes, it was," Hon said. "I'm doing well. Victoria is resting."

"I'm glad," Rowan said, lifting his basket. "Sorrow has a way of sucking life from the soul. I suspect she'll need plenty of naps over the next few weeks. Come with me. I'll leave these with Julia and we can walk down to the river."

The village of Newtown bustled with activity as it did every day. Many were involved in the chores of daily existence, moving back and forth across the square. Others were in their homes preparing bread and meat for their evening meal. Hon knew that for the next few days many of those meals would be arriving at Victoria's door as gifts of sympathy and expressions of love. The two men headed toward the river, talking as they went.

"Something is troubling you," Rowan said. "How can I help?"

"Rowan, I think you know that I love Victoria. She has become the most important thing in the world to me, even more so now that Abigail is gone. I want her to be cared for... no, I want to *be the one* to care for her for the rest of her life. But I also have to lead the fight against the dragon masters. It will take me far from home and into many dangers. There's a part of me that is eager to be in the grip of that danger. But then, when I think of Victoria being left behind, I wonder if I'm just being a selfish boy who craves what seems heroic?

"What do I do? If I leave, Victoria will be here alone. If I don't, the dragon masters will be left to their evil schemes, unmolested." He sighed. "Rowan, as a soldier you had to make this kind of choice again and again. How did you decide?"

Rowan smiled.

"It *is* a familiar situation. Julia and I have had countless conversations about this exact thing. For a man who cares for his loved ones as he should, it's a very real struggle. I don't doubt your calling or God's appointment to go after the dragon lords. And I know the responsibility you feel toward Victoria is real and true as well.

"You want to know how to determine what you need to sacrifice, and for what reasons. Love requires sacrifice. You know that. But it's not a one-sided thing. Any sacrifice you choose to make will have to be mutual.

"What do you mean?" Hon asked.

"The two of you have to decide what should be done *together*. If you decide that you should go, don't think that you're the only one making a sacrifice. Victoria will not only have to overcome the physical and emotional void caused by your absence, she will also have to learn to manage the anxiety of daily uncertainty concerning your safety. If you take that step, it's a test of faith for both of you." He paused, a new thought appearing to dawn in his mind. "It's interesting to me that you are facing this decision on the day we have laid Abigail to rest. Hon, do you have any trouble trusting that Abigail is now in the arms of her Savior?"

"None," he said with confidence.

"Does Victoria?"

"Not at all," Hon replied.

"Why not?"

Hon hadn't considered the thought before.

"Because we both know that her faith was genuine and that her death has happened according to God's plan."

Rowan cocked his head to the side.

"You've both got to be able to give the same kind of confident answer regarding the decision to move against the

CHAPTER SEVENTEEN

dragon lords. Both of you have to be certain it's the right thing for you to do and both of you must be able to trust that it is God's plan for both of you, despite the risks and pains involved. Hon, if God is calling the two of you to this, then there is no risk, only the opportunity to trust."

*****†*****

Hon peeked through the cottage door. Victoria was not on her pallet as he had left her. Swinging the door wide he found her seated on a crude bench near the hearth, her head in her hands.

"Victoria? Are you alright?"

She looked up with a smile.

"Yes. I'm just clearing my head, and missing mamma."

Hon strode across the room and took her into his arms. She cried again as she had many times over the last few days. Pulling away from him, she looked into his eyes.

"Hon, I know she's with Jesus and I know I'll be alright without her. But her absence reminds me that I will soon be losing you."

"You are not going to lose me."

"How can you say that?" Victoria responded, getting up from the bench. "You don't know what's going to happen. The first dragon you face could cover you with that black filth like it did Mamma, or scorch you to nothing like the other did my Papa and brother. Don't you dare try to comfort me with nice sounding assurances about things you can't control!"

"I was only trying to…"

"You were trying to be nice, but it's not nice. It's cruel. It's building hope out of wishes instead of dealing with reality. Don't do that to me, Hon. Not now, not ever."

"Victoria, I'm sorry. I didn't mean…"

"Hon, you're going to hunt down dragons! Dragons, Hon! Doesn't that frighten you? Don't you know that you might never come back to me?"

"Yes. I'm afraid. I know all those things could happen," Hon said, "and I'll do everything in my power to come back to you, but…"

"Hon, I don't want you to go!" she interrupted. "I can't lose you, too!"

Victoria collapsed beside him in tears. He took her in his arms.

"I thought we'd decided it was the right thing to do? Didn't we?"

She stiffened in his arms but did not pull away. After a long silence, she replied.

"I know what I said, but I still don't like it."

Hon smiled.

"Then maybe you'll like this... I want us to be married."

Victoria turned to him wide-mouthed.

"Married?"

"I don't think we should wait. Brother Philip is not leaving until tomorrow. Let's go talk to him."

"Hon, I don't know, I, I want to be married but it seems so quick."

"I know it is, and it's probably not what you dreamed of for your wedding, but if I am to leave it will have to be very soon. I don't want to put this off."

Victoria bit her lower lip.

"But what if you don't go? What if you decide you should stay here?"

Hon took a deep breath. He could see from the hopeful look in her eye that they would need to talk through everything again before she would feel comfortable.

"Then let's talk about it. I just spoke with Rowan because I've been feeling torn between the calling to go and the desire I have to be here with you. You are more important to me, without a doubt. But Victoria, this feels like something I'm meant to do."

She looked away as anger flashed across her face.

"What did Rowan say?"

"He said that we need to make the decision together and if we think I should go, we have to commit ourselves to trust the Lord."

CHAPTER SEVENTEEN

She walked to the fireplace and began nervously picking at mortar between the stones. Her shoulders rose and fell, accentuating a large breath and she turned to face him.

"Hon, I told you at the start that I know you're supposed to do this. But I'm afraid you'll be killed, that I'll be alone," she waved her arm toward the door, "that I won't know what's happening to you while you're out there. I'm just scared, Hon."

Hon took her in his arms again.

"So am I. The fear will be the hardest thing we have to conquer."

She looked up at him.

"I still don't like it."

"Neither do I," Hon answered.

Victoria stepped away, stretching their joined hands between them. He tugged her back in his direction.

"Let's go find Brother Philip," he said with a smile.

She smiled and nodded.

*****†*****

Ancient elms stood tall, presiding dominantly over the small glade of trees near the community of Newtown. Aspen and fir dotted the space between their massive roots with scrub oak and wild flowers lying low across the rolling ground. In the center of the grove was a small clearing, one of Victoria's favorite places to walk and think, and it was there that she had chosen to be wed.

The entire village was gathered as they had been the day before, but this time for a very different reason. Hon and Victoria stood before the crowd with Brother Philip officiating and made their vows to each other and to God. The Redpoll and Siskin projected their birdsongs across the glade, the soft wind in the leaves serving as the chorus. It was a day of confident joy, a day when the young man committed himself to love, protect, and care for his bride, and the young woman promised to honor, obey, and love her husband. The bright sun pierced the leaf canopy, dotting the guests and participants with dancing spots of gold.

Far to the east, just cresting The Ridge a dark cloud loomed, its westward motion restrained by the rocky spine that intersected the land north to south. The cloud hung low over the rocky peaks, waiting for its trailing companions to join it, amass atop the stony ridge, and tumble down the side to overtake the sun drenched plains below.

Chatting gaily with friends and neighbors, receiving their congratulations in earnest, Hon looked to the east, to the darkness that loomed over The Ridge. For him it was a portent of days ahead, a sign of dark battles and dangerous ventures.

He turned to find his bride, radiant among her companions that day. He would enjoy her beauty and the delights of her love now, while he could. He put the thoughts of dragons and evil men out of his mind. It was a day to delight in the gracious blessing of his God.

Just as he was turning back to the festivities a movement on the road caught his eye. A rider was just entering the town. Hon corralled a neighbor boy, pointed out the rider, and sent him to lead the man to the grove since nobody would be in town. Within minutes the boy returned with the rider who dismounted from an obviously exhausted horse.

"Hello," Hon said, walking to meet the man. Sandip and Hector strode up behind him. "Looks like you've been riding some time."

"Yes, from around the southern end of The Ridge. I'm looking for Hon."

"That's me," Hon volunteered. "You've come on my wedding day."

"Wedding day? So sorry to interrupt such a joyful time, especially with the news I have to give."

"What is it?"

"Your father, Stewart. He's been taken by Rajic's men. They say the only way you'll see him alive again is if you surrender yourself to the kingdom of Rajic and confess that you are a spy."

CHAPTER EIGHTEEN

Preparations at the estate of Lord James Kendrick were moving at a furious pace. Every worker knew that any evening the dragon might be upon them. Kendrick forced himself to work in spite of his injury, moving among the men to oversee the work and boost morale. He moved among the craftsmen and soldiers as if he was one of them and felt that on a certain level, he was. They were comrades, building and preparing as one for the defense of their homes as well as his.

After the dragon's attack they immediately set to work rebuilding the walls and towers that had been destroyed in the first attack. Lord Kendrick, the captain of his guard, Rupert, and his chief engineer Lucius worked together to make sure the rebuilt towers could accommodate the size of the new weapons.

The primary weapon was an oversized version of a traditional crossbow, with two modifications. Since the six foot width would prevent the weapons from being easily handled, they were permanently placed on a rotating wooden platform that would allow side to side adjustments. The front of the weapon sat on a fulcrum just beneath the "bow" so the back end could be lifted or lowered to make vertical aiming possible. Construction on the trial model had begun simultaneously with the first tower repair. When finished, Kendrick watched with pleasure as Rupert and another man made use of it for the first time.

The "iron cross" as Kendrick called it, could be operated by two men, one to control the aiming and the other to be responsible for loading and firing. Once the weapon was deemed usable Kendrick ordered construction of five others. Within two weeks all five were built and mounted. Ten crews were trained in their use. Kendrick instructed Rupert to drill all iron cross crews for at least six hours each day. He wanted to be ready and knew that the new weapons would not only have to be tested thoroughly, but able to be put to good use should a dragon attack come.

The smiths had been hard at work as well. Every foot soldier was provided his own standard crossbow. The production schedule was demanding but the crews set themselves to the task with vigor. Every man knew that their lives and those of their families depended on the weapons being ready.

Lord Kendrick stood atop the central tower looking on as teams took turns aiming and firing the new weapons. Below him, group after group of soldiers flowed through the courtyard, each one taking their turn perfecting their aim with crossbow, longbow, and javelin. Rupert had been present all day, walking among the soldiers, distracting them, forcing them to fire with handicaps of various sorts. The goal was to see that the soldiers could adapt to any and all circumstances. Kendrick knew that Rupert's experience with him in the northern mountains had sobered him. He had seen the beasts personally and had heard Hon's first-hand account of confronting one of them. Rupert wanted his troops to be ready for the terror they would face, and he knew it would be worse than they imagined. Kendrick raised his eyes to look across his lands, the bony spine of The Ridge rising in the distance. Storm clouds gathered there. A chill ran up his spine.

"James?" Patrice's voice broke the silence.

"Yes, love?" he said, turning to face his wife of 23 years. She was lovely in mind, heart, and appearance. Her long, dark hair was drawn up and back, secured with a gold clip at the crown of her head. From there it streamed down behind her ears and over her shoulders in gentle waves. The sky blue gown she wore was stunning.

"Do you think we are ready?" she asked, a look of concern very evident in her deep eyes.

"Absolutely," he answered, not as confident as he sounded. "Rupert has been very thorough and the men have

CHAPTER EIGHTEEN

responded well. There is nothing more we can do except to hone our skills, and wait."

"James, do you think he is alright?"

He knew immediately she was speaking of Cedrick.

"I'm sure he is, though I expected his return before now. There could be all kinds of valid reasons for it, though. Perhaps Hon or Gerrard has run into trouble and Cedrick has been prevented from coming. Were my legs healed you know I would have already been on the road after him myself."

She snuggled under his strong arm.

"Yes, I know. He's blessed to have you as his father. I hope he sees that, though we often don't see things as they are. It reminds me, Camille and I have been talking about her years away, and what happened in both of us as a result of that whole, horrible ordeal. It's strange to say, in fact, it sounds quite mad, but we both feel that we would not change a thing even if we could."

Lord Kendrick was surprised.

"What do you mean?"

"Well Silas, for instance; he intended to do us great harm, and he did. I still hate him for it," she said, with an embarrassed glance at her husband. "For eleven years we agonized over our lost daughter, fearing her abused, violated, even dead. By the end of it I think I had almost resigned myself to the belief that she was dead. But James, now that she's back and the raw pain of the injustice and loss are no more than distant aches, I see so much good that came of it, so much in myself that has grown and that would never have come about any other way."

Lord Kendrick raised his eyebrows as he stroked his beard.

"And if that surprises you," she continued with smirk, "you won't know what to do with the next part. Camille feels the same way." She paused, looking curiously at him. "James, do you understand what I'm saying? We bore the pain of loss and uncertainty. But Camille bore the true pain of abuse and privation, of being taken from her home as a little girl and mistreated in cruel ways. She was the most vulnerable, the most abused, the most unjustly treated of anyone. If any person has a right to begrudge her past, it is Camille. But James, she has told me... let me think, what were her exact words? Ah, yes, she said, 'I am not thankful for what I had to endure, but I am thankful that I had to endure it.' "

His wife was right. He didn't know how to think about Camille's attitude, except to be thankful.

*****†*****

Camille sat by the window in Quinn's dimly lit room, pouring over notes he'd jotted down in the middle of the night. He was a peculiar man, keenly intelligent but strangely devoid of the life habits of a normal person. She believed he was intentionally so.

Quinn viewed sleep as a waste of time and preferred to arrange his life such that he slept only four hours a night, usually from just after sunset until midnight. The rest of the time he was wide awake; thinking, reading, planning, writing, talking to himself, and testing his theories. The amount of energy he was able to generate on such a small amount of sleep astounded her. But what he produced in his waking hours baffled her even more.

Quinn's thoughts and theories about human nature, social interactions and conventions, societies, political systems, and commerce were more than she could fathom. And the way he applied and combined the knowledge from each of those areas caused her mind to spin. His notes were so thorough and deep she had to work on them in small chunks, two or three hours at a time. Then she'd step away to take a walk or visit the garden; anything to allow her mind to rest.

When she needed to ask for clarification regarding what he'd written, which was often, she'd first receive a blank stare in response, as if he thought her to be the most imbecilic person alive. That was followed by a rapid explanation of the subject in concepts and vocabulary she struggled to understand. But understand she did. Little by little, the often abrasive and always harried contact with Quinn's razor sharp

CHAPTER EIGHTEEN

mind was enabling her to grasp concepts and implications she'd never have imagined on her own. She was hopeful that her time under Quinn would benefit the rebellion against the dragon masters in great ways.

A timid knock at the door interrupted her reading.

"Come."

The door cracked open and her mother's head peeked around the edge.

"Mother? What are you doing up here? Come in, come in, it's alright."

"I hope I'm not disturbing," Lady Patrice apologized, glancing nervously about the dim room. "I wanted to see if you'd like to join me for tea."

"Definitely," Camille said, tossing the parchment on the table. "My brain was about to erupt. I could use the diversion."

The two regal women walked arm and arm down the hallway, chatting as they descended the curving staircase that hugged the tower wall.

"I'm glad you came, mother. I have been thinking about the future and could use your counsel."

"Oh?" Patrice said with a pleased look on her face. "Camille, you don't know how much good those words do to a mother's heart. You are such a lady now and I missed so much of your life. It's good to know that I'm still needed."

"You most certainly are," the younger woman insisted. "I'd have been lost these past months without your guidance."

"What did you want to ask me?"

"I'm truly enjoying what I'm learning from Quinn, though I must admit it's overwhelming at times. He has a capacity for knowledge and thinking that are beyond me. So I take it slowly and learn what I can, at my own pace. But what I am learning mother, it's amazing and wonderful!"

Lady Patrice smiled in response.

"It's good to see you so happy and fulfilled. What exactly is it that you're learning, my dear?"

"I'm learning about people." She stopped and giggled. "It sounds funny to say it that way, but really, that is what I'm doing. I'm learning how the human mind works and how things like ambition, and desire, and injury, and disappointment affect us. I'm learning how we take things for granted, so much so that we overlook vitally important things. And I'm learning that all of that can be used to put our dragon slayers in places where they can gain advantage without being noticed."

"My, my Camille, such intrigue and mystery. I'd never have believed my daughter to be so wily."

"Mother, I come by it naturally," she said with a wink.

"Whatever do you mean?" Patrice said, pretending to be dumbfounded as they walked into the bedroom.

"Mother! Don't pretend you don't know what I'm talking about. All that time you and father played along with Silas' game and he never knew. The two of you are skilled at subterfuge and mystery whether you know it or not."

Lady Patrice looked her straight in the eye, an amused look on her face. She turned her attention to gently stirring her tea.

"So, you mentioned your future. How do you see all that you're learning fitting in?"

"I think... no, I know that I can be of great help to Hon's cause. The things I'm learning are the knowledge and skills that he and his band of men are going to need in order to covertly make their way into a place where they can strike effectively. From the start I knew that I wanted to play a role in it, and I think I assumed that I'd be able to do that from here. But I'm beginning to see that I won't be able to."

Her mother looked up from her tea cup, stone faced.

"Why not? You know your father will provide all the space and weapons and resources that Hon and his group need."

"I know he will, mother, but this is not a safe place for them to train. First off, if they are here and a dragon attacks, they could be destroyed. But even more importantly, they need to be away from curious eyes, someplace tucked away and unsuspected. We are anything but that here." She paused, seeing the pain in her mother's eyes. "I know that you want me here and I do want to be here with you. We have a great

CHAPTER EIGHTEEN

deal of rebuilding still to do between us. But wherever Hon chooses to make his base of operations, I need to be there."

Patrice sat down her cup and raised her head, her straight jaw set firmly as she looked into her daughter's eyes.

"Camille, it was a motherly wish to have you to myself. But these are disturbing times and you are not a child. You have a life of your own to live, though in heaven's name I can't understand why you'd want to be in the middle of all this intrigue and deception. But regardless, I will support you in whatever you do." She paused, a tear forming in her eye. Raising the billowing sleeve of her dress to her eye, she continued. "Where do you suspect Hon will want to locate his little band of secret warriors?"

"I don't know," Camille answered. "But Gerrard has offered his forest home as one option. Or perhaps it will be somewhere near Newtown, though I would caution against it."

"Why? It is an out of the way place," Patrice offered.

"Yes, but it is also a populated place. Should the base be discovered everyone there would be in danger. I wouldn't want that and I'm sure Hon wouldn't either, especially since it's his hometown."

"That does make sense," her mother agreed. "Do you have any ideas?"

"I think Gerrard's suggestion may be the best one. We'll have to wait and see what Hon thinks."

She looked up to see her mother staring at her.

"Camille, you are an amazing young woman. I am so happy, so blessed to be your mother."

A knock on the door interrupted their conversation.

"Come," answered Lady Patrice. Her maid, Madeline entered.

"Excuse me m'lady, but a message has come for you and Lord Kendrick, from the woodsman."

"Gerrard!" Lady Patrice said excitedly, extending her hand for the message. Breaking the seal she read it aloud to Camille.

Me dearest Lord and Lady Kendrick,

Upon me arrival at The Boar's Head, where I was to meet our young dragon slayer, I did not find him, but was instead provided a message by the hand of the Innkeep. An urgent matter has occurred at Newtown, taking Hon away. Rest assured, yer lad Cedrick is with him, safe as a mother bear's cub. Put yer mind at ease on that account.

I have found another man here who is willing to join our escapade. I am sending him on to Newtown to join Hon and the men he's already collected. I believe him to be a trustworthy man and will entrust yer message to him. We shall do our best to get yer' lad home to you. Me own plan is to return to yer castle to get the pigeons trained.

Signed,

Gerrard Reginald McGreggor, the third.

CHAPTER NINETEEN

Hon looked across the table at his "council," the people whose advice mattered most to him. Next to him was his new bride, Victoria. He felt for her. Just a day earlier she was immersed in the joys of becoming a bride and here she sat in a somber, anxious meeting to discuss the fate of her new husband. It didn't feel right or fair, but it was their reality.

As always, Rowan was ready to lend a hand or give counsel. His wife, Julia, sat beside him, tears in her eyes as she looked across the table at Victoria. Hon's long-time friend, Rowan and Julia's son, Frederick, was present as well. Lord Kendrick's son Cedrick, who had just turned twelve a few days earlier, was seated on Hon's other side.

Over the last few days Hon had come to believe that something was on the boy's mind, but hadn't had time to explore it. Hampton, the quirky old steward was present, though still suffering from the loss of Abigail. His mop of hair hung low over his ears, a visual representation of the heaviness that covered his heart. Standing in the corner was brother Philip. The monk had planned to begin his journey to the monastery in the northern mountains but told Hon he would wait until the meeting was over, on the chance that he might be of some use.

Seated along the wall on a short bench were the men newest to the group, Sandip and Hector. He'd had little time to spend with them since the trip to Newtown, but was encouraged by the fact that they had come along on such short notice. He hoped that they were men willing to lay down their lives for the protection and safety of others. As he remembered the night spent in the stocks alongside Hector, he wasn't too sure.

"I received a message yesterday that my father, who lives over The Ridge, has been taken by Rajic's troops. I'm believed to be a spy for Kendrick and they are forcing me to give myself up."

Victoria gripped his hand. Cedrick looked from face to face. Sandip's head dropped.

"Obviously, this changes things, but I'm not sure how. I wanted to begin our training right away," he said, nodding in Sandip and Hector's direction. "But I can't do that now. Most of you know my history with my father. I've only seen him once since I was very small, and that only for a few days. I cannot let him wither away in a prison cell because of me."

"I am new heer," Hector said. "I want to know why thees Rajic wants you. *Are* you Kendrick's spy?"

"It's a misunderstanding," Hon began. "When I was on the way to see my father the commander at the southern crossroad suspected me of being a spy for Lord Kendrick because I rode alone and was of fighting age. He allowed me to pass, but required me to return to his checkpoint within three days. That never happened. While I was at my father's home I received word of the dragon attacks that were happening here so I came directly home instead of returning to the crossroad. The commander must have remembered where I was headed and decided to use my father to find me."

"Hon, do you know where they are keeping your father?" Rowan asked.

"No. The message says I am to surrender myself to any of Rajic's troops."

"Are you considering a rescue?" Sandip asked.

"Considering it, but I don't know if it's wise."

Sandip nodded.

"I understand, and advise against it. Any attempt to rescue your father would bring you and possibly the rest of us, to Rajic's attention. The problem is with the commander, you see?. If you can deal directly with him, you may be able to remain hidden as far as Rajic is concerned. Who's to say the commander will not be appeased by your appearance and release your father, as he has promised?"

"Agreed," Hon said. "If our move against the dragon lords is to succeed I must not come to Rajic's attention. But I

CHAPTER NINETEEN

cannot allow my father to remain as he is, either. From my experience with Commander Eadric, I'm not so confident that he'll keep his word. Besides, once I'm there, he'll assume me to be a spy and I'll probably wind up before Rajic in the end, anyway."

"I served with a man called 'Eadric' under Thurmond," Rowan said. "Is he a stocky man? Hairy, with scarred forearms?"

"That's him," Hon answered.

Rowan released a loud, long breath.

"Eadric is not a bad man, but he is ambitious. My guess is he's trying to move up in the ranks and he's using you and your father to do it. I agree with Sandip. Eadric will release your father if you turn yourself in to him. Besides, what other choice do you have?"

Hon sighed.

"None."

Hampton spoke, his head held low, wild hair in his face.

"It appears to the astute observer, which I am, that the situation before you is precisely what you desire."

Hon looked to Rowan, who shrugged his shoulders.

"I don't understand Hampton."

The older man raised his head, extended his lower lip, and blew the hair from his eyes.

"Your goal is to infiltrate the inner circles of the dragon lords, so as to bring calamity upon them. You have before you an invitation move among them. I concede, it does not appear to be such, and has its disadvantages, but such it is."

Hon was amazed. Victoria squeezed his hand and gave him a hesitant nod.

"I'm content to do it," Hon replied, "and trust the Lord for the outcome. But what of our plans? What of the rest of you?"

"What of us?" Hector slurred. "We are barely eenvolved at thees point, anyway."

"What were you planning before all this came about?" Sandip asked.

"There are a number of things. First, we need to find at least one more man, though two would be better. Next, we have to find an out-of-the-way place where we can strategize and do some training together. I was hoping we could all meet with Quinn, Lord Kendrick's spymaster. His instruction would be very helpful. I think the two of you could still meet with Quinn, without me," Hon said, looking to Sandip and Hector. "Lord Kendrick would be happy to receive you, and Cedrick could make the introductions."

Cedrick fidgeted on his stool.

"Cedrick, is something wrong?" Hon asked.

"No, I can do that," the boy replied. "I need to return home, anyway."

Hon looked at him curiously. Cedrick's chin rested on his chest.

"I left without my parent's permission."

Hector chuckled.

"Excelente! Your father weel be so angry weeth you, he won't care about me at all!"

Cedrick ignored the comment and turned to Hon.

"I've got to go home and make it right."

"I say we leave tomorrow morning," Hon suggested. "We'll go to Lord Kendrick, then I'll travel on to the southern crossroads. As soon as I can I'll send word."

CHAPTER TWENTY

The dragon lords had agreed. It was time for their beasts to meet. They would so in the far, southeastern region of Rajic's land on the evening of the next full moon. It was a region of open, sage-covered fields, devoid of cities and roads. It was an isolated area so they were unlikely to be seen. Some referred to the landscape as "high desert" terrain and looking around the area in the bright moonlight, Hugo had to agree.

There was nothing but sage, cactus, and twisting mesquite trees for as far as he could see. He was the first to arrive, purposely so. He had calculated every aspect of this night just as he had planned every detail leading up to it. He wanted his Boreas to be there first, waiting for the others like a king receiving his subjects. The only uncertain thing was how having all four beasts together in the presence of their masters would impact the dominance he and his white beast had attained. He was certain that Boreas would eventually reign over them all, but wasn't sure how easily or quickly it would come. From the north he heard the unmistakable beat of dragon wings.

Silas or Rajic. Good. Either will be fine as the next arrival. Silas' red is the most submissive to Boreas, and Rajic's black is the one longest acquainted with him. Their arrival should make the situation more stable from the outset.

Peering into the moon-glow sky from the back of his monstrous steed, Hugo saw the glimmering red of Hestia's crimson scales. Silas brought his dragon to earth a hundred feet to the east, clearly concerned that the first meeting of their beasts might produce an unwanted conflict.

The young red was radiant, almost glowing in the moon-drenched night. Its graceful form was characteristic of the dragon tales through the ages; a large, triangular head perched atop a strong, thick neck. From its muscular shoulders the mighty fore-claws hung menacingly, its thick, powerful wing arms extending regally from its mighty back. Massive legs supported the huge body with a powerful tail swaying behind.

A loud screech echoed from the sky as Sanniya and her green beast, Gahlib, landed to the south in a puff of desert dust. The emerald dragon, though obviously of the same species, was entirely different than the red. Whereas the red was distinguished by a powerful form, the green's shape was characterized by grace. From its thin, shapely head all the way to the tip of its extra-long tail, the beast was a lithe and nimble serpent, its four agile legs seemingly thrown in as afterthoughts. Upon landing it immediately folded its wings alongside its twisting torso, almost camouflaging their existence. Gahlib was unsettled by the presence of the red dragon, shifting his weight back and forth, swinging its long, graceful neck side to side. Soothing words from its master, spoken in a hypnotic foreign tongue soon had the green monster settled and calm, though its breath still puffed out and in heavily.

Looking back to assess the red's reaction to the arrival of Sanniya and her Gahlib, Hugo recognized the angular silhouette of Rajic's black dragon as it descended against the outline of the rising moon. Everything about Raat gave the impression of chaos come to life. Bony protrusions ran up its tail and spine, ending in a flurry around its head. Sharp, zigzag scales covered its stocky body. Its form was one of hard lines and harsh symmetry. Each of the masters had their own reservations about the meeting. Hugo knew it to be true. None truly knew what to expect. But Hugo had the advantage. He dismounted his beast determined to take initiative where he knew the others to be leery.

Leaving his Boreas lying obediently atop a rocky outcropping, he walked to the central point between the four beasts and raised his thick, fleshy arms above his head. With a loud clap of his meaty hands and a shout of "Down!" all four dragons snapped their heads in his direction and settled

CHAPTER TWENTY

onto their bellies in the dirt. He smiled as astonishment registered on the other dragon lord's faces.

"A trick my father taught me." Hugo shouted the lie in his irritatingly high-pitched voice. "I thought our introductions would go a bit easier if things were controlled from the outset. Will your beasts be content to stay as they are so we might have a word together?"

Each of the dragon masters dismounted, obviously disconcerted by the influence Hugo had over their dragons. He chuckled to himself.

This is going to be good.

All agreed that the first introduction of the beasts should be arranged between the black and the red, since they were already acquainted. The hope was that their example might set the tone for the introductions to follow. Hugo was impatient but he played along. As suspected, Hestia the red and Raat the black were immediately friendly toward each other, exchanging the characteristic sniffings and nudgings that familiar dragons do.

Hugo noticed Boreas shifting nervously across the field. With a snap of his fingers his white beast settled. Upon sending the red and black dragons back to their respective places, the green was allowed to approach the white. As Hugo expected, there was no difficulty.

The apprehension among the masters waned with each interaction. Rajic suggested that they bring all of the beasts together. Everyone agreed. Each of the four was summoned to its master who stood in the middle of the clearing. Instinct and the struggle for male dominance erupted with a fury even Hugo did not expect. The white dragon immediately asserted itself, positioning its body menacingly over the top of Hestia, the only female in the group. It was the posture of a dominant male claiming a female as its own. The black rushed the white unexpectedly, sending the masters scrambling for cover. Their commands were drowned in the growls and hisses emanating from the two males. They barred their teeth at each other and their huge bodies slammed together in a game of intimidation and strength. Their long necks were drawn back as they pressed their mighty chests together, pushing against each other with their mighty hind legs. It was soon evident that neither would easily give way to the other.

Vicious swipes with their powerful fore claws landed repeatedly upon rock-hard scales. Their powerful necks darted in and out, aiming razor-teeth at vulnerable spots on the neck and head of their counterpart. The howls of the two opponents mixed with the manic hissing and rumbling of the other two, who seemed to be rooting the pair on. Blood flowed as teeth and claws found their mark.

Hugo glanced to his left. Rajic was clearly concerned for his beast and fuming that things had gotten so out of control. Hugo laughed to himself. He knew that neither dragon would be killed. It was a fight for dominance, nothing more.

Boreas was the larger and stronger of the pair and soon gained the advantage. Hugo smiled as the black dragon flinched and cowered under his white's repeated blows. In a matter of minutes, Boreas stood menacingly over the black as it lay prone, head and neck lying flat between the outstretched fore-claws of the great white dragon. Boreas dropped his head low over his opponent and released an earth shaking howl. Raat did not move, ready to submit to the authority the white dragon had earned. Raising his head, Boreas erupted with another great roar in the direction of the other two beasts and lumbered back toward the red female.

"Your beast is out of control!" Rajic screamed at Hugo.

"We all knew this was a volatile recipe, Rajic!" Hugo responded with equal volume. "Didn't you realize that we are trying to control wildness itself? Such things are to be expected. Besides, how would you feel if another man approached your queen with the intent to make her his mate, Rajic?" He let his words sink in. "It is clear that your black had more to do with the red than raids on unsuspecting villages. They were mates, until a stronger male was added to the recipe. There must be a leader of the pack and now we know which of them it is to be. "

Rajic was silent.

CHAPTER TWENTY

"It is over now and the four will be friends," Hugo concluded.

"Is the way of the beast," Sanniya agreed. "The four are one."

Silas had not spoken since arriving and it made Hugo curious.

"Your Hestia is a coveted jewel among the brutes," Hugo said to him.

Silas nodded, eyeing Hugo carefully.

"It appears so. We are fortunate it was no worse."

"See them," Sanniya interjected. "They become one."

The four beasts had come together, sniffing, grunting, and posturing, but displaying no further aggression. They were strangely peaceful, like old friends. Hugo laughed to himself again.

"The difficult step has been taken and we are on the other side," Hugo said. "It's time for us to determine our first strike."

It was time for the dragon lords to rise.

CHAPTER TWENTY-ONE

Five riders moved through the small village tucked neatly at the foot of Lord Kendrick's estate. They drew no attention to themselves, mounted on horses entirely unremarkable and were moving slowly, None of them spoke and not one showed his face, the hoods of their cloaks pulled low over their foreheads. They traveled west, past the village and up the rocky road leading to the east gate of the castle. Upon their arrival at the front gate the smallest rider moved to the front and briefly lifted his hood for the benefit of the guard on watch. The gate rose and the small band entered.

  Dismounting at the stables, Hon removed his cloak and looked around. A great deal had changed since he was last there. The walls and towers were entirely rebuilt, most with more substantial buttressing and masonry work than before. Atop the towers were the oversized crossbows Kendrick had proposed. The complement of watchmen and soldiers was at least double what it was previously. Cedrick stood beside him, his eyes also raised, but his face revealed that his mind was elsewhere.

  Hon placed a firm hand on the boy's shoulder.

  "We should go in and get it over with, don't you think?"

  Cedrick nodded. Hon motioned Frederick, Sandip, and Hector to follow. The ornate double door opened to a wide stone hallway running deep into the keep. In a few moments they stood before another ornate double door.

  "The great hall," Cedrick said. "They've probably already sat down to supper."

  Stepping to the door Cedrick paused, the rest of the men remaining a comfortable distance behind. His shoulders raised and lowered with a large breath and he pushed the doors open. Firelight and torches illuminated the expansive hall. A long, intricately carved rectangular table was its central feature. Seated at the large table was the royal family, Lord Kendrick, Lady Patrice, and Camille. A loud clank greeted the men as Lady Patrice stood, her utensils dropping into her plate. She rushed across the room.

"Cedrick! I'm so thankful you are safe," she said, her voice trembling. The two remained in a tender embrace as Lord Kendrick limped forward alongside his daughter to greet the group.

"Hon, thank you for watching over Cedrick and for returning him to us."

"I'm happy to have found him, Lord Kendrick. But honestly, he was no trouble at all."

"The important thing is that he's home now," Lord Kendrick said. "I see you have brought friends?"

"Yes, these three are considering our cause, and this," he said, pointing to Fredrick, "is Fredrick, a long-time friend who I think you met when you were with us at Newtown."

"Yes, of course," Kendrick said, reaching for Fredrick's hand. "Rowan's son, am I correct?"

"Yes, sir," Frederick responded.

"Every bit a man yourself, though. It is good to see you again, Frederick," Kendrick said genuinely. "I'm sure you make your father quite proud."

Frederick blushed.

Lady Patrice had taken Cedrick aside and the two whispered in the far corner of the room. Hon continued with the introductions to Lord Kendrick and Lady Camille.

"May I present Sandip, a new acquaintance and one who has some very interesting family connections as far as we are concerned."

Lord Kendrick took Sandip's hand and nodded.

"I look forward to hearing more, sir."

"And finally Lord Kendrick, I present Hector, a man I'm convinced will be of great help to us."

Hector looked nervously at Hon before taking the hand Kendrick extended.

CHAPTER TWENTY-ONE

"I am truly happy to make your acquaintance," Lord Kendrick said as he shook Hector's hand vigorously. "Join us," he invited. "We welcome you to our home."

Servants brought additional plates and food without being asked. The aroma of pheasant and potatoes set the hungry men's mouths watering. Lady Patrice, still holding Cedrick's hand led him to the chair beside her.

"If you don't mind Lord Kendrick, we would like to seek the help of Quinn while we are here," Hon said

"He is at your disposal," Kendrick said. "I doubt I could keep him from the venture even if I wanted to. It's the greatest challenge to his abilities that has come along for some time."

"Hon, it is good to see you again," Camille said. "And I am pleased to meet the rest of you." Hector's eyes nervously met Camille's for a moment and then looked away. "I've been working closely with Quinn while you've been gone and father is right, he is eager to make some headway. He is peculiar, but an amazing man all the same. Father, did you know Quinn has a flawless memory? One look at a parchment, for just a few seconds and he has its contents etched in his mind."

"Yes, I've seen him perform the same feat many times," Kendrick answered. "It's one of the many reasons I procured his services. There's not a mind to rival him, I venture."

"I wish it were only one mind we were up against," Hon said.

"Yes, well, Quinn will relish the opportunity to help you outmaneuver those who oppose you. Each time I've seen him over the past few weeks he's been mumbling under his breath about them. You can be sure he's worked out any number of scenarios by now."

"I'm thankful to hear that," Hon said. "I hope he won't mind me leaving these three with him. I have some urgent business across The Ridge." Kendrick's brow furrowed. "My father has been taken by a commander named Eadric. He has demanded my appearance before my father will be released."

"I see," the older man said. "Naturally, you must secure his release. Do you think there will be trouble?"

"I don't see how it can be avoided. They suspect me of being one of your spies so I'll have to make my way from here secretly. I'm hoping that my voluntary appearance will enable them to see me in a different light."

"Godspeed to you," Kendrick replied, "and I pray for your safe and soon return."

Looking across the table Hon saw Hector seated at the table. His new friend clearly enjoyed the food but was noticeably uncomfortable.

"Lord Kendrick, may I beg your favor in regard to a rather delicate subject? It has to do with my friend here?" he said, motioning toward Hector. The Spaniard's head snapped up.

"Hon, ask anything and it shall be yours."

Hector's eyes grew large.

"Hector is willing to join us and I believe him to be an honest man who will serve well. But he feels that the association with you could pose a difficulty," Hon said with a smirk.

"Oh?" Kendrick replied.

Hon decided to have some fun with his new friend.

"He's had his share of difficulties with your troops over in the Twins and other places. He's concerned that his reputation may not meet with your approval and that you'll clap him in irons."

Hector shot a glare Hon's direction. Kendrick stifled a smile and turned toward Hector.

"Tell me sir, what is the nature of these difficulties?"

Hector fidgeted in his chair, picking at a crust of bread with his unwashed fingers.

"Eet is a hard thing, señor, sir, Lord Keendrick." He dropped the crust and raised his head to meet Lord Kendrick's gaze. "I do not mean to make troubles, but troubles find me. I drink too much, wheech I admeet is most of the problem. Because of eet I have done wrong in many ways. But eet is not only that. I do not like bullies or to see the helpless suffer. Wheen I see your troops being bullies, I fight theem. Wheen I am drunk," he flashed an embarrassed look in Camille's

CHAPTER TWENTY-ONE

direction, "I do not leesten very good and I fight harder. I am no stranger to your jails."

Kendrick frowned.

"I can see why you are nervous. A man with your background would normally be of great concern to me. But there are three things in your favor. First, I sense that you regret your past behavior. Am I right?"

"Yes señor, I do," Hector said with a nod.

"That carries great weight with me. A man who sees the error of his ways and openly admits them as you have done, is fertile soil for a new start. I am willing to give you the opportunity to make that new start.

"The second thing in your favor is of greater importance to me, Hector. You despise injustice, as I do. Few men are brave enough to stand up to it and even fewer will speak to me about it when it concerns my own men. I thank you for that, truly. I clearly have work to do in the discipline and training of my troops."

"Finally, you are a companion of my good friend," Kendrick placed his hand on Hon's shoulder, "a man to whom I owe my life. If Hon says you can be trusted, then I trust you too. But let me be clear. I trust you today with no marks against you. It is up to you to make sure that it stays that way. Comprender?"

The look of befuddlement on Hector's face almost set Hon laughing, but he restrained it for the sake of Hector's pride. Hector nodded.

"Good," Kendrick said, extending his hand. "We will shake and be friends and say no more about it."

Hon smiled at Hector and could see that his friend didn't know what to think of his newly received pardon. The man looked nervously again at Camille, who smiled kindly in return, and resumed eating his meal. Hon leaned forward to look down the table. Cedrick and his mother were still engaged in a hushed conversation, their food untouched. Just beyond Lady Patrice was an empty place, set as if ready for another guest.

*****†*****

Rupert, Captain of the guard moved atop the highest rampart of Lord Kendrick's castle, making his evening rounds before retiring. The heightened state of alert was wearing on the troops and it concerned him. The men were well trained and ready, of that he was sure. But the knowledge that the attack of the dragon lords would surely come but with no assurances as to when, produced a weariness that he could not combat. But he tried nevertheless.

A thick fog rose from the trees in the surrounding forest but the air bore no chill or dampness typical of a fog. In fact, the evening was uncommonly warm and still. Stepping closer to the edge of the mighty wall Rupert peered into the haze and felt as much as saw that it bore a greenish tinge. Reaching to his right Rupert patted the shoulder of a soldier, and using hand signals, gave the command to take up arms.

Silently but swiftly, like a wind-stirred ripple across the treetops, the signal was passed and men responded.

Rupert peered into the woods, searching for anything that might reveal the presence of their enemies. A large, fog-shrouded movement caught his eye and was gone. Another motion to his right and then all was still. His keen ears could hear the sound of the gears at the front gate, lowering the portcullis and raising the drawbridge. The silent order to arms had made its rounds.

What is out there? Rupert wondered, knowing all the while that he had seen the answer months before, atop a mountain far to the north.

*****†*****

Sandip pushed back from the table with a large burp, a sign of deep satisfaction with the meal. Camille snickered behind her hand as she looked toward her mother. Hon was just beginning his explanation of Sandip's connection to Rajic when a powerful sound from above and a massive vibration shook the room with a force that caused Hon to grip the table. Every eye went to the ceiling.

CHAPTER TWENTY-ONE

"The iron cross," Kendrick said. High overhead an unearthly screech moved rapidly from south to north. The sound of the mighty weapon registered again, but more distant and without the accompanying vibration. Lord Kendrick spun to face his wife.

"Patrice, Camille, to the tunnels as we rehearsed. Send for our guest to meet you there. Men," Kendrick said, as he reached for his sword and glanced knowingly at Hon, "gather your courage. You are about to face the fury of hell itself."

*****†*****

As Hon emerged from the keep the mixture of dark and light that is twilight engulfed him. Its dull glow muffled his senses and gave the sensation that everything was moving at a snail's pace. An eerie fog shrouded everything. Soldiers called across the courtyard, the iron crosses with their ear-splitting "*SHHUUUKK!*" sounded repeatedly from all directions, and in the midst of it, from multiple directions at the same time came the hideous screeches he dreaded. The dragons were upon them.

The heavy stroking sounds of dragon wings shot through the gathering darkness overhead. The southeast watchtower was already a heap of rubble and two of the iron crosses burned, their crews battling the flames with blankets and buckets.

Hon bolted up the stairs to the main battlement where men were rapidly firing crossbows into the deepening haze. Out of the darkness a lithe green form, long and powerful emerged, belching a heavy green-tinged fog across the top of the wall. Within seconds of being covered by the cloud, soldiers fell to their knees, retching up their supper in great heaves. Hon held his breath and turned away just as a man to his right emptied the contents of his stomach.

Running down the stairs to escape the dragon's breath, a monstrous howl from the far side of the courtyard pierced Hon's ears. He turned just as a scaly dark form shot out of the darkness, spewing a foul, black mucus across the men posted atop the eastern wall. Within seconds the men fell, writhing in pain. Seconds later, they lay still.

Just like Abigail.

Following close on the tail of the black beast came a larger white one, its mighty rear claws extended like an eagle snatching a fish from a river. Through the haze Hon saw a large man astride the mighty shoulders of the white monster. The top ten feet of the rear-most tower broke from its place and men, stone, and the oversized crossbow were carried into the night. Moments later he heard the screams of men and the crash of the iron cross as they dashed together on the ground below.

As the beast vanished, Hon recognized Sandip's lean form hurtling up the stairs toward the destroyed tower, bow in hand and arrows flying one after another toward the retreating dragon. From behind him Hon heard the shouts of Hector. He was speeding down the length of the parapet walk atop the curtain wall, a rapid stream of unintelligible screams flowing from his lips. As he neared the end of the walkway he did not slow, and with a great leap hurled himself from its edge just as the black beast sped past.

He collided with the dragon's rider, almost knocking him from his scaly perch. With a firm grip on Raj's hairy coat, Hector pulled himself atop the monster, his heavy punches landing hard on the dragon lord's head and shoulders as he did. Hon saw Rajic pull a katar from his belt just as the monster melted into the darkness.

"Where is the red one?" Hon asked himself. He knew that the dragon he'd met in the northern cave had to be engaged in the battle. It was the only beast he knew to have the fiery breath, and fires were blazing all around. Then he saw it, far up in the sky, circling like a vulture searching for carrion. It was waiting, selecting the most vulnerable place to strike. On its back he could see the small form of the wicked old man, Silas.

Hon's eyes darted from side to side until he found what he sought, a crossbow lying on the cold stone beside the body of its fallen owner. Snatching up the bow and pulling the

CHAPTER TWENTY-ONE

quiver of bolts from the belt of the dead man, he steadied himself against the outer wall. Raising his weapon, Hon peered down the shaft, lining up his shot with the red dragon's rider. The beast was moving swiftly, making it difficult for Hon to synchronize his movement with its flight. The beast suddenly dropped toward the far northern wall, spinning like an arrow as it hurtled toward its target.

Hon pulled the trigger and the bolt took flight. The old man jerked backward as the bolt found its mark, passing entirely through his extended forearm. Silas slumped over the dragon's back clutching tightly to the leather harness he sat upon as the dragon continued its run over the north wall. In an instant its fiery breath ignited the top of the wall. The screams of its victims filled Hon with anger.

He felt a hand on his shoulder and turned. It was Lord Kendrick, with Frederick at his side. The younger man had taken it upon himself to see that the still-crippled ruler was not left to himself.

"Hon, they are too much for us."

"Have we even hit one of them??" Hon asked.

"Not that I can see, and we only have one iron cross still operable, and only one of its operators is still alive. We have to sound the retreat."

Hon nodded, watching as his friend limped away leaning on Frederick's shoulder. The brave man still bore the wounds of his last encounter with a dragon. The loss of his home and kingdom would be another heavy blow. The castle walls lay in ruins, smoke filled the air. The moans of the injured melded with the crackling of flames to create an eerie tune of devastation.

Out of the darkness, Rupert's horn sounded retreat and men abandoned their posts, emptying their bows and crossbows at the circling beasts as they did. The soldiers headed into the keep, lifting fallen comrades as they went. Hon followed. Descending a wide stairway, the growing crowd of men filed into deep passageways, torch-lit tunnels constructed long ago as escape routes.

"Señor!" the distinctive voice of Hector rang out. Hon turned to see the stocky man coming toward him. Pushing their way through the crowd, the two met against a wall. Hector was shirtless, the garment now serving as a bloody bandage wrapped around his forehead. His wide, muscular frame showed the scars of many battles as well as a few fresh ones.

"I am glad to see you alive," Hector said. "So many are keeled."

"I'm surprised to see you at all," Hon answered. "Last I saw, you were riding a dragon!"

"I deed that?" Hector replied with a wry smile as he wiped away a trickle of blood that was running down his cheek. "I saw a beeg man who needed to be made small, that is all."

"*Did* you make him small?" Hon asked.

Hector shook his head.

"No. The dragon shook me loose before I could feeneesh."

Hon motioned to the bloodied and burnt men helping each other past them. The weight of the loss was beginning to settle on his soul.

"It's terrible. There is no way they could have been ready for four dragons. Have you seen Sandip?"

Hector was straining to look over Hon's head, "Here he comes, señor."

The lean eastern warrior moved down the stairs, only recognizable by his fluid gait. His clothes were smoldering and his face was burnt on the right side. Noticing Hon and Hector, he moved to them.

"Do not be alarmed my friends," the man offered, "the time of pain will come but for now I feel nothing. We must escape so we may fight another day, you see?"

The three men joined the thinning crowd and disappeared into the dark tunnels.

CHAPTER TWENTY-TWO

Silas cradled his right arm against his body. It was wrapped tightly in clean linens taken from Kendrick's keep. He had stopped the blood flow the only way he could, by removing the arm completely through the use of a tourniquet.

Two of his fellow dragon masters stood next to him atop the central tower of the castle, looking down on the destruction their beasts had wrought. The four beasts were feasting on the dead men and animals that remained in the courtyard below. Silas smiled. The day he had promised had finally come. It gave him great satisfaction to think of Kendrick's body being dug from the rubble by one of the beasts.

"The last obstacle has been removed," Hugo was saying, "there are no more rulers to stand in our way."

"People will resist," Sanniya replied. "Great cities must be taken. All the land must be ours."

Silas looked around.

"Where is Raj? Did he fall in the battle?"

"Inside," Sanniya answered.

"What is he doing?" Silas insisted.

The brown-skinned woman from the south shrugged her shoulders. Silas continued despite Raj's absence.

"We must dominate the rest of the region to solidify the victory. Each of you has a realm to keep, so I will take this castle and see to it that the rest of Kendrick's lands are subdued."

"Agreed!" Hugo said.

*****†*****

Rajic rushed through the lower floor of the keep, searching frantically for Queen Amla. His anger burned hotter the longer he searched. There was no one inside. No cowering women and children. No servants. Clearly, Kendrick's people had escaped. Amla had to be among them, beyond his grasp.

He hurled a vase down the hallway, its crash echoing from one end of the corridor to the other. One last hallway remained, beyond the stairs he'd come down. Rounding the corner he saw the unbelievable; sconces hung from the walls every 20 feet, smoldering torches faintly lighting the hallway for as far as he could see. The passage sloped downward, disappearing in a gradual turn to the left.

The way of escape. I must tell the others.

Just as he turned the corner someone barreled into him. The familiar smell of jasmine told him all he needed to know.

Amla.

His bulk had stopped her progress immediately, knocking her to the floor. He towered over her, watching with pleasure as the terror or recognition spread over her lovely face. A strong backhand met her cheek, sending her backward across the hallway.

"You will never have the opportunity to betray me again, witch. You will beg for death before I am finished with you."

CHAPTER TWENTY-THREE

The dark tunnels extended underground for a deceptively long time, eventually surfacing far to the south, a mile away from Crystal Lake. The women and children were already there, awaiting news of the battle. Grateful cries greeted the men as they emerged from the tunnels. Elation was soon followed by wailing as many discovered that their husbands and fathers had fallen in the battle. Hon stepped into the darkness outside the tunnel with Hector and Sandip close behind. They soon found Lady Patrice and Camille.

"Where are James and Cedrick?" Lady Kendrick asked immediately.

"We didn't leave the battle at the same time," Hon volunteered, "but I spoke with Lord Kendrick just before the retreat was sounded. He was with Frederick and both were well."

"And Cedrick?"

"I didn't see Cedrick at all during the battle, m'lady. I didn't even consider him, to tell the truth. I assumed he was with you."

Lady Patrice rolled her teary eyes with a huff.

"With me? He is too much like his father to remain with the women and children. As soon as he saw us safely into the tunnels he bounded away, and..." she paused, noticing Hector and Sandip's injuries. "Forgive me, prattling on about my own concerns. You men are injured. We must tend your wounds."

She motioned to a boulder and the two sat down. Reaching into a bag, she produced a jar of ointment and helped Sandip remove his shirt and head-wrap which clung to his charred skin. Camille moved to Hector's side, obviously concerned about the blood that dripped from his bandaged scalp. Hon watched for the three missing men and noticed Quinn stepping out of the tunnel and into the black night.

"Quinn! Over here!"

The short man raised his eyes just enough to pinpoint the location of Hon's voice and began moving toward him, hands clasped behind his back, his head down. Upon reaching the group he stopped and raised his head to look into Hon's face.

"I heard you had returned. Who's survived?" he asked in his no nonsense way.

"The women, myself, and two companions who came with me. I was watching for Lord Kendrick and Cedrick when I saw you."

"He will be the last to come through. It's the kind of man he is," Quinn said, as if it was a fact of nature that none could contest. Hearing a commotion near the tunnel entrance, Hon looked to see Lord Kendrick emerging from the dark hole, still leaning on Frederick's shoulder. Cedrick was with them.

"Lady Patrice, here they come," Hon called over his shoulder. He waved his arm to get their attention and the three made their way through the crowd.

"We've made sure everyone was safely out," Lord Kendrick explained. Quinn playfully bumped Hon's chest with the back of his hand, an eyebrow cocked high.

"Thankfully, we found Cedrick and he has seen his share of the battle."

The boy was covered in blood, but very little of it was his own. He had been thrown from one of the southern towers just as the great white beast had demolished it. A man who fell next to him was crushed by a falling stone.

"I know I look frightful mother, but I am fine," the boy consoled as his mother rushed forward. The youthful eagerness that once characterized the lad was gone. In its place was the sober reality of war.

"James, is it a total loss?" Patrice asked.

"They've destroyed us without the beasts being so much as scratched. We weren't prepared, even though we thought we were. Those creatures are unearthly, beyond defending

CHAPTER TWENTY-THREE

against. And the way they surprised us… we simply weren't ready."

"What are we going to do?" Camille asked. Lord Kendrick surveyed the gathering of injured and frightened people, less than half of the residents of his estate.

"The only option we have is to head west, to the Rocky Point. I believe it remains hidden to our enemies and there is room enough for everyone who has survived." Kendrick looked at the stars, calculating the remaining hours of night. "First we must be away from here. The dragon masters will discover our escape route soon enough."

"Lord Kendrick," Hon interrupted, "As much as I want to be with you, I cannot stay. I have to find my father."

"Do what you need to do. You men," Kendrick said, motioning toward Frederick, Sandip, and Hector, "are welcome to accompany us if you still wish to learn from Quinn." He looked at the spymaster who was silently counting on the fingers of one hand and waving the other hand back and forth, absorbed in his own assessment of what had happened. "He'll have a head full of ideas by morning."

"If it's alright with Hon, I'd like to go with him," Frederick said. "I don't like the idea of him going into the unknown alone and I remember commander Eadric from my childhood. Perhaps he will remember me, too."

"I'd like that, Frederick. Thank you," Hon said.

Hector and Sandip looked at each other. Sandip spoke first.

"This night has shown what will come of all lands if my brother and the other dragon masters are not stopped. I have made my decision. If Hon believes Quinn has things to teach us, I will learn them."

"Your brother?" Hector said. "I don't understand."

"The rider of the black dragon, he is Raj, my brother."

Hector's eyes grew wide.

"I was just beginning to explain that to Lord Kendrick when the attack began," Hon said.

Lady Patrice interrupted, panic in her voice.

"Amla! Where is Amla?"

Sandip's head spun around.

"Who did you say?"

"Queen Amla. I forgot she was even here!" Patrice answered.

Without a word the lithe warrior from the east took up his sword and dashed into the tunnel. In an instant, Hector chased after him.

*****✝*****

Hector huffed after Sandip, barely able to hear his footsteps in the tunnel ahead. Sandip was built for speed. The torches on the walls were almost used up, filling the tunnel with smoke. He hoped they'd last long enough for them to reach the keep. A shout ahead spurred him on. With every stride the sounds of battle became evident; threats, metal on metal, the unmistakable sounds of men locked in combat. The darkness gave way as he approached the end of the hallway. Sandip was battling furiously with one who could be his twin, were it not for the stranger's larger build and taller frame. It was the rider of the black dragon.

Sandip's sword clanged again and again against the gleaming scimitar and katar brandished by Rajic. Sandip was a master swordsman, equal in skill to Hector though different in approach and style. The agile easterner parried and thrust against his opponent with the speed and grace of a tiger. But Rajic was every bit his equal. Though drawn to admire the artistry of their swordplay, Hector forced himself away to search for Amla. He found her motionless against the far wall of the tunnel.

Rajic's cruelty was evident in her once-lovely face. She lay unconscious, her nose bent to one side and bleeding profusely. Her cheekbones were swollen already, her eyes blackening. Hector bent over, scooped her up and took a final look at the dueling brothers. A quick glance from Sandip told him what to do. He vanished into the dark tunnel bearing his precious cargo.

*****✝*****

CHAPTER TWENTY-THREE

The sound of Hector's retreating footsteps encouraged Sandip. Amla was safe. That was what mattered. Refocusing on his brother, Sandip steeled his mind for the grueling battle he knew lay ahead.

"I should have killed you before I left," Rajic said through clenched teeth.

"I *would* have killed you but you fled like the coward you are," Sandip responded.

"Ahhhhh!" Rajic shouted as he rushed his elder brother, their weapons clanging loudly within the narrow passageway. Sandip countered the blow and responded with a quick fist to the chin. Not allowing Rajic to recuperate from the blow, he swung forward with a wide arc of his sword. The strike was deflected, but not stopped, cutting a wide slice away from the top of Rajic's left shoulder. The injured man pulled away, wincing and cursing. Sandip pushed forward and with a strong kick to the chest he sent Rajic stumbling backward into the wall, his katar clattering to the floor. Sandip raised his sword to deliver the deathblow.

He watched in disbelief as his own sword fell to the floor in front of him. A hot pain in his right hand told him that Rajic was not his only opponent. A small, thin dagger impaled his hand, the blade protruding from the front of his palm. At the foot of the stairs was an older woman who was just straightening up after delivering the dagger throw. Behind her were two men, one old, the other obese.

The dragon lords.

With a last glance at Rajic, who lay helpless at his feet, Sandip spun around and sprinted down the tunnel.

*****†*****

Running as fast as he dared in the dark tunnel, Sandip made his way out to rejoin the others. As much as he wished he could have finished Rajic, it would have been more than foolish to make the attempt. Four-to-one odds would still be to his favor against average fighters, but the dragon lords were not average. Pushing the pain aside, his mind rushed ahead, thinking of Amla, wondering if she would survive the beating Rajic had given her.

The soft air rushing past his face had almost obscured the faint sound of leather on stone behind him. He was being followed. Focusing his attention he heard it again, the footfalls of pursuit, swiftly gaining ground with each step. Sandip tucked his head and increased his speed.

*****†*****

With Amla safely in Patrice and Camille's care, Hector turned back toward the tunnel. Hon and Rupert followed close behind. Just before diving into the darkness, Sandip emerged at a run, blood dripping from his hand.

"The dragon lords come!" he cautioned in a whisper, spinning to face his pursuing foe.

Within seconds a lithe, cloaked figure emerged, skidding to a stop in the dust outside the cave. An old but graceful woman, her eyes burning with the flame of adrenaline shot glances from face to face. She seemed barely winded in spite of the sprint through the tunnel.

Lord Kendrick immediately took charge.

"You have no place to flee."

Hon and Hector moved to flank her on either side but in a whisper she was gone, swallowed by the dark mouth of the tunnel.

"Let her go. We have to get moving," Kendrick said. "They'll be coming for sure now. Everyone! Gather your things as quietly as you can and disperse into the woods. Get as far from here as possible then stop and hide yourselves before dawn. When morning breaks, wait an hour then make your escape. The dragons will not be about during the daytime. Travel in small groups and stay to the main roads. If you are able to meet us at the fortress at Rocky Point we will welcome you. Godspeed!"

Hon moved to help Sandip who's hand was bleeding profusely, but he was brushed aside. Sandip hobbled to Amla's side.

CHAPTER TWENTY-THREE

"She will be alright?" he asked.

"I believe so," Patrice answered. "She has been battered mercilessly. But she will mend in time."

Sandip knelt at the side of his beloved and pulled her close. The warrior wept.

CHAPTER TWENTY-FOUR

A grueling day's travel was behind them. Hon and Frederick would reach the southern crossroad of the kingdom of Rajic next morning. Frederick lay awake in his bed, roused by a feeling of deep apprehension. It seemed foolish to intentionally venture into hostile lands where Hon was certain to be captured or killed, but he didn't know what else they could do. From the location of the moon and a handful of recognizable constellations that peeked through the cloud-scattered sky, Frederick knew it was well past midnight.

The place they had stopped for the night was one Hon had used before, a lonely camp tucked inside a scattering of boulders. The large log they'd left burning was now only a chunk of glowing ember. In an effort to get back to sleep, Frederick rolled onto his side. Hon's bedroll was empty.

He's probably gone to check on the horses.

After ten minutes and no sign of his friend, Frederick decided to investigate. Rising from his bed, he peered into the darkness. Years of his father's careful instruction came to his aid as he knelt beside Hon's bed. He found what he was looking for, fresh tracks leading away from the camp. He lit a small torch from the remaining coals of the campfire. The prints led away from the camp toward the south, toward a large boulder standing apart from the rest. Moving carefully and quietly he listened.

The muffled sound of labored breathing seized his attention. He heard it again, and again. Frederick eased his way around the boulder. Sitting atop a flat rock, ten feet away he saw Hon. His knees were drawn toward his chest, his arms wrapped tightly around them. He rocked back and forth with his head dropped low between his knees. His shoulders heaved to the heavy rhythm of his breathing. As Frederick stepped into the open he thought he saw sweat on Hon's forehead.

"Hon? Is everything alright?"

The jerk of his friend's body told him that his approach had not been heard.

"Ye… Yes, Frederick. I'm fine."

Frederick hesitated, sure that Hon's words were not entirely true.

"I woke and found you gone. I wanted to make sure…"

"I am fine," Hon interrupted. "Thank you."

Frederick stood dumbfounded, unsure what to say next.

"Alright. I'll be at the camp."

*****†*****

The sun rose over a sky so blue and free of clouds it seemed that God had polished it with a mixture of ocean water and sunlight. It was a good day for travel. The horses were nearby and saddled, ready for the day's journey. The campfire blazed brightly. Frederick wondered if Hon had even slept. The events of the night had disturbed Frederick. He'd never seen Hon so out of control, so fragile. He warmed himself by the fire and tugged on a piece of dried pork as Hon came from the direction of the road.

"We should make good time. I expect we'll reach the crossroads before mid-day," Hon said. "There's not a soul on the road so far."

"That's good," Frederick said, as Hon began heaping dirt on the fire. He was surprised to see Hon so upbeat. "Are you alright this morning?"

Hon stopped in the midst of kicking another pile of dirt on the fire.

"What is it you want to know?" Hon asked, a tinge of irritation in his voice. Frederick wasn't sure he wanted to venture into the subject but felt he had no choice.

"What was wrong last night? I've always known you to be confident and self-assured, well, except for when you were very small."

CHAPTER TWENTY-FOUR

"What do you mean?" Hon asked, the irritation still evident.

"The nightmares," Frederick said. "They plagued you back then, and I understand that. But that was a long time ago. Since you've grown up you've seemed pretty secure."

Hon released a deep breath.

"Exactly. I may have *seemed* secure, but I'm not." He turned to face Frederick. "The nightmares still come, Fred, at least a couple of times a month. And they're just as intense and real as ever. When they do," he paused and looked away, "they set me back. What you saw last night was the struggle to move forward again."

"I don't understand," Frederick replied.

"Every time it happens I drown in fear. I can't control it. Panic rises like a wave and overwhelms me."

Hon clenched his fists tightly. Frederick noticed tension in his jaw.

"Hon, you don't have to talk about it,"

"No," Hon interrupted, "it's alright. I need to let it out. Last night it was the same nightmare again, only more vivid than it's been for a long time. They come on more intensely when something important or dangerous is on the horizon. The night before Victoria and I married was terrible."

"What was it *that* night, something important or something dangerous?" Frederick joked, trying to lighten the mood.

Hon smiled.

"Probably both. What I'm saying is that it makes sense that the nightmares were so powerful last night. We just left a horrendous scene behind us and I don't know what I'm going to face ahead. I don't know if my father is alive or if I'll be able to do anything to help him. The dreams seem to express the helplessness I feel about such things."

"So, what do you do? Just grit your teeth and sweat your way through it? That's what it looked like to me," Frederick said.

"Sometimes that's all I can do," Hon answered. "Emotions have no substance, nothing to touch or grab onto. Yet, they dominate us. They have power to make us believe something is real when it is only a thought, or a concern, or a possibility. I don't understand it myself. What I do know is this; in those moments, the battle I have to fight is a battle for truth. I have to take control of my mind. I have to fill it with truth that can oppose the lies the emotions are presenting. I have to *will myself* into a place of sound thinking." He paused, then continued.

"You remember Abigail's funeral? When father Philip spoke?" Frederick nodded. "He was doing the same thing, fighting for truth to prevail, but he was doing it on our behalf rather than his own. It was us who were wracked with grief, unable to think clearly. He was trying to cut through the fog of emotion to show us the truth, to help us fight the power of the emotions we felt.

"I've thought about that a lot over the years and I think that's what good preaching is. And we all have to learn to preach to ourselves because much of the time there's no one there to do it for us. We have to learn to fight fear and anguish and hopelessness with truth. If we don't, we'll be ruled by something that isn't real."

Frederick was stunned. He didn't know the waters of his friend's soul ran so deep.

"Does Victoria know?" Frederick asked. Hon waited a long time before answering.

"She knows *about* the dreams, but she doesn't *know* about the dreams. We've only shared a bed two nights since being married, so she's not experienced it herself. And, more important things were thrust upon us so quickly, I haven't had the time to bring it up."

"So, back to my question… are you alright this morning?" Hon rose and moved to his friend's side. He clapped his hand on Frederick's shoulder.

"As alright as I can be, and it will have to be enough." Hon's horse, Storm, stomped impatiently. "I think they're ready to go," he said, gesturing toward the horses. "Are you?"

*****✝*****

CHAPTER TWENTY-FOUR

Gerrard stepped outside just as the glow of morning was appearing over the eastern horizon. Bongani and Fiona were awake and preparing the morning meal inside. He breathed deeply, thankful for the crisp morning air after being cooped up inside the dank back room of the poulterer's shop. But there was something strange on the wind, an uncommon scent.

Scanning the horizon, his eyes were drawn to a small column of smoke, rising far to the southwest. It rose a hundred feet then dispersed, driven in his direction by the wind. It was the odor the smoke carried with it that caused his stomach to turn. Bongani came out the side door, his eyes darting about curiously.

"You smell?" the dark-skinned man asked.

Gerrard raised his arm, pointing to the southwest. For a full minute Bongani stood, examining the smoke as it spread into the sky, sniffing the wind.

"Flesh," the giant said.

"We've not a second to waste," Gerrard said.

Throwing their meal into sacks, Gerrard and his two new friends mounted their beasts and headed north, for Newtown.

*****†*****

After two days of hard riding, Gerrard, Bongani, and Fiona rode into Newtown. It was the same idyllic place Gerrard had left over a month earlier. Victoria was crossing the square with a bucket of sloshing water when she spied them. Letting her bucket fall, she ran to Gerrard, throwing her thin arms around him in a warm embrace.

"I am glad to see you, Gerrard. Hon," she hesitated and smiled sheepishly, "I mean, my husband, has gone to see to his father's release."

"Yer husband, lassie? Our young dragon slayer must be the happiest man alive, then."

"Thank you. It was hard to let him go but it couldn't be helped," she replied.

"I feared such would happen but didn't know exactly how," Gerrard said. "We can talk on it more bye the bye, lassie. Fer now, we've terrible news to bring. Something's happened down Kendrick's way. From the Twins we saw smoke and smelled a stench to beat all. Methinks the dragon masters have made their move."

Victoria's delicate hand covered her mouth and her eyes grew wide as Gerrard spoke.

"That's where Hon was headed!"

Pounding hooves sounded from the road behind them. A rider wearing Kendrick's colors approached, his horse dripping sweat and blowing hard. Gerrard raised his hand and the man reigned in his horse, coming to a stop in a flurry of dust.

"I bear a message from Lord Kendrick for a man named Gerrard."

"Gerrard is me, man," Gerrard said.

"Our lord has been routed," the soldier said, extending a parchment to the woodsman. "Four fierce beasts attacked just three nights hence. Only a handful of the manor's residents have survived."

*****†*****

"They won't be coming here fer their training after all," Gerrard said to the small group. He dropped the parchment on the table. "The beasties have found them out, or at least made it difficult fer 'em to stay hidden. Yer hubby continues on to Brookhaven as planned and Frederick goes with him."

Victoria released a pent up breath.

"Thank the Lord he's safe! And I am glad Fred will go with him. I've not liked the idea of Hon being left to himself all alone in that dark land."

"Aye lassie, seems a prudent move to me as well."

"The rest of the folk head west in small bands so as to avoid notice. Seems Kendrick has a hidden fortress somewhere out there. But Kendrick's lot will try to pass this

CHAPTER TWENTY-FOUR

way first. Seems Hon's other two are coming back here to join you, Bongani."

The black man sat motionless at the table.

"Darkness falls. If others fight, Bongani will fight also." He looked at Fiona, sleeping in the corner. "She cannot go with Bongani.

"I will care for her," Victoria offered. "We both need the companionship and she will be safe here."

Bongani clasped his hands against his chest and bowed his head.

"Bongani, thank you."

*****†*****

A day later, a group of seven travelers rode into Newtown. They were dressed as tradesmen. An old mule pulled a rickety wagon full of hay and wood. Hampton met them as they entered town, his wild hair dancing in the gentle wind. After a smattering of muted conversation the old man led the party to the stables where the wagon and riders were taken inside the barn.

Lord Kendrick slipped from his horse, still favoring his injured legs. He turned to help his wife and daughter from the back of the wagon. Cedrick, Quinn, Sandip, and Hector all dismounted as well.

"I find myself appreciative to see you among the living," Hampton was saying, "appreciative to the Lord God Almighty, indeed. Your message was received just yesterday, and though not as regal as you deserve and as we'd like to provide, we've prepared lodgings for you here," He motioned toward the pallet beds that had been made in the barn. "I apologize profusely for such humble arrangements."

"No need to apologize, Hampton," Lord Kendrick assured. "We are making do with quite a bit less than regal these days and are no worse for it."

After unburdening their animals and setting them to feed in the stalls, Hampton led them to Victoria's cottage for the evening meal. Lord Kendrick made introductions and upon hearing the news of Hon and Victoria's recent wedding, extended warm congratulations. The conversation centered on the next day's travel. Kendrick and his party were hoping to make Rocky Point within two days. The secluded retreat, lodged in the foot of the mountains far to the northwest was little known and would serve as a safe place to gain strength and determine a course of action.

"Once there," Kendrick continued, "our dragon slayers can begin their training. There is much to learn, isn't that right Quinn?"

The aging spymaster replied without the twitch of a muscle.

"Yes, indeed. But Rocky Point is not the place."

"What do you mean?" Kendrick asked.

"A central location is needed. Someplace where they can reach the dragon lords with only a few day's travel."

"What do ya' need in such a place?" Gerrard asked.

"Hidden. Not regularly traveled," Quinn barked. He looked deliberately from Hector, to Sandip, to Bongani. "A place where these three and myself, and perhaps a few more could bed down. From the looks of them, they know how to handle themselves in a fight so we won't be needing lots of space. The training we'll be about is all in here," he said, knocking his forehead with his knuckles.

"Well the good Lord works in mysterious ways, that's for certain," Gerrard replied. "I've wondered long and hard why He's plopped me in the midst of the forest, and now me eyes see the answer. As I've offered before, I've a place, deep in the woods on the other side of The Ridge. 'Tis exactly as you describe, secluded and quiet. Yer all welcome there, though we'd have to erect another shelter before winter is upon us."

Quinn's rolled back eyes betrayed the depth of his thought as he muttered, "Yes, yes, that should do."

"May I offer something?" Camille asked. Lord Kendrick nodded.

"I believe I am to be a part of this secret order of dragon slayers." She laughed at her father's expression. "Of course, not to be the one hunting down the beasts, but behind the

CHAPTER TWENTY-FOUR

scenes, directing communication, organizing, making sure things are not being overlooked. I know it sounds strange and perhaps even improper for a young, unmarried woman to be among so many men, but I feel I should go with you into the woods."

Lady Patrice was the first to respond.

"You might expect me to be opposed to such a suggestion Camille, and in my heart I am. But I have known almost since the day you came back to us that I would not have you long. You have become a grown woman quite apart from me. The years together as mother and daughter have been lost and it would be wrong of me to insist upon having them now. The choice of what to do with your life is yours. I have resigned myself to it. It is part of the price we must pay to see this dirty business done."

"And it will be an advantage to have a woman among us," Quinn added. "We need the perspective of the fairer sex."

"Excuse me," a timid voice interjected. All eyes turned to Fiona as she looked up from a cushion tucked against the wall. "I know you said that I could stay with you, miss," she said, nodding at Victoria. "I am grateful, ma'am — Lord knows I am. But I aim to be of use." The room's occupants shuffled uncomfortably. "I know I am a cripple. I know it best of all, Lord knows. But cripples can do things what nobody else can. We who are lame become invisible. Important folk walk past without a look our way. If they do see, they assume us ignorant. But not so. I hear them and I understand every word'."

Bongani smiled broadly, his arms crossed tightly across his chest. An awkward silence hung over the room until Quinn cleared his throat.

"Brilliant!" he declared. "An advantage I had not considered. Not only could we use her, we need her."

Camille smiled at Fiona.

"And if you come along Fiona, I won't be the only woman among this motley crew of men," she joked.

CHAPTER TWENTY-FIVE

Memories of his last encounter at the southern crossroad formed a hard knot in the pit of Hon's stomach. The checkpoint looked all too familiar and the uncertain nature of what would come made the knot tighten. They approached slowly, giving the guards plenty of time to observe their approach and see that they were no trouble. The armed men who stepped onto the road to meet them were unfamiliar.

"Ho!" the leader shouted as Hon and Frederick reigned in their horses. "What is your business in the land of Rajic?"

"I come in response to a message I've received," Hon answered, as he extended the parchment to the guard. The man eyed the two carefully as he stepped forward to take the document. Two other soldiers stood ready. After scanning the parchment the man tossed it in the dirt.

"Off your horses," he said. Hon and Frederick complied, raising their hands once on the ground. "To your knees, hands on your heads," the man barked, and the two friends complied. Walking behind them, the man put a firm boot in Hon's back and pushed him onto his face. Frederick landed in a puff of dust beside him. The man moved to face them, kicking up an extraneous amount of dust as he did.

"So you are the spy, but who is this other?"

"He is a friend, and I am no spy," Hon answered. "Why would I return if I were a spy? I come to redeem my father and to clear up this misunderstanding."

"Hold your tongue before I cut it out," the man threatened. "Gaylon! Their weapons!. Bind them and set them back on their horses."

The soldier obeyed as the leader retrieved the parchment and went into the tent beside the road. By the time Hon and Frederick were in the saddle again the commander returned with a parchment of his own, sealed and bound with a strand of twine. He looked into the eyes of the one he'd called Gaylon.

"They are to go to the palace. When you arrive, ask for Commander Eadric. This is his affair. You'll be wise to keep them as they are. I don't care if they have to piss or are dying of thirst, get them there quickly. If for any reason they are lost, your head will be too."

"Yessir," Gaylon replied.

*****†*****

Hon's heart was torn as the trio pounded past Brookhaven on their way north. It was his childhood home and where he'd first met his father, Gerrard, and many others who had come to mean much to him. As the last visible hut flashed past him Hon recommitted himself to finding and freeing his father at the journey's end. Neither he nor Frederick had said a word since leaving the crossroads. Gaylon had only spoken twice, once when he'd interacted with the sentries at two new checkpoints along the road and again when he spit out permission for them to relieve themselves beside the road. Though it was a mercy to empty their bladders, it was also a deep humiliation. Gaylon did not remove their bindings, forcing them to do the deed fully clothed.

Evening came, darkness fell, and still they drove on. Turning to the east, another sentry station forced a halt to their incessant travel and Gaylon wisely traded out the horses. Hon and Frederick were seated against a large tree and a young soldier stuffed a small crust of bread into each of their mouths. The stale morsel was washed down by a short gush of water from a coarse wooden bowl. After only fifteen minutes they were back on their horses, galloping toward a dark castle that loomed in the distance.

The front gate was alive with activity. Five to six guards manned the entrance while others paced the tops of the walls above and beyond. Gaylon slowed their approach and raised a one hand in salute, the other held his horse's reins high. When

CHAPTER TWENTY-FIVE

he produced the sealed document, he was allowed to lead his prisoners inside the fortress. Reaching the stable, men pulled Hon and Frederick from their horses and pushed them into line behind Gaylon and another man, who led them into the keep. They were taken to a dark, dank smelling room, locked inside, and commanded not to make a sound.

*****†*****

Two days after their arrival Hon and Frederick were separated. A week later Hon awoke to the creaking of the heavy door that concealed him from the outside world. The same toothless young man who had served his meager meals kicked the tin cup on the floor across the room at him.

"On yer feet ya' bums! You'll be whipped if ya' ain't outta' here in five second..."

Hon got to his feet and moved to the door. Toothless eyed him warily. In the hallway three guards waited. A burlap sack was thrust over his head and his hands were bound behind his back. He was led down a twisting hallway and through a clanging metal door. The sack was removed and he was shoved toward a small window in a rough wooden door. Peering through the dust-filled light streaming into the small room, Hon recognized his father seated against the far wall, head down.

"Father!" Hon called. The older man raised his head, a smile on his face. He rose and hobbled toward the door.

"You did come," Stewart said calmly. "Thank you son, but I am hardly worth the trouble."

"You know I had to come," Hon answered. "You are well?"

"I've not been harmed if that is what you mean. I seem to have caught a cough in this damp place., but I fare well, overall."

The sack was thrust over Hon's face again and he was jerked away from the door. After five minutes more lumbering through the echoing hallways and up two flights of stairs, he was thrust hard into a chair. The bindings around his wrists were cut and the sack was removed. He found himself in an opulent room that felt eerily familiar. Though he didn't recognize anything specific, he assumed he'd been in the room as a child. It was the throne room of Lord Rajic.

The powerful frame of the ruler dwarfed his large wooden chair. Though dimly lit, Hon could see the last traces of bruising around Rajic's eyes. Standing next to him was Commander Eadric.

"Your father has been released. Two of my best soldiers return him to his village even now."

Hon stared at him in disbelief.

"I just saw him. He was still in his cell."

"It's being done as we speak," Rajic replied. "Do you doubt me?"

"Wouldn't you?" Hon said. Rajic glared at him. "What of the friend who came with me?" Hon asked.

Rajic spoke with no acknowledgement of his question.

"The selfless attitude you've displayed is to be commended. It is uncommon. Even family ties do not mean so much to most men."

Hon stared in disbelief, knowing that Rajic was the prime example of his own comment.

"What do you know of me?" Rajic asked bluntly.

"Not much," Hon lied. "You came to power here after Lord Thurmond's passing. I was only a boy then. I live across The Ridge so I don't hear much of this land."

"But you do hear things?"

"Some," Hon answered.

"Tell me."

Hon took a deep breath.

"You rule with a firm hand. You're not one to be trifled with."

Rajic chuckled.

"Is that what they say? Well, gossip isn't always filled with lies then."

"What about my friend?" Hon repeated.

"I haven't decided yet. I've allowed Commander Eadric full reign in your case. If he determines you are a spy, then so be it. You and your friend will suffer in that case. You've

CHAPTER TWENTY-FIVE

already admitted that you live in Kendrick's land. We'll see what else he can pry out of you."

Commander Eadric chuckled.

CHAPTER TWENTY-SIX

The journey to Gerrard's forest hut was anything but easy. The woodsman had insisted they were better off going over The Ridge instead of around it to avoid any of Rajic's troops. The "Widows Way," the only known pass, was known by Gerrard to be impassable so he led them to the south and then east, forging a path of his own. After three days of arduous travel over boulder strewn ground that ranged up and down over the shoulders of the craggy peaks, seven weary travelers arrived at the small hut tucked into the thickest part of the woods. Camille and Fiona were given the only bed in the hut and both fell into an exhausted sleep the moment they arrived.

Morning came and Camille woke to the smell of smoke and the crackle of fire. She spied Gerrard hunched over a pot that hung over the fire pit in the center of the small room. He hummed a playful tune as he stirred its contents.

"Thank you for the use of your bed," Camille whispered, just loud enough for the lanky woodsman to hear. "I don't think I stirred all night."

"Aye, yer welcome me lady, welcome indeed!" Gerrard thundered, apparently unconcerned about waking Fiona. "Sleeping as still and quiet as a rock *is* a sign that you slept well, lass."

The heavy bearskin that covered the entrance to the hut was drawn back and the other four members of their company entered.

"Eet is about time the ladies woke," Hector joked, winking at Camille, "My stomach is aching for food." She blushed, uncomfortable yet pleased with his attention.

"Only one of us is awake," Camille answered softly, nodding her head in Fiona's direction. "I suspect she's never been on such a journey before."

"Only as child," Bongani volunteered, "Her father was tradesman. Much traveling for her then."

"How did you come to be responsible for her care?" Camille asked.

A cloud fell over the countenance of the otherwise smiling man. His black skin appeared even darker as he struggled to speak.

"Painful to speak it. Her family come to Bongani's country, far beyond great desert. They come to sell, to make living. Bongani then was young, training to be Queen's soldier. I serve on main road, stopping all coming into the land. Each must pay tax to bring goods to our people. My Captain was very heavy over men. Unkind to travelers. Fiona's family arrive, the captain abuse them. He demand her older sister as payment. Her father refuse.

"Her father speak strong words to Captain, tell to repent before God of heaven. Bongani's heart warmed but Captain very angry. He push father who is holding baby Fiona." He looked beyond Camille to the sleeping girl.

"They fight. Fiona fall. Other soldiers force father down and tie hands. Bongani afraid. Bongani do nothing. Captain make father to watch. He hurt family. He tell us kill them. Bongani not want them die, but soldiers obey. Fiona crying. Captain stands over her. She crying still. He curse her father and crush her legs." Tears pooled in the giant man's eyes. "What happen then hard to remember. Bongani standing over bodies of Captain and other soldiers. Their blood on Bongani hands."

A somber mood filled the room, all eyes on the tall, muscular man. Hector finally broke the silence.

"You were right to do eet. Boollies do not deeserve to breathe."

"Bongani believe this," he replied, striking his own chest forcefully, "but does not free the heart."

The tone of the conversation turned as a loud belly laugh burst from Gerrard.

"If ya don't mind me saying so me lads, it seems Providence has smiled on our young dragon slayer. He sought

CHAPTER TWENTY-SIX

hardy souls, men ready to take on hell itself for the sake of others. From what I've heard of yer tales the three of you fill the need and then some."

Camille watched as the men made their own assessments of each other. Gerrard was right. Bongani clearly cared deeply for others and was ready to stand against injustice. Sandip, though motivated mainly by the treachery of his own brother also seemed willing to make hard choices for the sake of what was right. And Hector, though roughest of the band, had a good heart. She liked them all. She changed the subject.

"Sandip, did you get to spend enough time with Amla before we left?"

The easterner shook his head.

"It will never be enough. We have long been apart, you see? The pain of it still grips my heart," he said as he placed a lean hand against his chest. "Leaving her now was harder than losing her."

"I'm sure so," Camille said. "I know about being away from the ones you love. But I did not choose it. That must have been a hard decision for you."

"Yes," Sandip said, "but Rajic must die if she is ever to be safe. I must see to it, you see? It is my place."

Camille nodded. The crackle of the fire and Angus' snoring were the only sounds. A smile broke across Sandip's face.

"What is it, Sandip?"

He looked up, the contagious smile still beaming.

"She is as beautiful as a flower in the desert. Do you agree?"

"Yes, very beautiful," Camille nodded. "You are a blessed man."

Sandip nodded.

"It is a wonderful thing to find a companion, one to love and care for. I must do what I must and then return to her. We will not part again."

Camille looked at the other men in turn. Bongani smiled, obviously happy for Sandip. As much as she could tell Gerrard was smiling through his thick beard. Quinn sat deep in thought. She wondered what he was thinking. She turned to Hector and their eyes met. Something in the way he looked at her caused her heart to flutter and her stomach to twist. She looked away.

*****†*****

Quinn's training regimen proved grueling, even for men as capable as Hector, Bongani, and Sandip. Though some physical training was involved, including tactics designed specifically for combating their reptilian enemies, the primary strain was mental. Quinn pushed the entire team, including Camille and Fiona. He forced them to think, strategize, and learn skills of observation that were common sense once learned but hardly noticed before. The odd little man was not easily satisfied with their progress.

"Again!" he shouted as Hector gave an unacceptable response to one of his mock scenarios.

"I answer you seven times already," Hector complained.

"And you will answer another seventy if that is what it takes for you to get it right!"

"Eet ees too much," Hector said, turning toward the door of the hut. "I cannot think so much."

Quinn scrambled forward, placing himself between Hector's formidable body and the doorway.

"Yes, it *is* too much, which is exactly why you must continue! If you can learn to think clearly under the strain of fatigue you can face anything."

Hector was about to push the small man from his path when Camille stepped in.

"Hector?"

The flustered man looked her way in a huff.

"We must be ready for the worst. Would you try it again?" She smiled broadly at him.

The deep creases in his furrowed brow vanished as he looked into her eyes.

"For you señorita, I will."

Hector fell to his seat atop a large rock.

CHAPTER TWENTY-SIX

"Again!" Quinn demanded.

*****†*****

The day came when, with a hesitation characteristic of his odd ways, Quinn announced the team ready to begin their work.

"We can wait no longer. Rajic is first, for two reasons. One. His realm is nearest. Two. Hon and Frederick are by now prisoners somewhere within his borders. We can neither wait for them nor let them remain as they are."

Camille smiled at the curt nature of Quinn's comments.

"So you think us ready?" she interpreted. "That's high praise coming from you, Quinn."

"You are as ready as I could make you in the time that was available," Quinn quipped, clearly uncomfortable giving the affirmation Camille sought.

"I've been waiting too long already," Sandip said. "It is time for Raj to pay for his treachery, you see? But I warn you all, as I remind myself, he is strong, cunning, and will not be unguarded."

"Guards or not, I owe heem a beating," Hector said, rubbing his jaw. "You weel have to wait your turn, beeg brother."

"How do we begin, Quinn?" Camille asked, hoping to divert attention from the good natured rivalry that had developed between Sandip and Hector. Wasting no time, Quinn launched into his plan.

"Bongani and Hector, you must acquire uniforms of the armies of Rajic for yourselves and return here immediately."

"Si," Hector answered, "I hope we can find a man large enough to clothe our friend," he said, clucking his tongue at Bongani. Absorbed in thought Quinn continued without acknowledging the comment.

"You will be our way into the throne room Sandip, the prisoner of our two guards," he said, waving at Hector and Bongani. "The capture of his brother is sure to gain an audience with Lord Rajic."

"What then?" Sandip asked.

Quinn's eyes narrowed.

"I want you all to come out alive, but Raj must be slain. *Everything* else is secondary, even your safety." He looked from Sandip to Hector, sure to catch their eyes in turn. "And what is important is that he dies, not who does the deed. The first and clearest opportunity must be taken."

Sandip and Hector nodded to each other as Quinn continued.

"Without its master the black beast will be directionless, a mere beast. Then you will hunt it down and kill it."

"Ees that all?" Hector joked.

Quinn furrowed his brow, missing the humor entirely.

"Kill Rajic. Kill his beast. I believe it is enough for now."

CHAPTER TWENTY-SEVEN

Hon stirred from his comatose state and found himself lying on the cold stone floor of his prison cell. Weeks of beatings and torture at the hand of Eadric and his men had taken a toll on him unlike anything he'd experienced. Every muscle ached as he raised himself to sit against the wall. The crusted cuts on his face were stiff and hard. His head spun. As he fought to free himself from the surreal fog caused by the abuse, keys rattled in the lock of his cell door. The regular day guard stepped into the dank room.

"Up with you," the guard commanded. "You're to be taken before Lord Rajic."

His hands were bound and he was led once again through the winding passageways of the castle, a bag over his head. Two flights of stairs up, multiple turns down various hallways, the sounds of others passing. Then, with the slam of a heavy door the sack was stripped from his head and Hon found himself in a small room where two male servants stood behind a large wooden barrel, laid on its side and split sideways. It was filled with steaming water.

"Off with your clothes," the guard demanded as he cut Hon's bindings. "You'll be clean if you're to stand before the Master."

Hon stepped into the tub with some difficulty and sat in the freshly boiled water. Though a bit too hot for comfort it relieved his aching muscles considerably. The two male servants roughly scrubbed him from head to toe and redressed him in clean servant's garments.

The guard led him by the arm without the customary sack over his head, out the door and down the wide hallway. His head pounded with each step and his vision blurred. Arriving before a large double doorway, two guards opened it to allow the pair entrance. Seated on the platform was Rajic, king of the realm. The massive chair was completely filled with the man's muscular body. Standing next to him was Commander Eadric. Hon was led to the foot of the platform and forced to his knees.

"Your friend has been quite cooperative," Eadric began. "You should save yourself further pain and admit that you are a spy. It's pointless to hide it any longer."

Hon's head was spinning, his eyes still unable to focus. He could hardly make sense of Eadric's words.

"My friend? Who… oh, Frederick. Where is Frederick?"

Rajic chuckled as Eadric continued.

"He's being released as we speak. He's made it quite clear that you are the one we want. Just admit it, boy. You are a spy for Kendrick."

Hon shook the fog from his head as the last sentence bounced around inside his skull. Squinting his eyes and focusing his thoughts he finally made sense of what was going on.

Good, Frederick held out. They know nothing of our knowledge of the dragon slayers.

"He couldn't have said that because it's not true. I came into this land for the sake of my father," Hon stammered.

Just as Eadric was about to respond, a commotion at the door behind him drew Raj's attention and the dragon lord thrust a wide palm in Eadric's face. A soldier hurried from the back of the room, bowed before Raj, then spoke in a hushed tone, but loud enough for Hon to hear.

"Sorry to intrude, my lord, but we have a prisoner you will want to see immediately. He claims to be your brother."

Hon's heart sank.

Has Sandip had been captured?

Raj's eyes were drawn to the door.

"Return to your post, Commander," Rajic snapped at Eadric. "You can finish with this one later."

Eadric stepped off the platform and grabbed Hon by the arm, jerking him to his feet.

"Leave him," Rajic commanded. "I want him to see what happens to those who resist me."

CHAPTER TWENTY-SEVEN

Eadric laughed quietly and left via the side door. Flashing a vicious grin in Hon's direction, Rajic called out.

"Bring in the prisoner!"

Two soldiers entered, accompanied by the sound of rattling chains, dragging Sandip between them. His hands and feet were shackled and his nose was bleeding. The guards stationed in the outer passage pulled the heavy wooden doors closed behind them. Raj's lips curled into an evil grin as Sandip was forced to his knees fifteen feet in front of the platform. The guards remained on either side of the prisoner. One was dark skinned and extremely tall, so much that his muscular arms and strong legs stretched noticeably clear of his uniform. He held a gleaming short sword at the ready. The other was thick-chested and sturdy, a man of obvious strength. Hon's eyes moved to his face and their eyes locked.

Hector!

"Lord Rajic," Hector spoke, "thees man was captured at the southern crossroad station. He was trying to sneak hees way into your lands. We have compelled heem to admit that he ees your brother. Other than hees weapons he only carried thees." Hector held up a large leather case covered with ornate stitching. Raj rose from the throne and extended his hand, never moving his smoldering eyes from Sandip. Hector moved to the throne with the case. He handed it to Raj who immediately unbuckled the clasp and looked inside. Hector stepped to the side and bowed his head.

"You are still the fool," Rajic scoffed. "You bring these into my lands, hoping to keep them hidden from me? How pitiful."

Sandip struggled for words.

"Silence!" Rajic screamed. "I will not hear even a breath of your insolence." He descended the three steps down the platform, stepping forward. His eyes burned with hatred.

"You *will* hear me," Sandip screamed in return. "Someone must speak for our slain parents!"

With a bloody scream, Rajic drew a katar from his belt and rushed Sandip. Hector moved behind him and in a swift, fluid motion, he simultaneously clamped a strong hand onto the back of Raj's thick leather belt and threaded his right arm through the elbow of his weapon hand. He used Rajic's own momentum to thrust him forward, driving him toward his kneeling brother who held the sword of the second guard. The flailing dragon lord hurtled toward the point of the shining blade, eyes wide, until it disappeared into his chest. Sandip shoved hard on the blade, causing it to emerge between Rajic's shoulder blades. With a spit and a shove, Sandip toppled the dragon lord into a bloody pool on the stone floor.

The tall soldier had moved to the door, listening intently. With a shake of his head, he indicated that the commotion had not been heard. Hector smiled.

"That was eesy."

He and Sandip lifted the body, carried it into the small room behind the platform, and returned with a large rug which they spread over the bloody spot on the floor.

"We met Frederick on the road," Sandip whispered. "He told us you were dead."

"I'm happy to disappoint you," Hon joked weakly. "Where is he?"

"He's going to meet us when we're finished, you see?" Sandip answered.

"You don't look very good, Señor," Hector interrupted, helping Hon to his feet.

With a humor he didn't feel, Hon said, "I've never felt better."

*****†*****

The two soldiers made their way through the dark hallways of the keep, winding in the direction they believed they'd find the outer doors. Between them were two prisoners, bound and sullen, both with canvas bags over their heads. As they exited the front entrance of the manor another group of men was entering, Commander Eadric in the lead. He stopped them short.

"What are you doing with this man?" he insisted, ripping the bag from Hon's head.

CHAPTER TWENTY-SEVEN

"Lord Rajic has commanded us to keel these two in the forest," Hector responded.

Eadric eyed them cautiously.

"Do you have a problem with eet, commander?" Hector asked. He stepped forward, moving close enough to Eadric to intimidate the smaller man with his size. "I suggest you step aside," Hector said, tapping the tip of his blade on rank insignia emblazoned across his own tunic. "Lord Raj was insistent that we do eet right away. You would not want him to hear that you have delayed us."

Eadric was clearly not impressed, but capitulated all the same.

"Fine, but I'm coming with you." He took a handful of Hon's tunic in his hand and pulled him close, ripping the sack from his head. "This one is mine. Isn't that right, boy?" Hon replied by spitting in his face. A strong backhand flew hard across Hon's cheek. "I will enjoy watching you die, boy."

*****†*****

Hector and his tall companion, whom Hon had yet to meet, played the part of calloused soldiers well, shoving Hon and Sandip deeper into the forest. The soldiers who had accompanied Commander Eadric rambled along at the rear of the column, jabbering about what they planned to do once off duty. Eadric was a different matter. He walked close to the four of them, watching every move. Hon knew there would be no choice except to fight it out and he knew he didn't have the strength for it.

"This is far enough," Eadric insisted. "Why waste time going any farther?"

"Fine," Hector relented. "Move aside so we can geet on with eet," he said with a shove to Eadric's chest.

Eadric moved quickly into Hector's path.

"Where did you say you were stationed?" he asked.

"I deedn't," Hector answered, stepping again into Eadric's space. "You know what I think? I think someone should slap your mother for raiseeng such a fool," Hector snapped. The tall man slipped behind Eadric's men who were clearly surprised at the row that was developing between Hector and their commander. "When I'm feeneeshed with you, I'll see what I can do to find her," Hector quipped.

Hon laughed aloud. The commander spun around to confront him.

"I'm gonna' kill you myself, you miserable…"

Eadric's words were cut short by the impact of Hector's rock-hard fist as it landed behind his right ear. Another blow pounded into his kidneys. Hector continued his assault, landing punch after punch on the commander's head and shoulders until he fell to his knees. Eadric managed to free his sword from its scabbard but Hector stomped hard with his heavy boot, snapping it in half. Just as he was about to deliver the deathblow, one of the soldiers deflected the strike so that it plunged into Eadric's left shoulder instead.

Hector's companion was doing his best to keep the remaining three soldiers at bay but was clearly in need of help. His hands still tied, Sandip threw himself into the legs of the middle attacker. The tall man took advantage of the distraction, delivering a rapid upward slice that passed through the first soldier's bicep, severing his arm. The blow continued its upward trajectory until it came down hard on the sword of the second man. Rolling to the side, Sandip thrust a foot into the back of the man's knee, causing it to buckle. It was the only advantage needed for their tall friend to drop the soldier with one stroke.

Sandip screamed. The hilt of a dagger protruded from his side. The man he'd taken down at the beginning of the fight was propped on one elbow about five feet away, his arm still extended from the throw. Hon tried to rise from the needle strewn forest floor but his head spun in a dizzy whirl and he collapsed. The last thing he saw before passing out was Hector's thin, flashing blade.

*****†*****

Cold water from a nearby stream stunned Hon back into the realm of consciousness. All was quiet. Sandip knelt over

CHAPTER TWENTY-SEVEN

him as Hector and the tall man dragged bodies into a thick hedge.

"Who is he?" Hon asked, nodding toward the tall man.

"Bongani," Sandip answered with a quick glance. "Gerrard found him at The Twins, you see. He's one of us now."

"Good," Hon said, "I'd hate for him to be an enemy."

Sandip chuckled.

"I, as well. You've been badly treated, my friend. You are weak. Darkness comes soon, so we will conceal ourselves. But before daylight we must be well away from here, you see?"

Hon nodded.

"Get me something to eat then I'll rest. I can be ready by morning."

The skeptical look on Sandip's face wasn't very reassuring to Hon, but he rose to fetch provisions from a nearby pack. Behind him Hon could see the thick body of what had to be commander Eadric. It was headless and riddled with at least ten sword thrusts.

"Here, Sandip said, offering Hon some food.

Hon snatched the dried venison from Sandip's hand and tore into it.

"So he was no match for Hector?" Hon asked, nodding toward the body.

"They were closely matched. Each held his own ground for some time. But when the commander fell," Sandip turned to see if Hector was within hearing, "it was not enough, you see? Our friend stabbed the body again and again, even after he was dead.

CHAPTER TWENTY-EIGHT

The still night was a pleasant relief to Victoria after the hot day. It had been unseasonably warm; a sure sign that summer was still very much with them. Adding to the discomfort of the heat, she hadn't felt well all day. Strolling along the river with her shawl draped over her shoulder, she looked into the brilliantly starlit sky. She had come away from the town to be alone, to examine the jumble of feelings that compiled the knot in her stomach. She knew that she must unravel them before her God.

She wondered where Hon was and how he was faring. Did the same stars shine on him? Could he be looking up at them right now? The thought made her feel closer to him somehow, yet her heart was heavy, missing him terribly. The two days they were together as a married couple were wonderful, but far too short. What if he never came back? What would she do? How would she go on? Her faith was strong and she knew that God was good, but the possibilities of what could happen were bearing down on her.

As she walked, she dreamed of the future in spite of the fear she felt. She was afraid to allow her hopes to rise too high, but she couldn't help it. She dreamed of their life together, with many children and a simple but happy existence in Newtown. What would Hon do for a trade once the dragon masters were no more? Would their children look like him, or her? Her hands moved to her stomach. She couldn't imagine bringing a child into the world, yet she would. Enough time had passed that she knew for certain. She looked again to the stars and thought of the God who had taken such care in placing each of them against the black canopy of the night.

"Lord, I know you look down on Hon. Whatever danger he faces, I know he is in Your loving hand." Her shoulders lifted, then quivered as she released a trembling breath. "I can say that and know it's true in here," she said as she raised her fingertips to her temple, "but I don't feel even a touch of it in here." Her hand moved to her chest. "Every morning the first thing I feel is fear. Every night, even as I pray myself to sleep, fear is there as well. Please Lord, keep him safe. Bring him back to me. And calm my anxious soul. I am afraid of facing the future alone, of raising our child alone. I don't think I could do it."

She turned back toward the flickering lights of Newtown, feeling no better than she did when she left.

CHAPTER TWENTY-NINE

Rounding a large boulder, Hon spied Frederick, seated alone against a large oak. The young man rose and ran to them, relieved to see Hon with the group.

"I am so thankful you made it. Did everything go as planned?"

"No," Bongani answered bluntly, "but we are here. Hon, he was there when we see Rajic."

Frederick turned to Sandip.

"And what of Rajic?"

Sandip raised his head, a pained expression etched on his normally peaceful face.

"He is dead."

Hon shook his head, prompting Frederick to leave the subject alone.

"Now we have to find the black dragon," Hon said. "It can't be far, but that's not our only concern. Our search is likely to become even more difficult when Rajic's body is discovered. They will come looking for us."

"And you are weak," Bongani stated.

"Not as weak as I look," Hon said with a smile. "It's amazing what decent food and a night of peaceful rest can do for a man."

"I think you're right about the dragon," Frederick said. "I'm sure it's nearby. I've scouted the area. There are large, rocky outcroppings to the south and east of the estate."

Hon turned to Sandip, "How is your wound?"

"Tolerable," he answered, wincing from the pain. "We must go."

*****†*****

The five men worked their way through the woods, staying far from the roads. There was nothing to indicate that Raj's body had been discovered, but they were a few miles away and behind the estate so it would be hard to tell. When the terrain turned rocky they began their search in earnest. Though they knew that small tunnels or crevices might serve as the entrance to a dragon's lair, there would have to be a larger opening as well, so they didn't waste time exploring smaller openings. Midday came and only a large pit that descended straight into the earth had been found.

"It has to be the pit," Hon said. "There's nothing else that is remotely possible."

Removing a rope from his pack, Bongani tied one end to a large tree trunk near the gaping hole and tossed the other end over the side.

"How do we proceed?" Frederick asked.

Hon peered into the pit after the rope, which disappeared into the blackness 50 feet down.

"We go quietly, one at a time," Hon said. "At the bottom we should wait until everyone has made the descent. From there, we'll decide on our next step based on what we find."

In spite of Frederick's protests that he was still too weak, Hon was the first to go over the edge. He wrapped the rope around his back, gripped the tree-fastened end in front of him with his left hand, and leaned backward over the pit, keeping his feet extended against the wall. With the rope threaded around him, he held the other with his right hand and worked it around his waist as he walked himself carefully into the darkness. One by one the others followed until all five were safely at the bottom.

They had descended 100 feet and a small dot of light poked through the darkness from above. Hector produced a torch and inquired of Hon with a curious look. Hon nodded and Hector lit the torch with a few strokes of flint upon steel. The others produced torches of their own and lit them from Hector's. Holding the torch before him, Hector led the way into the darkness of a massive opening in the pit wall. The

CHAPTER TWENTY-NINE

men drew their weapons and stepped gingerly into the darkness behind him.

Fanning out across the width of the tunnel, the dragon slayers moved ahead. The familiar fears of childhood rose like specters in Hon's mind, urging him to turn back. His chest grew tight and he had to force himself to breathe in a slow, measured pattern. The stale stench of death grew stronger with every step. It was the dragon's lair. He knew it.

The tunnel opened to a larger cavern. Hon stopped short and raised his hand in a fist as they paused to listen to the darkness. The rhythmic sound of the dragon's breathing was unmistakable; a heavy sound that echoed eerily from the cold walls. He motioned to the others that the dragon was asleep and indicated they were to stay where they were while he investigated.

Step by step he moved forward. He tried to follow the sound but found it difficult to locate in the reverberating cavern. Every step seemed to shout his presence, but the sound did not change. He strained for any sign of movement but saw none. After traveling deep into the cave he moved alongside a rock formation that rose from the cavern floor and knelt to assess the situation.

It's nearby. But where?

*****†*****

Frederick and the others watched anxiously as they saw the light from Hon's torch grow smaller, until finally it was a fluttering pin-prick in the distance. They waited, wondering what their friend had found.

*****†*****

Hon jerked to attention as a shuffling noise echoed from behind him. His head snapped around as he thrust his torch into the darkness. There was nothing but the jagged shapes along the top of a large stone, their shadows dancing in the torchlight. He watched and waited, but saw nothing. Moving as quietly as possible he took step after painfully slow step toward the area where he believed the sound came from. As he did, the dragon's breathing became louder. Looking back toward the entrance, he could see the other four torches, dancing spots in a black void.

Spreading his legs wide, he extended his torch as far to one side as he could, then quickly transferred it to the other hand and stretched in the opposite direction. He repeated this motion again. He hoped that to his friends it would serve as a sign that he'd found something.

*****†*****

"Do you see that?" Frederick whispered. "He's trying to tell us something."

The men stared into the blackness as Hon's torchlight floated back and forth. Hector stepped forward and moved his torch back and forth in a similar fashion.

"To show heem we have seen hees message," he whispered in explanation. The dancing dot stopped, then vanished and reappeared, vanished and reappeared.

"He wants us to come, you see?" Sandip said. "If his intention was for us to leave he would have simply returned."

The men looked askance at one another and agreed with a nod of the head. One at a time they inched toward the distant speck.

*****†*****

Seeing the forward motion of his friends' torches, Hon breathed a sigh of relief. They had understood his message. While he waited, he searched the darkness again, but there was nothing. While the approaching flames were still a good way off, a wet, smacking sound echoed from the darkness nearby. Hon's heart almost stopped. He was very close but still couldn't see anything. Looking back in the direction of the torches he could see that his friends must have heard the sound as well because they had stopped where they were.

CHAPTER TWENTY-NINE

He waited, knowing that he'd need the additional light their torches would provide if he was to see more of the cavern. Finally, they resumed their slow trek. He huddled down next to the rock to wait.

The first to arrive was Hector, who hitched his shoulders in a silent question. Hon shook his head and the two waited for Bongani, then Frederick, then Sandip. With each arrival, the surrounding area grew brighter, extending the illuminated circle. As Sandip stepped forward, he stopped suddenly. Even in the dim light the look of terror on his face was evident. He pointed past them.

Turning slowly, Hon saw the impossible. The torchlight revealed a symmetrical, zigzag pattern, stretching across the top of the rock they were huddled against. Their eyes traced row upon row of raised ridges that could only be one thing; scales.

As recognition dawned on each man's face, all eyes went to Hon. He indicated the direction he believed the head to lay and motioned for the men to spread out and follow. Stepping away from the now-evident foreleg of the beast, Hon inched forward. With each step the bony protrusions of the black monster's spine came more into view, towering some ten feet above them along its back.

Hon assumed the black beast would have the same thick scales as the red and doubted that their swords would be of much use. He stopped and indicated to Frederick and Sandip that they should prepare their crossbows. He hoped Hector and Bongani would make better use of their blades due to their size and strength.

The tiny circles of light extending from each torch provided a combined circle of illumination 40 feet wide, by which they were only able to see the beast's massive shoulders and head. But it was enough. Hon motioned for the men to surround the beast; himself, Hector, and Bongani gathering on either side of the muscular neck, and Sandip and Frederick further out and in front, crossbows loaded and ready.

Each man lodged the end of his torch into a crevice or rock pile on the cavern's floor and prepared for the attack.

The three men nearest the dragon raised their blades high overhead. Assured that every man knew his part, Hon pushed down the lump in his throat and said a trembling prayer. With one hand he silently counted down: *one - two - three!*

CHAPTER THIRTY

A feeling of dread gnawed at Victoria. The fear she'd been battling ever since Hon's departure was stronger than it had been for some time and she had been unable to banish it. Her appetite was gone, her heart ached, and she could not keep herself from worrying. She was certain that something vital was happening, out there, somewhere.

She knocked on the door in front of her and Rowan's wife, Julia opened it to greet her.

"Victoria! I was just thinking about you and… what is it dear? What's happened?"

Victoria burst into tears, collapsing against Julia. The older woman pulled her close.

"I have this terrible feeling that something is about to happen, or is happening; that Hon is in danger," Victoria answered through her sobs.

Julia rocked the new bride and expectant mother gently.

"Oh my dear, there, there. I understand. So many times Rowan has been gone from home, in harm's way somewhere out there, fighting a battle I didn't understand. My heart ached then as yours does now."

Victoria's soft sobs continued as she pulled Julia's arms closer around her.

"I miss mother. I, I… still need her so much… especially with Hon gone."

Julia said nothing for a long while, rocking the young woman back and forth there on the front stoop. When Victoria's sobs became quiet, she spoke again.

"It is hard to share our men; to allow them to risk their lives for the good of others. I hated it for a long time but came to see that it is what Rowan was made to do. When he's home, he gives his life for us in less obvious, but important ways. And when he must, he gives his life for us and others out there," she waved her arm toward the west. "I wouldn't want to hold him back from being that man."

Victoria sniffed, wiping her eyes with the edge of her apron.

"I know, but I need him, Julia. I'm alone. I feel so helpless."

"I know you do," Julia responded. "I know you do. But you must strengthen yourself with what is true, dear. You are not alone and you are far from helpless."

Victoria pulled away and looked into Julia's eyes. The older woman continued.

"You've told me many times how the Lord is with you. It is no less true now, when you have such feelings of doom and dread. He is with you in spite of how you feel. And who's to say that He is not the source of such feelings?" Victoria's nose wrinkled in confusion. "My dear, perhaps the good Lord gives you such feelings to motivate you to prayer on behalf of Hon." She smiled down at Victoria. "That is far from helpless, isn't it now? You can do for them what they may not be able to do for themselves at this moment. I've thought that many times when Rowan was out on some battlefield. Perhaps at the moment when I was most fearful, he was defending himself against some barbarian or was the target of an arrow in flight and did not know it? At such times he's unable to pray for himself. Victoria, I resolved myself to help him in those moments by praying *for* him. I called out to the God of heaven and earth, the Ruler of the hoards arrayed against my husband. I was all I could do, so I did it."

Victoria wiped her eyes again and got to her feet.

"May we go inside?" she asked. "We need to pray."

*****†*****

Three blades glimmered in the torchlight, descending as one across the back of the black dragon's thick neck. The beast lurched violently and quickly into the world of consciousness, its head jerking upward as it struggled to its feet. A deafening screech bounced along the walls of the

CHAPTER THIRTY

subterranean cavern. Hon withdrew his sword for another strike, unable to see Hector or Bongani because of the dragon. He landed a second stroke, this one cutting a thin, shallow swath across the left shoulder of the dragon. The blow had little effect on the diamond-like scales that covered the animal's body.

The familiar sound of a crossbow echoed from his left and a bolt flew high overhead, missing its mark. In response to his last stroke, the beast flailed blindly in his direction, catching his shoulder with one toe of its massive claw. Though not a full impact, the blow was still enough to send him sprawling painfully across the rocky cavern floor. A second scream burst from the beast. He hoped it meant that a second shot had better success than the first. Hon saw Frederick raising his bow while Sandip hurried to reload. The beast was occupied with something on the other side of the cavern.

Hector and Bongani!

Hoping to serve as a distraction, Hon charged the beast, holding his sword forward as a knight would wield a lance. With all the strength of his legs, back, and upper body, Hon drove the sword into the beast's flesh as deeply as possible. The thick scales deflected the blow, lessening its impact significantly before the sharp point was able to find where the scales crossed and penetrate. But the dragon cried again in pain as it recoiled in his direction.

If we can keep this up, we may be able to do more damage to it than it is able to do to us.

Hon's head spun as he flew through the air, the flickering torches, rock walls, and distant faces of his friends careening around him. He landed hard on a pile of stones pushed against the cavern wall. Breathless and dizzy, he tried to gather his wits. He was forty feet away from where he was just moments earlier. The dragon had whipped its tail around, sending him flying like chaff.

The beast's attention was entirely on Hector and Bongani who were looking bravely into the face of death itself, swords ready. Hon discovered a wide gash in his right thigh where the dragon's tail had struck him; the bony spines had done what they were designed to do. Blood had already soaked his trousers and he could feel the hot, sticky trickle going down his leg and into his boot.

Another crossbow released and immediately the dragon shrieked. The bolt had caught the beast just behind its jaw, embedding deep into its neck. The beast flung its head wildly from side to side and turned in the direction of the bowmen. Another bolt flew, finding its mark in the lower portion of the beast's neck. The monster stumbled and fell to the ground. Hon ignored his pain and pressed the attack alongside his friends.

Across the back of the beast he could see the bloody face of Hector as he also rushed the wounded monster. The two met underneath the dragon's chest as it struggled to its feet. Hector had a dagger in one hand, his sword in the other and began a relentless and powerful assault against the beast's underside. Hon joined his efforts, thrusting his sword tip-first into the dragon's hide again and again.

A vicious, cutting slice from one of the monster's foreclaws came down hard on Hector's shoulder, crushing him to the ground like an insect. Hon saw the other foreclaw flashing toward him and was barely able to flatten himself to avoid its impact.

The dragon screamed again, another bolt from the crossbows finding its mark. The beast flung its head from side to side, spewing a combination of blood and black, tar-like goo. The ebony and crimson drops fell around Hon like rain. He heard the splatter as they struck his thick leather tunic. Rolling away, Hon sought refuge from the poisonous saliva of the beast, feeling a burning sensation begin on one ear and along his scalp.

"Avoid it's spit!" Hon cried in warning. "It's poisonous!"

Hector did not move from the place he'd fallen beneath the monster. The crossbow echoed from behind him and Hon heard the loud "thwap" of its bolt penetrating the dragon's scales again. The beast rose to its full height, tottering precariously on its massive hind legs.

CHAPTER THIRTY

"Keep at it!" Hon screamed into the echoing darkness. "It's almost finished!"

A blade flashed in the torchlight to his left, and the deep red blood of the beast splattered across him as two toes from the beast's fore claw flew in his direction. The monster screeched in torment yet again. Hon raised his sword, driving it hard into the beast's underbelly. He scrambled away as its massive body fell, and all was silent.

The only noise was the heavy breathing of a handful of brave men, each collapsed in exhaustion. Hon dragged himself to the place where Hector lay, only inches away from where the dragon's heavy body had fallen. He was still breathing, but did not move. He was covered with the same black slime that had first paralyzed and then poisoned Abigail.

"Frederick! Sandip, Bongani? Are you alright?"

Each man answered in turn, acknowledging that they were alive.

"Hector took a full dose of its poison. We have to get him out of here, quickly."

Hon tore off his tunic and began frantically wiping the sticky black saliva from his friend. His three companions came to assist. Bongani opened a flask and poured its contents over Hector's exposed skin. Due to their position as bowmen, Sandip and Frederick had avoided direct contact with the beast, but were weary from the tension and adrenaline of the fight. Bongani had a variety of cuts on his face and arms but his bleeding was minimal. His main injury was a slice across the cheek that was already crusting over.

"You hurt," Bongani said, dropping to his knees. The tall man worked with speed and care, binding the gash in Hon's leg tightly. Hon and Frederick continued to remove the goo from Hector.

"I'll be able to make it out with some help, but Hector will have to be carried," Hon said. "Sandip, see if you can find anything we can fashion into a litter." In no time his friend was back and shaking his head.

"There's nothing. Only rock."

"Bones." Bongani said with a matter of fact tone.

Removing his sword from its sheath, the tall man began the hard work of slicing through the scales on one of the beast's forelegs. Sandip understood his meaning and began work on the other foreleg. It took well over 15 minutes, but they were finally able to expose the whiteness at the core of the leg and begin trimming away the flesh. Once the long bones were extracted, two cloaks were stretched and tied between them.

Hector was loaded into the makeshift stretcher and Bongani and Sandip silently lifted it and moved toward the cavern entrance. Frederick and Hon followed behind, holding torches to light the way. Minutes later they stood at the foot of the pit, looking up the length of rope into the quickly darkening sky. Bongani struggled to lift their unconscious friend to his shoulders, bound him there with leather and rope, and laboriously began the ascent with Sandip close behind.

Watching his new friends grow smaller as they climbed toward the sky above, Hon spoke.

"We never imagined this when we were growing up."

Frederick laughed.

"That's for sure. And the unbelievable thing is that we have to do this three more times."

Frederick turned to his friend and motioned toward the rope.

"But not today. You're next."

CHAPTER THIRTY-ONE

Gerrard rushed into the small hut to find Camille and Quinn immersed in a game of chess.

"'Tis a pity to interrupt such a contest, but news has come from our band of warriors," the woodsman said as he waved a parchment in their direction.

Camille leapt from the table.

"What is it?"

Gerrard broke into a jig as he spoke.

"Rajic is dead and so is his beastie!"

Camille squealed with relief as her hands clasped over her nose and mouth. Quinn's attention never left the game.

"Good news, indeed," the spymaster said drolly. "Where are they now?"

"In the woods, still near Rajic's castle. They'll be headin' this way soon, but slowly due to their wounds," Gerrard answered.

"Who is hurt?" Camille asked. "How badly?"

"Says here that Hector took the brunt; sprayed by the beast's black poison. The rest bear marks of the battle but move under their own power."

Camille's countenance darkened noticeably.

*****†*****

Two days later, on the western side of The Ridge, Victoria sat with a parchment unrolled across her lap, tears of relief running down her cheeks. Though injured, Hon was alive. She cried softly for some time, surprised at the amount of pent up emotion that flooded out. She stepped outside to pass the news along to her friends and felt suddenly tired. Her legs and lower back ached as if she'd climbed a hill.

I'm not handling this very well, she said to herself, *and it's not over. I've got to let go of the worry, to give it to the Lord.*

Rowan and Julia received the news from Victoria gladly, genuinely relieved and delighted, though concerned for Hector. They stopped to pray for him and ask for speedy healing for the wounds of the others. They thanked God for the first step of success in their dangerous quest.

"You must be very relieved," Julia asked.

"It's good to know they are safe," Victoria answered, "but my stomach is still in knots knowing there are three more dragons."

"I can imagine," Rowan said, glancing at her stomach which was just beginning to show evidence of the growing life within her. "Being with child must make it even more difficult."

"Of course it does!" Julia said with a playful slap across Rowan's arm. "The poor dear has so much emotion coursing through her it's a wonder she's as well as she is."

Victoria smiled, trying to appear hopeful, but the gnawing ache in her stomach reminded her of the depth of her struggle.

"Would you let everyone know?" she said, extending the parchment toward Rowan. "I'm suddenly very tired. I should go home and lie down."

"Happy to do it," Rowan answered with a sympathetic smile.

Victoria smiled back at him and turned to go. Julia and Rowan watched as she shuffled out the door, staggered, and collapsed in the dusty street.

*****†*****

Blurry shapes moved in front of her as Victoria heard her name spoken. A voice seemed faint and far away.

"Victoria? Just relax, now. Everything is going to be alright."

CHAPTER THIRTY-ONE

"Mother?" she said in confusion. "Mother? I miss you, mother..."

The voice responded unintelligibly, sounding like a child speaking from under a blanket.

She felt familiar hands on her shoulders, pushing her gently backward.

"Lie down dear, you're too weak to sit up just yet," the voice answered again, clearly.

A foggy, distorted face appeared, grizzled and deeply lined. It was Leechy, the retired troop surgeon.

"Lay down now, little Miss. We want to keep that little one if we can."

"What? Leechy, where's mother? I just heard her..."

"No dear, your mother's not here, don't you remember? She's been..." his voice turned to mush in her ears. The disorienting sounds melted into the blur of his face.

A second set of hands, stronger than the first forced her to lie down. Her heart began to pound.

"Who is with you, mother? Why won't you let me up?"

The voice answered in a garble of words she couldn't understand.

"Hon! Help me, Hon, help me!"

The fuzzy images dimmed as darkness closed in.

*****†*****

Victoria awoke in pain. Her stomach felt as if it were twisting a thousand directions at once, her mouth was dry and cold. Julia ran to her bedside at the sound of her groans.

"What is it Vickie? What is it?"

"My stomach... ohhh...." she moaned.

Julia called to Rowan, whispered something to him, and he raced out the door. She reached for a cloth and dipped it in a bowl of water sitting at the bedside. Patting Victoria's forehead and face with the damp cloth she spoke again.

"Rowan's gone to get Leechy, dear. Please, hold on a little longer."

"Hon... is he back yet? Ohhhhh...." Victoria cringed as another cramp seized her abdomen.

"No, I'm sorry. We haven't heard from them since the message came. Rowan says they're either delayed for some reason or it was harder to travel with an unconscious man than they thought it would be."

"Owwww!" Victoria cried. "It's getting worse!"

"Bite down on this," Julia said, doubling a leather belt and holding it to her mouth. Victoria clamped her teeth onto the leather as the next wave of pain began. Blood flowed, soaking the bed instantly. The door flew open and Leechy rushed to the bedside.

"She's begun bleeding," Julia said, pointing to the bed. "The pain's worse by the minute."

"Get some towels my good woman," Leechy said. "Clean it up as best you can. Victoria, can you hear me? Listen carefully…" Her eyes bored into his as another pulse of pain hit her. "I wish it weren't so and I hate to say it, but you're losing the baby. There's nothing I can do to stop it so you'll just have to ride it out."

Shock overcame the pain and Victoria tried to sit up.

"No!" she shouted through tears. "No, it can't happen this way!"

"Victoria, lie down," Leechy insisted, gently pushing her back into the bed. "Moving about will only make it worse."

"Hon… where is Hon!" she screamed as the cramps overtook her again.

Leechy looked to Julia questioningly.

"I'm sure he's doing the best he can to get here. You just trust to old Leechy now, I'll take good care of you."

Pain surged. Blood flowed. Leechy and Julia took turns comforting Victoria while they cleaned her as well as they could. Within half an hour it was over. The pain was gone, as was the child she'd already come to love.

*****†*****

It was days before Victoria was able to get out of bed. Her body ached almost as much as her heart. Though she'd

CHAPTER THIRTY-ONE

yet to feel the baby move, there was a distinct sense of emptiness in her stomach and in her soul. Excitement was replaced with deep regret, anticipation with dread.

How will I tell Hon? He didn't even know he was going to be a father.

Julia suggested that fresh air would do her good and helped Victoria to the door. Her legs and back were weak, as if she'd walked for days with no rest. The afternoon sun felt good on her face as she stretched her weary muscles. She leaned heavily against her friend and sighed.

"Has this ever happened to you, Julia? I mean, have you ever lost a child like this?"

The older woman shook her head.

"No dear, I've not had to bear this kind of burden. It must be terrible."

Victoria began to cry

"I can't describe it," she stammered. "It's too horrible. It's like my heart's been pulled out, squeezed dry like a dirty old rag, and stuffed back inside. Hon not being here makes it all the worse."

Julia pulled her closer.

"You just cry it out, dear. It's alright, I don't mind."

"I'm scared Julia. When Hon gets home he's not going to understand. He never knew I was pregnant." She dabbed her tears with the sleeve of her dress. "The loss is real to me because the baby was real to me. But it wasn't real to him. It will all seem like a fairy tale or something. He won't understand."

Julia squeezed her shoulder.

"I don't know what he'll think, dear. But I know he loves you and will want to help you through this. Now listen to me young miss dragon slayer…" Victoria began to cry harder at the thought of the danger Hon faced.

"I'm sorry Vickie, I didn't mean to…"

"No, it's alright," Victoria insisted through tears. "We chose this. I just didn't know…" her throat clenched. She gritted her teeth and choked out the words, "I didn't know I'd have to contend with this too. If I'd known I wouldn't have let him go."

Julia patted Victoria's shoulder, rocking her side to side.

"Now *that* I understand," Julia said. "Once, when Rowan was away soldiering in who-knows-what land, I received news that my mother had passed. Mother lived far to the west and I didn't know when Rowan would return, so I decided to make the journey on my own. Well, not exactly alone. Frederick was due in a few months, but I went anyway. I carried the burden of grief along with my child, who didn't wait the two months. He came while I was away.

"Victoria, unexpected things like this happen throughout life and we don't know why. Some are harder to bear than others. It's hard to judge what's what when you're under the cloud, dear. Everything looks gloomy. Wait for the sun to come out. Then you'll be able to see clearly." She stepped away and looked into Victoria's green eyes. "There's enough burden for you to carry without getting all bothered about whether Hon's gonna' understand your loss or not. You just remind yourself of his love and leave it at that."

Victoria smiled at her friend.

"I'll try."

"That's all you can do now, isn't it?" Julia replied.

CHAPTER THIRTY-TWO

Silas paced the floor atop the central tower of his new home. His hands were clasped behind his back, a small parchment dangling from his hand.

"The fool," he said aloud to himself. *My only regret is that I didn't have the pleasure of killing Rajic myself.* His pacing slowed. *The loss of his beast is the real tragedy, though with his death we lose our grip on an entire region. This is regrettable indeed.*

The haggard old man looked down into the courtyard where a handful of his newly acquired slaves did their work. Mercenaries stood watch along the ramparts of the castle walls, dutiful out of fear for their lives rather than the salaries they had expected. Silas had put out the word that men were needed and they came in droves. But when they were gathered, he had introduced them to Hestia and told them they would serve as his guards or become the beast's next meal. Nothing could have been easier.

Who has done this? How could we have not gotten wind of them before now? he wondered. His mind drifted back to the night he encountered Lord Kendrick in Hestia's lair. The memory nagged at him. His instincts told him he was onto something.

"The other man. Who is he?" he mumbled again. "Who is he?"

After a few minutes of motionless thought the dragon master sprang to life again. Stepping to the doorway that led to the stairs he called for a servant. He met a cowering village girl at the top of the stairs.

"Yes sir?"

"Send up my captain. Do it quickly!"

The girl rushed down the stairs to carry out his wishes. When the captain arrived, Silas wasted no time.

"Form a squadron and set out in search of Lord Kendrick. Spare no expense or measure. He must be found."

The rough looking man grinned, revealing a mouth containing only half its residents, and those remaining being far from pearly.

"Yes m'lord, immediately. I value yer guidance in the matter so anything you can tell that would be of help is 'preciated."

Silas despised such patently pandering responses from those around him. It was much of the reason he'd remained alone over the years. But it was necessary for the moment.

"He was last seen moving north, but I know nothing more." Silas glared at the man. "Prove yourself an able captain, Ligon and you just might accomplish something with your miserable existence. Find him."

Ligon bowed his head and departed. Silas called down after him.

"And send up a scribe immediately!"

"Right away," returned the echo of Ligon's muffled voice.

Silas resumed the conversation he'd been having with himself.

If this mystery man has already had this kind of success, who's to say where he'll show up next. He could even be... Silas rushed to the edge of the tower and called across to the rampart. "Double the guards at every gate immediately!" A man near the stairs rushed down to carry out the command. Stepping away from the wall, the paranoid dragon lord jumped at the voice coming from the doorway.

"You sent for me, sir?"

"Yes!" Silas nearly shouted at the frail old man who had spoken. "Take down this message!"

The old man nodded.

"Write exactly this: 'R is gone, as is his pet. I believe it to be the cave man. Be cautious. We must meet immediately.' Now, read it back to me."

The old man obeyed.

CHAPTER THIRTY-TWO

"Make another copy exactly like it, seal them separately, and send them to me along with two messengers as soon as you're done."

"Yes sir," and the scribe departed.

CHAPTER THIRTY-THREE

Deep in the woods, three miles northwest of Rajic's estate, Hon, Frederick, Bongani, and Sandip had found a secluded hideaway in the rocks where they could recuperate and nurse their ailing friend. They had expected to head toward Gerrard's a day earlier but found Hector's dead weight made it impossible to do so with any stealth, so the decision was made to wait out his sickness.

Hon knew from Abigail's slow decline that it could be weeks before they had any sign of whether he'd recover, but he saw no other choice. So far the large man showed no onset of weakness or fever as Abigail had. He slept corpse-like, his rhythmic breathing undisturbed no matter the activity around him. Perhaps cleaning him of the dragon's black spittle so quickly had saved Hector from its full effect. Only time would tell.

The men made good use of the inactivity, treating their wounds and regaining their strength. Other than the necessary jaunts into the woods to kill game, none of them had ventured far. Finally recovered enough to feel useful to the group, Hon stood the night watch for the first time. He gazed into the starlit sky, remembering a night long ago when he first saw the stars for what they were; beacons of hope to a hopeless world.

Though he'd just endured the most dangerous event of his life and had three more just like it ahead, he felt that hope still. The half-moon illuminated the rocky shelf where he sat, giving the surrounding woods a dream-like hue. He was sure Victoria must have received his message and was thankful to think of her heart's burden being relieved by it. He longed to be with her, to hold her, to never leave her alone again, but knew that their next reunion would require another goodbye. It wasn't what he wanted, but it would have to be.

The moon dimmed as a gust of wind tousled Hon's hair. He looked up just in time to see a massive, spiny beast swoop toward the east. It covered the distance between Hon's lookout post and the dragon pit in a matter of seconds. It momentarily rose upright in mid-air then dropped into the trees like a wisp of smoke. Hon rushed down from his rocky perch and woke the others.

"One of the dragons! I think it's over at the pit now."

"The other dragon lords must know," Frederick said, rubbing the sleep from his eyes.

Sandip was on his feet, arming himself for battle.

"We cannot wait," he snapped. "Strike now and we will not have to hunt it down later, you see?"

"But we are short a man," Frederick protested, looking in Hector's direction, "one of our best men."

The reality of their disadvantage bore down on them heavily.

"Fred, we've got to try," Hon answered. "It's an opportunity we can't miss. But I say we move on the dragon master first, not the dragon. We're more likely to succeed there and if it's all we can do, it would help our cause greatly."

Bongani nodded.

"Four fighting one is good. But beast will defend master."

"We have to try," Hon said. "Let's go."

"What about Hector?" Frederick asked.

"He is going nowhere," Sandip said with a wink. "We will return to him, and if we are unable, he will continue to rest, you see?"

*****†*****

Moonlight and two days of rest made the return trip to the dragon pit short work. In a relatively short time the foursome came to a halt within the edge of the trees surrounding the pit. The white dragon was perched atop a large outcropping of rock to the east, its nose high in the air,

CHAPTER THIRTY-THREE

sniffing the wind. For a moment Hon thought the beast had smelled them, but the wind was in their favor. They were safe for the moment.

"It's bigger than the black one," Frederick whispered.

"Yes," Bongani answered, the whites of his eyes glowing in the moonlit night.

"Hugo must be in the pit. By now he's found the black dragon." Hon said. "He could be out any minute so we need to get ready. Sandip and Fredrick, take your crossbows and get as close to the dragon as you can without him getting wind of you. You've got to keep him busy once the action starts."

The lithe warrior nodded and vanished into the woods. With a jerk, Frederick realized he'd been left behind and darted into the woods after him.

"Can you see the rope?" Hon asked Bongani, pointing to the same tree they had used to secure their rope. "That's where he'll come up. We've got to get as close to that tree as we can without the dragon seeing us.

"Yes," Bongani answered.

The two spread out until they were twenty feet apart and began inching along the ground on their bellies. At that distance Bongani's dark skin made him indistinguishable from a rock or downed log. The dragon's nose was still tilted skyward, its sniffs rising above the sound of the gentle wind. Five feet from the tree Hon noticed movement at its base; the rope was trembling. His heart skipped as his eyes returned to Bongani. His new friend was nowhere to be found. He resumed his slow trek toward the tree, hoping to reach it before the dragon master finished his ascent.

A deep rumbling sound stopped Hon cold. He slowly turned his head toward the beast. It was looking in his direction. The wind had shifted. Remaining as still as possible, he waited. Did the beast see him or Bongani? Either way it wasn't good. A scuffling noise emanated from the pit. The top of a massive head attached to an enormous body was emerging from the edge of the pit. Hugo was just six feet away, his large hands grasping an exposed tree root, beginning to heave himself out of the hole.

The sound of tumbling rocks joined the deep rumble of the dragon's throat. Hon looked to see the dragon step down from its perch. The graceful white head was extended, its eyes focused intently on him. Uncontrollably, his body trembled. Terror gripped his throat and his hands lost their strength.

Move. Get up!

His will insisted but his body was unable to respond. Chains of terror that had threatened to enslave him his entire life bound him. In a second his mind raced through hundreds of images, stretched out before him as a limitless scroll. Victoria. His father. Flames consuming Brookdale. Rowan and Julia. Lord Thurmond. Abigail. The bloody eye of the red dragon, full of malice and rage. A river of blood pouring from his dead mother's gaping mouth. He was frozen with fear. The dragon moved toward him, the hard flesh of its lips pulling back to reveal daggers of bone, its deep rumble growing louder and more menacing. Lord Hugo's shrill voice sliced the darkness.

"Boreas! It is me you foolish beast! Back, back."

The dragon hesitated, confused. Instinct grappled with conditioning, the hunter inside the scaly skin warring with the pet it had become. It was a millisecond of struggle, but it was enough. The distinctive snap of a crossbow was instantly followed by the loud "thwap" of the bolt meeting flesh. The dragon's head jerked to one side and another snap-thwap combination caused it to lurch in the opposite direction.

The reality of what was happening broke through and Hon's mind began to clear. Willing himself up, he rose to his knees. The motion drew Hugo's attention.

"Boreas! To me, to me!" Hugo screamed.

In a blur to Hon's left, Bongani charged the dragon lord as he rose to his knees on the edge of the pit. Clearly, he intended to knock Hugo back into the pit. His timing was perfect. The tall warrior met Lord Hugo with a force that would have easily sent any other man to his death. For a moment the dragon master teetered precariously on the pit's edge but by sheer strength regained his balance and thrust his

CHAPTER THIRTY-THREE

weight back in Bongani's direction, his large hands clamped like a blacksmith's vise around his attacker's biceps. Gaining his feet, Hon drew a dagger and ran at the two combatants. At the last moment Hugo twisted Bongani into Hon's path and the two friends wound up in a pile on the ground.

A shriek from the dragon indicated another crossbow had found its mark and Hon looked up from the dust to see the dragon whirling around in search of its attackers, showering the area with a foamy solution that chilled the air instantly. Hugo lumbered toward the dragon at a surprising pace. Bongani was already in pursuit, closing the gap rapidly.

"Boreas, down, down!" the dragon lord yelled. In spite of its confusion and pain the dragon dutifully obeyed, flopping its body to the ground. Hugo leapt astride the powerful shoulders of the dragon and commanded it skyward. As the enormous wings of the beast began pumping, Hon pulled the bow from his back and knocked an arrow. Lord Hugo's size made the shot almost too easy.

He let fly. The dragon master lurched over the dragon's neck as the arrow struck high on his left shoulder. By the time Hugo sat straight again a second arrow was on its way, striking lower and to the right, very near the spine. The white beast struggled into the air, its wounds posing an uncommon difficulty to the beast.

"Keep firing!" Hon yelled to Sandip and Frederick. "Keep firing!"

Bolt after bolt trailed after the departing beast and at least two of them found their mark. In a blaze of speed and grace Bongani pulled himself from branch to branch up the pit-side tree. In seconds he was at the top, his eyes following the retreating pair.

"Very low, badly hurt," he called to the upturned faces of his fellow dragon-slayers. "It falls."

Bongani scampered down the tree. The crack of timber echoed on the wind. Without hesitation the four men darted into the woods in search of their prey. Bongani and Sandip led the way, both naturally faster and stronger than Frederick and Hon. Bongani stopped occasionally to listen and smell the wind and in those few pauses Hon and Frederick were able to make up ground, only to be left behind again almost as soon as they'd arrived.

When Hon reached Sandip and Bongani for the final time it was at a narrow gash in the otherwise thick forest. Many stout trees had given way to the careening descent of the white dragon. Lying huddled at the far end of the devastation was the beast, still alive and fiercely self-protective. It snarled and hissed like a giant cat, baring fangs and claws, ready for any attacker. Its mighty wings bore tears and gashes from its haphazard descent into the close knit trees.

"Where's Hugo?" Hon asked between breaths as he came up beside Sandip.

"He has not been seen. We must be careful, you see? He could be anywhere."

Bongani stepped along the edge of the clearing, painstakingly searching every fallen tree and smashed shrub. Sandip stepped in the opposite direction, mirroring the actions of his friend. Frederick arrived in a huff, gasping for breath.

"It's not dead," Hon warned, "and we don't know where Hugo is. Be careful."

Hon stepped through the center of the tree-strewn scar, eyes darting side to side as he moved in the dragon's direction. The beast growled menacingly at his approach, its foaming saliva spewing toward him. He halted just beyond the reach of the dragon's venom, feeling the chill from the pools a few feet ahead. Bongani and Sandip halted as well, Sandip shrugging his shoulders and Bongani shaking his head in indication that they'd found nothing.

Focusing his attention on the dragon, Hon could see two of the bolts, one lodged deeply underneath it's jaw and another protruding from the opposite side of its neck. Though there was no shaft evident, a crimson river flowed from high on its chest as well. Hon looked around the edge of the clearing and saw nothing. Though Hugo could have been nearby, chances were he wasn't in any condition to mount an attack on four men, so Hon threw caution to the wind.

CHAPTER THIRTY-THREE

"It was injured badly enough to come down," he yelled over the dragon's raging, "and it doesn't seem able to rise. It's only a matter of time before it bleeds out. We should wait it out. No need to get in harm's way if we don't have to!"

"Yes," Bongani agreed.

Sandip waved his hand in agreement. Hon turned to make sure Frederick had heard him. His friend stood almost exactly where Hon had left him, but he was not alone.

Lord Hugo's thick arm was wrapped around Frederick's shoulders and chest from behind, holding him immobile. A thin dagger was pressed firmly against his throat. The dragon master's piercing voice cut through the dragon's threatening growls.

"Boreas, quiet!"

The wounded dragon reluctantly obeyed.

"Drop your weapons now or he dies!"

Hon looked side to side at his friends, nodded, and everyone complied.

"The bows too!" Hugo commanded.

Hon and Sandip slowly removed their bows from their shoulders and tossed them away.

The fleshy, bleeding face of Lord Hugo grinned grotesquely over Frederick's shoulder. The growing daylight revealed jagged gaps where teeth had once been. The fat man drooled blood down the front of Frederick's tunic.

"On your faces! All of you."

Hesitantly, Hon, Bongani, and Sandip complied. The sound of halting footsteps crunched through the underbrush until Hon caught sight of the duo, awkwardly coming toward him. Hugo had tightened his hold on Frederick and a trace of blood was evident on his friend's neck where the dagger's edge was leaving its mark. Lord Hugo shoved Frederick in Hon's direction.

"Lie across him, face down, now!" he shouted. " You other two don't move!" Hugo screeched to Bongani and Sandip.

Frederick did as he was told, making it nearly impossible for Hon to see what was happening. The unmistakable sound of metal on metal and the shuffling of feet told Hon that a sword was being unsheathed and Hugo was approaching. Bracing himself for the killing blow, his mind went to Victoria, so far away. Her greatest fear was about to become reality. He clinched his eyes and set his jaw. The blow would come any second.

Nothing happened.

"Drop the sword, you fat peeg," a familiar voice commanded.

"Fred, get off me," Hon said.

Frederick rolled to the side. Hon scrambled to his feet and gaped in disbelief at what he saw. Hector's left hand clutched a handful of Hugo's beard, his right arm wielded his rapier, its point pressing into the skin above Hugo's Adam's apple.

"What should I do with thees fat one, Señor? I almost just keeled heem without asking."

Hon chuckled.

"I'm impressed with your self-restraint," he answered in a joking tone, though he really meant it.

"Sandip, Bongani, it's alright!" Hon called over the dragon's rumbling.

"Go ahead you slug! Kill me!" Hugo shouted. "Our rise has been foreseen and planned since the days of the great flood. You can't stop it!"

Hon stepped closer to Hugo, staring him down.

"That long, eh?" Hon mocked as a perfect response came to mind. "You've staked your future on the unwise choice of one of the survivors of that flood, but there was One who carried them through it. He's the one who has raised us up for this very time."

Hon reached into his vest. He unfolded a tightly woven red and green cloth.

"You remember the one who wore this?" Hon said, extending the ornate seal for Hugo to see. The dragon master's eyes burned with hate.

"What of it?" he screamed with a look of uncertainty in his eyes. "I saw to his death long ago."

CHAPTER THIRTY-THREE

"Gerrard lives and he's my friend. What you've done to him and countless others is being called to account... now."

Hon stepped forward, draped the sash around Hugo's neck with a jerk and firmly patted the dragon master on the chest. As he stepped away, Quinn's cryptic words whispered to his mind.

If one of you gets close enough to strike, you must. It is the only way to deal with someone who is truly evil.

He saw nothing but pride and defiance in Hugo's eyes. Even in defeat his arrogance blinded him.

Hon nodded at Hector.

As the oversized frame of Lord Hugo fell, the white dragon released its final roars of defiance. The deafening sound echoed over the trees, across the forest, and toward the icy lands of the north country. Each man stood motionless in the eerie silence, the weight of the last two weeks bearing down on them in a rush of reality. Tears flowed down Hon's dirty cheeks. Sandip eased himself onto a huge fallen tree trunk and lay back, staring into the sky. Hector wiped his rapier on Hugo's coat, pulled the sash from the dead man's neck, tossed it in Hon's direction, and walked into the forest. Frederick sobbed.

Bongani walked purposefully toward the dragon corpse, careful not to step in the pools of saliva. Hon watched the surreal scene for some time as the muscular dark man diligently carved off large stretches of scale-covered skin. When he was finished he moved to Hon's side, carrying the 5 armor-like swaths of hide. His presence stirred Hon from his stupor.

"We should get to cover," Hon said, hardly feeling the strength to actually do what he said.

"Yes. It is good," Bongani replied. Frederick came up from behind.

"What's that for?" he asked, scrunching up his face at the bloody skins.

"Strong armor."

Hon shook his head at the irony. They'd be wearing a dragon's natural armor to bring about the extinction of its own species.

CHAPTER THIRTY-FOUR

A lonely pair traveled the narrow road across forsaken lands, cutting cross country. They were an odd combination; a small, quiet man of middle age, and a young woman who was even more silent than the man. With hardly a word they moved, the man afoot and the woman astride a swaybacked old cob that seemed hardly able to support its own weight, much less the woman's. But the haggard old horse stumbled along dutifully through the blowing sand and barren land, headed south.

As darkness fell they came to a dome-shaped wayside hut set back from the road. The two approached cautiously. A sapling-thin man with ebony skin stepped from the dwelling, the neck of a broken flagon gripped tightly in one hand, a torch in the other. The traveling man held his hands up, palms forward and carefully pulled back his hood.

"Look carefully. You know me, Kofi?" the man asked.

The desert dweller raised his torch and squinted his eyes, clearly trying to place the face and voice. After 10 seconds he lowered the jagged flagon, nodded, and went inside. The traveler turned to his companion.

"We'll be safe here for the night. Kofi can be trusted."

He led the horse behind the shack where a donkey was kept in a broken-down corral. The beast of burden looked up from its meal of straw temporarily to investigate its new stable-mate, then resumed its eating. The man turned his back toward the young woman. She placed her arms over his shoulders, curved her fingers and hooked her hands together in front of his chest. The man eased away from the horse, pulling her off its back and headed inside.

The one room mud hut offered few comforts. A pallet on the floor and a small stool were the only things resembling furniture. A few pots lined one wall. Kofi poured dried millet into a bowl that already contained a smattering of beans.

Using a large pitcher, he poured a small bit of water into the mixture and stirred it with his finger. Turning to his guests, he handed it to the man.

"A precious gift," the man said. "Thank you." The traveler gave the bowl to his companion and whispered, "This will do for both of us." The woman nodded and began to eat.

"It is long time," Kofi spoke. "Why you come?"

"We head to the Araati river and beyond it to the great city," the man answered cryptically. Kofi's eyebrows raised. "It is all I can say," the traveler offered in response to the unspoken question.

Kofi shrugged and handed a small cup of warm, cloudy water to the man, who in turn handed it first to the young woman.

"Tell me of the land," the traveler said, "and of your queen."

Kofi glanced cautiously at the man as he busied himself with his own food.

"Kofi no call her queen," he answered.

The traveler laughed.

"You know what I ask."

"Sanniya is Sanniya. What more to say?" Kofi answered.

"Then nothing has changed," the man replied.

"Only for worse," said Kofi.

They ate in silence for some time until the traveler spoke again.

"When did you last visit the great city?"

"Two weeks," Kofi said. "Trading."

"We could reach it tomorrow?" the traveler asked.

Kofi's lips stretched into a wry grin.

"Not on that horse."

The two laughed. The young woman smiled.

"Do beggars still sit at the palace gate?" the traveler asked.

Kofi shrugged again.

"When not driven away. Your questions. They are odd."

"How else am I to learn things?" the man replied.

CHAPTER THIRTY-FOUR

Kofi smiled.

"You always learn things, questions or no."

"Yes, I do," the man said.

Silence swallowed the three again. Outside, sand blew, producing a persistent clattering sound on the mud encased structure. Kofi rose, took the bowl and cup and put away what was left of the meager meal. Pointing at the young woman, he waved toward his pallet.

"You rest. Very tired."

The young woman smiled.

"Thank you."

The man looked at his companion and she nodded. She rode on his shoulders again and lay down on the pallet. When her breathing slowed, Kofi spoke again.

"You come to bring good?"

"I hope so. It is dangerous," the man said.

"And you bring her?" Kofi said, nodding toward the pallet with a confused look.

"She is more than you see," the man said. "A sharp mind and sharper eyes. She is a great asset."

Kofi nodded.

"Why you come, friend?"

"It is better for you not to know."

"Yes. But I ask anyway," Kofi said with a smile.

"The queen," the man replied. "She is more evil than you know."

Kofi's expression was unchanged.

"You mean the Galib. Yes, very evil."

The traveler was shocked. Kofi nodded.

"How do you know?" the man asked.

"I see it. Many time. It hunts in desert often."

"How did you know the connection with the queen?"

"Kofi did not. But now you say it," Kofi said with a wink.

The traveler laughed.

"Only a spy could fool a spy, my friend," the man said.

Kofi smiled.

"As you say, Quinn." He paused. "Many try to defeat queen. None live. How you do this?"

"I don't know. Yet. But I will soon. She will help," the traveler said, jabbing a thumb over his shoulder in the direction of the pallet.

Kofi cocked his head again and smirked.

"She more than Kofi see."

*****†*****

The five dragon slayers hoped to turn off the road and into the woods toward Gerrard's hut soon. Their packs were heavy with the weight of the dragon skins and felt even heavier from the long journey, but they made good time.

The road running north-south through Rajic's land was busy. Many who had served under the dragon lord were already off to seek new positions, and none of them seemed too forlorn about his death. The night before, they shared a fire with an elderly cook and her husband. Neither of them had any idea how their master had been slain. From their perspective, nobody knew any more than they did, which was welcome news.

Sandip was in the lead, followed by Frederick and Bongani who chatted as they walked. Hon and Hector brought up the rear. Hon took the opportunity to learn more about his new friend.

"Hector, may I ask you something?"

"Si."

"After we left Rajic's keep with Eadric and his men," He paused to assess Hector's mood. His face was a blank. "Sandip told me that when you killed Eadric you were, well, out of control."

Hector glanced at Hon uncomfortably.

"He said so?"

Hon looked at him curiously, waiting for more. Hector shrugged his wide shoulders.

"What can I say? Wheen I fight, the anger, eet comes too. Eet always has."

"But to repeatedly stab a man when he's already dead… Hector, that's more than anger…"

CHAPTER THIRTY-FOUR

Hector bristled, clearly not used to having his actions questioned. He walked on in silence. After some time he shrugged again, stopped, and turned to face Hon.

"Wheen you ask me to join you, I told you I was trouble. Now you know. Eef you want me to leave, I will."

"That's not what I want," Hon said, shaking his head.

"What do you want theen?" Hector asked with a raised voice. The others turned at the outburst.

"Keep walking!" Hector yelled. Frederick started to turn away, but stopped when Sandip and Bongani didn't move. Hector stared them down, to no effect.

"Hector," Hon said, extending his hand, "I want to help."

Hector slapped away his hand.

"I don't need help."

Hon stood in the dusty road watching as Hector stomped into the woods in the direction of Gerrard's hidden forest home.

*****†*****

By the time Hon entered Gerrard's hut the others were already there. The atmosphere was tense. Camille approached him immediately.

"What's wrong with Hector? About five minutes before the rest of them got here, he appeared out of nowhere, grabbed two bottles of wine, and disappeared into the woods. Sandip said you'd tell me what's going on."

Hon smiled, intrigued by her concern for the Spaniard. He decided to have some fun with the situation, imitating her voice as best he could.

"Oh Hon, I'm so thankful that you're free from Rajic's evil clutches. I was so worried that you might be killed!" he teased.

Camille flashed an embarrassed smile. Bongani laughed aloud, his deep voice seeming to shake the little hut.

"I'm sorry, Hon. I *am* glad you are alive and well. I want to hear everything."

Hon chuckled and put his arm around her shoulder.

"It's alright Camille, I'm only fooling with you. We're all concerned about Hector. I was talking with him about something that happened while we were away and he didn't appreciate my questions. I think if we give him some time he'll settle down."

"Shouldn't we go find him? Who knows what kind of trouble he'll get into if he starts drinking!"

Gerrard laughed.

"Where's the lad going to go, lassie? Pick a fight with a bear? Me closest neighbor is Newtown. There be little damage the lad can do out here."

The concern on Camille's face did not fade.

"Where is Fiona?" Bongani's bass voice interrupted.

"Ahhh," Gerrard answered. "Our spymaster took a notion to do some work of 'is own. He believed the wee lass could be of help to 'im in it. The two of them left fer the south almost a fortnight ago."

Bongani was clearly unhappy but said nothing. Camille resumed the previous conversation.

"What happened? What were you talking to Hector about, Hon?"

Hon glanced at Sandip for help but he raised his palms outward, shook his head, and busied himself by tending the knife wound in his side. Hon sighed.

"Camille, Hector's a very angry man. In one of our battles after he killed a man, he couldn't stop there. By the time he was done the body was a bloody, mutilated mess."

Camille's eyes grew wide.

"What did you say to him?"

"I just brought it up while we were walking, that's all. He admitted that he gets angry when he fights, but when I pointed out that what he did goes beyond anger…"

"He got angry," Sandip interrupted with a laugh.

"How are we going to get through to him?" Camille asked.

"Lassie, there's an old sayin' from the days of me youth," Gerrard answered, "A nod's as good as a wink to a blind horse."

CHAPTER THIRTY-FOUR

"What is *that* supposed to mean?"

"It means it doesn't matter what we say to him if he's not ready to listen," Hon answered.

"Aye lad, that it does. But there may be ways we can make him want to listen," Gerrard said, motioning with his eyes toward Camille.

"What do you have in mind?" Hon asked with a smile.

*****†*****

An hour later, Camille had finally agreed to the plan, and just in time. Hector came stumbling through the door, obstinate and clearly drunk.

"I geev myself to thees cause as much as any of you," the Spaniard began, waving his arm wildly, the neck of an empty bottle clutched in his fist. "I do what needs to be done. I keel men and dragons, just like the rest of you. What does eet matter eef I am angry? What does eet matter! I do what needs to be done! That ees all that matters!"

Camille glanced at Hon, clearly uncomfortable with the situation. With a nod he encouraged her forward. Camille rose and moved carefully toward the drunken man.

"Hector, we are all very thankful that you've joined us. Hon tells me they would not have been able to defeat either of the dragons without you."

"That ees right!" Hector agreed loudly as drool escaped the corner of his mouth. "I am a man of action, a man who does what needs to be done!"

Hector stumbled to the table and fell into a chair.

"Hector," Camille said, moving closer and touching his shoulder, "We all see that in you. You've been a great asset to our cause and we are thankful." Hector looked up with her, a silly, awkward smile on his face.

"You are kind señorita. A lovely woman." He paused and began to tear up.

"What is it, Hector?" Camille asked.

"You have been greatly hurt and I hate the man who deed it. One day, I will keel heem."

Camille's eyes filled with tears. Standing over him, she placed an arm around his shoulder and pulled his head against her side.

"I am thankful that you care for me so much Hector. But I don't want you to hate him, because I don't. I know it sounds strange but I don't resent what happened to me. It's made me who I am and more than who I would have been without it." She pulled away and turned his chin up with a gentle hand. "Do you understand what I'm saying?"

Her words brought a torrent of tears from his strong, dark eyes. It was an awkward but touching sight. The large, hardened man, weeping against the side of the dainty daughter of Lord Kendrick, her smooth cheeks streaked with wetness.

"The past has also made me," Hector blubbered, "…a violent man, and a drunk. I hate eet. I hate myself."

Camille rocked back and forth as she held him close, looking at Hon through tears. She smiled and nodded at him and then at Gerrard.

"Come with me," she said, reaching for his massive hand. She led him to the door, placed his heavy coat around his shoulders, wrapped a thick shawl around her own, and led him outside.

Once they were gone, Gerrard laughed with satisfaction as he pointed toward the door.

"Mark me words lads; the bonnie lass will tame the beast, sure as the sun will rise come the morn."

CHAPTER THIRTY-FIVE

Debris blew across the road as a man pulled his mule-drawn cart toward the market. Thugs and criminals loitered in the streets watching for prey, a clear sign of the changes that had come with Silas' rule over the land.

The small village at the foot of the keep had been easy for Silas to control. The appearance of the red dragon, perched high atop the castle wall, and a few carefully chosen demonstrations of the beast's destructive power were all it took to put down any notion of resistance. Silas' was a power unlike any the villagers had experienced and nobody was willing to test it. Every breeze carried rumors that the new ruler was a warlock, or that he was a demon come to life. Silas had done nothing to discourage the tales.

The man limped down the dusty main street, a bent tree branch serving as a makeshift cane. Stubble darkened his dirty face, his eyes surveyed the town lazily. He attracted little attention. Hunched and unkempt, he was nothing to look at or fear. Just another soul decimated by the rise of Silas the Screw.

He turned down a narrow alley and disappeared through a nondescript door. As his eyes adjusted to the dimly lit room he made out a handful of tables, their random stools and chairs giving a thrown-together look to the place. A thin, toothless man sat at a tall table near another doorway, a bruiser of a fellow leaning against the wall beside him, arms crossed and scowling. Both judged their newest guest with a careful eye, watching for any sign of trouble.

Besides the mismatched pair of proprietors, there were two others in the room; a man of average build, in his 40s, and a smaller but fit hooded figure seated at the same table with the first man. The first man was clean-shaven, wearing shabby clothes, bearing a battered old blade that was tucked into his thick leather belt.

The newcomer locked eyes with the two and made his way toward the table where they sat. The trio waited in silence for the tavern keeper to approach. As expected, toothless waited on the new patron while bruiser lingered nearby.

"What'll it be?" the old voice inquired.

"Ale, for all of us," the visitor answered, extending a weathered silver coin toward the man.

Toothless tossed it to bruiser, who spit on the coin, wiped it across his smock, and bit down on it with yellowed teeth. Bruiser nodded a silent reply and toothless continued.

"Right. Anythin' else?"

The newcomer shook his head and toothless departed, returning shortly with three wooden tankards. Once the odd pair had returned to their post near the door, the clean-shaven man spoke.

"A long trip?"

"Yes," the newcomer replied, "many perils to avoid."

"I thought as much. What do you think of the village?"

The newcomer shook his head.

"A sad sight compared to what it was. I suspect there are ears everywhere?" he asked with a subtle hitch of his head in the tavern keeper's direction.

"No doubt," the hooded man replied. "What's the plan?"

"Watch. Listen. Wait. There's much to be learned still."

"Yeah," he replied, "We've heard some interesting things already."

"Oh?" the newcomer said, his eyebrows arching.

"It's said the neighbor up the hill is becoming paranoid. Never goes anywhere without his pet or his guards."

"Hmmmm," the newcomer said, taking a draw from his tankard. "That may be to our advantage in time. Any word?" he said, assuming the other men knew what he asked.

"Nothing," the clean-shaven man said.

"See what you can do to find out. Where are you staying?"

The man laughed.

CHAPTER THIRTY-FIVE

"There's only one place. Around the corner to the west, the 'The Goose and Gander'."

"Right. I'll secure my own room so we don't attract undue attention. Are the two of you lodging together?"

The younger man shook his head.

"Good," said the newcomer. He scanned the room. "Does this place fill up come evening?"

"Never seen it full," the first man replied, "but it does alright."

"It's good for now," the newcomer said, pushing away from the table. "Here, tomorrow at this time. And make sure you keep him out of trouble," he said to the younger man, pointing to the clean-shaven one. The younger man laughed.

"Don't worry, I will."

The two at the table nodded a silent good-bye and the stubble-faced man limped back through the doorway and into the dirty street.

CHAPTER THIRTY-SIX

The torrent of the chilly night air whipped Silas' robes as the beast beneath him glided through the darkened sky. He flew to a meeting long overdue; one he hoped would clear up a month-long mystery. Rajic's death had come unexpectedly and at the same time Hugo had fallen silent. It was not only unusual and mysterious, it was unnerving.

The rise of the dragon lords, planned for centuries had suddenly become uncertain. Who was responsible? How many of them were there? These and many other questions tumbled through Silas' paranoid mind. He suspected the unknown man alongside Kendrick in the cave was at the heart of it, and that is what nagged at him. How could he not know the identity of such a formidable opponent? How could a man like that rise without being noticed?

Ahead was a rock-strewn hillside just north of the desert sands. Sanniya had suggested the meeting place and it served well for their purpose. The queen from the south was already there, her lithe, serpent-like dragon rolling playfully in the sand at the foot of the hill. Silas directed Hestia in a wide, arching turn to descend along the upward slope of the hill. It was a calculated move, knowing that such a descent would silhouette his beast against the moon that was rising over the top of the hill. He counted on it to create an intimidating image in Sanniya's mind. He was ever the planner, the schemer, one to use mind tricks and settings to his own advantage.

His red dragon pointed its triangular head skyward and it extended its bat-like wings, catching the air to slowly glide to a stop. Gracefully as a cat, the muscular beast lit atop a large boulder.

"You are early," Silas called as he dismounted.

"You are late," Sanniya replied, not intimidated by his carefully contrived entrance. "What is problem?" she asked without hesitation. "You say something wrong."

"I've not heard from Hugo since Rajic's death. Have you?"

"No," the almond-skinned woman replied.

"His silence can only mean that he's dead, or captured," Silas offered. "He's not one to remain quiet."

Sanniya nodded, eyeing Silas curiously.

"You think same ones kill Rajic, kill Hugo?"

Silas scoffed.

"Is there any other possibility?"

Sanniya was silent. Behind her hazel eyes Silas could see a sharp intellect at work. He'd known for years that she was the most cunning of the group, and the one to be watched most of all. He'd done exactly that. His spies had reported her every move. Finally, it had come down to the two of them, equals in skill, ambition, and avarice.

"We rule two lands," she replied. "We must take others, while still time."

"Agreed," Silas said, "but first we must discover who has overcome our brothers. If we don't, we are likely to meet the same fate as them."

Sanniya nodded in agreement, in no hurry to speak. Silas smiled.

"What stirs behind those lovely, piercing eyes?" Silas asked. "You have always waited for others to reveal their plans, plotting quietly in response. I am not so easily fooled, Queen Sanniya."

Sanniya eyed him dispassionately. He could read nothing from her gaze.

"You have nothing to say?"

She released a long, even breath.

"Our enemies number small. Six, seven."

"How do you know?" Silas asked.

"Many, we would see, would hear. Smaller, we no see, no hear" she answered.

Silas nodded, rubbing his chin.

CHAPTER THIRTY-SIX

"Go on."

"They. Know tales travel like wind, so say nothing. Very cautious. Very wise."

"Agreed. Do you have any idea who they are?" Silas asked.

A glimmer rose in her eye.

"Maybe. Man Sanniya knows long ago is wise in such ways."

"Who is he?" Silas asked impatiently.

"He called Quinn. Was with Kendrick."

"With Kendrick?" Silas paced back and forth, his mind turning over and over. "Hmmm... the man from the cave, the one I told you about; remember?"

"Sanniya remember. Not Quinn."

"How do you know?"

Sanniya laughed.

"Quinn old, no fight dragons."

"Then we know at least two of them; your Quinn, and the man from the cave. And Kendrick is the connection between them."

Sanniya smiled.

"Do you have an idea how we find them?"

Sanniya gave a slow blink and a slight nod.

"Searching no help. No flock as birds. They like wolf, separate until ready."

Silas shook his head in disbelief.

"So what are you saying? That we wait for them to come to us?"

Sanniya nodded.

Her idea had merit, but Silas was slow to acknowledge it. He didn't like the thought of allowing his enemies so close.

"You not like?" Sanniya asked.

"No, I don't," Silas answered. "But I don't see another way."

Sanniya nodded, a slight smile curling the edge of her full lips, momentarily revealing her once-stunning beauty, then it was gone. The deep rumble of a dragon's purr drew their attention and both masters smiled at the beasts, playing in the sand like pups.

"We should meet here again, in a week's time," Silas suggested. "Each of us must know what is happening as soon as possible. It is the fastest way. Before I return home tonight, I will take a trip to the north to be sure of Hugo's fate."

Sanniya nodded, turned, and with a click of the tongue her emerald dragon was on its feet and ready to receive her. She gracefully mounted, darting from its foreleg to its shoulder onto its back. She nodded once again to Silas and with an indiscernible command to her dragon, was airborne, effortlessly climbing into the night sky.

*****†*****

The night air grew noticeably colder as Silas passed the northern mountains, heading deeper into the country of Lord Hugo Champlain. Though he secretly hoped that the silence was another of Hugo's conniving attempts at steering the group in his preferred direction, the further north he flew, the more he became certain that the dragon lord was dead. Remote villages dotted the landscape, shining brightly in the darkness. An unusual amount of their residents were awake even though the hour was late. Finally, curiosity overcame Silas and he swooped low over one of the larger villages to take a closer look.

Music met his ears and the sounds of laughter wafted high over the snow-covered plains. As he neared the village it became clear that the villagers danced around a large fire in the town square, celebrating. It was as if a great weight, borne their entire lives had been cast off their shoulders for the first time; as if the lame had been miraculously made to leap and dance for joy. Were he not within minutes of Hugo's estate Silas would have turned back. He was all but certain that his counterpart was gone.

Flying low over the estate his suspicions were confirmed. Doors and windows banged back and forth in the wind. Debris was strewn across the snow-covered landscape surrounding the castle. At the top of the highest tower Silas

CHAPTER THIRTY-SIX

thought he could see the sooty evidence of fire trailing upward from the narrow windows.

"So he is gone," he said to himself, turning his beast back toward the warmer climate of the south.

The reality of the situation grew with every flap of his dragon's wings. He and Sanniya were the only dragon masters remaining, the only remnants of the centuries old cult began just after the great flood.

If we are to rise...

The dragon lord stopped his own thought in mid-stream. It was the first and only time he had ever doubted the prophecies that had been passed down from their ancestors. Nothing had ever given him *reason* to doubt. Nothing before had ever threatened their rise. But things were different. Unforeseen, mysterious people were thwarting them from the shadows.

Ironic. We thought ourselves the only ones adept at moving in shadow and fog. But someone is beating us at our own game.

At that moment he knew what he must do.

Kendrick is the link between the man in the cavern and this "Quinn." He's at the center of everything. There's no other explanation.

Silas surveyed the land before him in the first light of the rising sun. Everything from The Ridge westward used to belong to Kendrick but was now his. Much had been accomplished, but he'd failed in one thing.

I made a promise to Lord Kendrick long ago. I've been delinquent in keeping it.

The great red dragon passed by the castle, dipping low toward a cluster of rocks far to the south. Knowing his beast would find its way home, he allowed it free reign. It lit gracefully in the same clearing where Kendrick and the castle refugees had escaped the tunnels the night the dragons attacked. Silas dismounted and removed the leather saddle from his beast. The dragon rolled in the clearing, rumbling with satisfaction, then stomped into the tunnel which served as its new lair. Silas followed Hestia inside the cavern and watched with pleasure as she nestled down in her newly made nest. With her large snout the beast nudged two smooth orbs against her belly and released a comforting purr.

"Take good care of them Hestia!" Silas said. "Your pups will be our advantage over Kendrick and his band of dragon slayers, and one day over Sanniya as well. They will be the key to my rise."

REVIEW THIS BOOK ON AMAZON

https://DragonSlayerBook.com/review2

**READ CHAPTER 1 OF BOOK 3
DRAGON SLAYER: SACRIFICE**

https://DragonSlayerBook.com/DS3-Preview

The Dragon Slayer Chronicles Series can be found at

www.DragonSlayerBook.com

Dragon Slayer: Beginnings – Book 1
www.CareyGreen.com/DS1

Dragon Slayer: Rising – Book 3
www.CareyGreen.com/DS3

More books by this author

NON-FICTION

The Marriage Improvement Project
a devotional study for couples
www.CareyGreen.com/mip

The Elder Training Handbook
a leadership assessment & training tool for the church
www.CareyGreen.com/eth

RECHARGE
Spiritual devotional methods to recharge your spiritual life, improve your spiritual health, & grow your intimacy with God
www.CareyGreen.com/rechargebook

Moving Toward God
a 19-lesson workbook covering the basics of the Christian faith
www.CareyGreen.com/MTGbook

FICTION

The Great Smizzmozzel Bash
a rhyming, rollicking adventure for kids
www.CareyGreen.com/Smizz

Through Heaven's Eyes
a Christmas drama for the local church
www.CareyGreen.com/heavenseyes

PODCAST

The Morning Mindset Daily Christian Devotional
A 7-minute mindset reset to get you started for the day. Over 100,000 daily downloads.
www.YourMorningMindset.com

Made in the USA
Monee, IL
20 July 2022